MW00626310

THE
CERULEAN
LOCKET

A NOVEL

JUSTINA URAM

Tilden Terrence Press

Tilden Terrence Press
P.O. Box 4124
Merrifield, Virginia, 22116
United States of America

This is a work of fiction. The characters, dialogue, and events portrayed,
with the exception of some well-known historical figures and places, are
the products of the author's imagination. Any resemblance to actual persons, living or dead, actual events, business establishments, government
entities, or locales is entirely coincidental.

Cover photography:
pixabay | unsplash | CC0 Public Domain
pixabay | stocksnap | CC0 Public Domain

ISBN-10: 0-9972959-2-9
ISBN-13: 978-09972959-2-4

9 8 7 6 5 4 3 2 1

FIRST EDITION

PRINTED IN THE UNITED STATES OF AMERICA

For my best friends—
my mother, Susan, and my husband, Deffy,
thank you for believing…

THE
CERULEAN
LOCKET

Chapter One

Most would opine that Yale Law School hosts one of the most illustrious graduation ceremonies in the world. Yet hours ago, as I forced my towering frame between the first two rows of the Class of 1992, I damned Yale to hell.

Sitting lodged between Seye Oluleye of Nigeria and Henrik Nilsson Tott of Finland for two hours was tedious to say the least. The commencement speaker was some mediocre American politician who didn't impress me. As I counted down the minutes until my liberation, I felt a hint of sympathy for the eager new lawyer seated directly behind me who was unable to see above, around, or through my broad shoulders. Still, I made no effort to move from the position in which I was so thoroughly wedged.

After my name was called and my diploma was in hand, I found myself enjoying the company of my favorite professor, Bertrand Fillon. A fellow francophone, Professor Fillon was a former judge of the European Commission of Human Rights. He listened with interest as I shared my plans for the fall—a year at the Paris Institute of Political Studies, which was to be the last leg of my decade-long transformation from playboy to politician. As he politely inquired about my parents, who opted not to make the transatlantic trip, I glanced away just in time to spot my Italian amore, Lisetta Visconti, and her entire Milanese clan bounding across the field in my obvious direction.

Last night's public interest awards ceremony nearly became a personal disaster. I barely escaped being barraged by Lisetta's fifteen closest relatives, who were just dying to meet me. While I took great pleasure in studying her sharp mind and soft curves during my time in New Haven, I had absolutely no intention to extend the relationship past our one year course of study. Throughout the spring, I dropped clues that my well-laid scheme for a relaxing and wine-filled summer at my parents' Bulgarian seaside estate would be spent alone. Lisetta, on the other hand, not so subtly intimated other aims, which included marriage, children, and the two of us settling comfortably into her father's law practice.

Like most attorneys, I enjoyed hearty intellectual debate. However, I avoided full on confrontations at all costs, especially pertaining to matters of the heart. Instead, I found it much neater to either take the diplomatic way out or, better yet, sidestep the occasion altogether. In this instance, I chose the latter approach.

As Lisetta's familial army descended for battle, I instinctually lowered my head, apologized as graciously as possible to Professor Fillon for my hasty departure, and ran like hell in the opposite direction. Normally, my American football player build made blending in practically impossible. Fortunately for me, today was not like most days. My graduation cloak allowed me to slip seamlessly into the sea of deep purple.

Lisetta likely deserved an explanation, or at least a proper goodbye, but I simply couldn't bear to be bothered with the display of emotions that would inevitably ensue after our long awaited breakup. In truth, I didn't intend for it to end quite this way, but I'd let it go on long enough. And who could blame me? I enjoyed Lisetta far too much. Feisty and attractive, not to mention intellectually and sensually stimulating, she diverted me from my otherwise listless life of studying and spending my fortune. However, despite any feelings I may have had for her, the fact remained that if I didn't act quickly, the situation would become sticky. I hate a mess.

Certainly, one might argue that I could have extended myself long enough to cordially engage her family for the duration of the graduation reception. And of course, it would have been entirely possible to excuse myself thereafter, promising to rendezvous with her later that evening and naturally never show. Still, though I could be cold, I wasn't dishonest. Dishonesty, and the disorder it invariably created, was something I detested more than confrontation. For that reason, I couldn't bring myself to look into Lisetta's face and meet her entire family knowing it would be the last time they ever saw me. Rather, I decided to sneak away to my awaiting town car and head directly to La Guardia.

Just before I slipped behind one of the many brick buildings that lined Yale's Old Campus, I glanced back at Lisetta's lovely face for the last time. She looked so disappointed. I may have even noticed a tear fall from her hazel eye and trickle down her well-defined cheek. It was at that point when I felt a small amount of guilt.

Was it the coward's exit? Perhaps. But everybody knows the importance of keeping up appearances. I avoided a spectacle and spared Lisetta's self-respect. Her pain would soon pass and she had her family to console her. Besides, she was better off without me. I was in no position to settle down just yet.

With graduation, America, and Lisetta now behind me, my legs were free to stretch in first class. My mind drifted to my family's sprawling estate on the outskirts of Varna, known as Bulgaria's summer capital and the largest seaside resort city on its Black Sea coast. As direct descendants of the noble House of Hartenau-Hesse, my family held various properties throughout Europe, including our manor in Versailles, our villa overlooking Lake Como, my grandparents' mansion in Sofia, our beloved Château de Savoy Blanc in the French Alps, and of course, my own pied-à-terre overlooking the Seine River in Paris.

This was to be my first vacation in Varna since the late eighties. By now, I was past my penchant for summers filled with debauchery. These days, the thought of lazy afternoons spent floating atop the undulating waves of the Black Sea had greater appeal.

Though born and educated in Paris, I was of mixed nationality—French and Bulgarian. Thus, childhood summers were spent shuttling between Sofia and Varna under the watchful eyes of my loving, yet traditional, grandparents. Stefan Alexander II of Hesse and by Rhine, Prince of Bulgaria, and the Princess Yuliana abdicated their thrones in the 1940's when Communist forces overthrew the monarchy. My grandparents somehow seemed to effortlessly balance lessons of aristocratic etiquette with ample allowances for careless youthful endeavors. My father's recipe for childrearing was quite the opposite, consisting of strict guidelines for success and severe consequences for failure combined with a pinch of lofty aspirations and a dash of constant pressure. In fact, my father and his friends commissioned the plans for my life's work when I was still a boy.

A modern aristocrat, the greatly revered, and often times feared, Stefan Konstantin Nicolai Hartenau-Hesse expected that his only son would enjoy a lengthy, high-profile political career. My father wasn't the sort of man to be questioned, so I dutifully followed his wishes all these years and excelled with ease. Although my father's desires were the primary inspiration for my chosen career path, I somehow managed to generate some degree of contrived conviction for public service. So, after Assas, I spent a few years as an officer in the French Army, then on to Yale, and after my much-awaited Balkan summer holiday, back to France to complete my studies.

When I arrived in Paris seven hours later, I was greeted with instructions from my parents via our staff as to when to expect them in Varna. The next day, I took the private jet to Sofia where Absolon was waiting for me, as always.

My mother's favorite servant, Absolon was a quiet, genteel, and trustworthy sort of man. Though I was pleased to see my old confidante, I wasn't in the mood to chat and figured there'd be plenty of time to inquire about his health later.

As the Mercedes-Benz S500 sedan tore through Sofia's Lyulin highway en route to Varna with Absolon at the helm, I closed my eyes, relaxed into the seat, and stretched out as far as I could, enjoying the smooth ride. We would reach my estate in no time and I desperately wanted a nap.

Chapter Two

VARNA, BULGARIA

If Varna is the pearl of the Black Sea coast then the Hartenau-Hesse estate is the diamond of Bulgarian seaside properties. Shrouded by vegetation, Aytos Manor lies at the edge of Varna and is completely undetectable until the gate is reached.

Once admitted to the grounds, a long, private drive lined with centuries-old oak trees leads the way to the eighteenth century sandstone mansion. A pair of wooden doors fit for a king's entry open to a grand foyer of whitewashed walls and dentil moldings flanked by identical winding staircases with ornate wrought iron scrolling up and down the oversized banisters. Suspended from the center of the cathedral ceiling hangs a massive crystal chandelier, its prisms twinkling like tiny rainbows across the Macedonian Sivec marble floor. Beyond the foyer towards the eastern wing of the estate lies the Grand Hall, a dramatic ballroom that hosted some of Eastern Europe's most magnificent celebrations. In less than one week, my parents were to join me at Aytos Manor for that very occasion—a spectacular party for the enjoyment of Europe's social and political elite.

A decade ago, I would have used the time before my parents' arrival to corral several stunning models aboard my yacht and party the days and nights away. However, as a respectable international attorney and budding politician, I now preferred to spend the days reading beside the sea and reflecting on the future course of my career. My father and his associates talked incessantly about grooming the next President of France, but I believed that such a duty would not be in my path for some time. However, one thing was certain. If I wished to make a bid for the Presidency one day, I'd first have to work my way up the ranks of France's ruling party, the MFF—Mouvement pour la France Fortifié.

Still, such power plays were of no present concern to me. While the idea of achieving such elevated rank was, indeed, plausible, it seemed far into the future. As I looked out at the Black Sea and back again at my family's summer escape, I felt remarkably content to simply let the days slip away as I delved into a deep state of complete relaxation.

The week passed quickly and my parents soon joined me in Varna to prepare for Friday's fete. Absolon left for Sofia on Thursday to fetch my grandparents. My mother, who relished nearly every aspect of event planning, flitted around Aytos to extend superfluous supervision to every servant she encountered. In addition to enjoying a good party, she also attempted to keep herself attuned to the most fashionable, though oftentimes controversial, social issues of the day. To the distain of my father, she frequently managed to champion her causes at the least appropriate venues. Friday night would follow suit.

Intrigued by the platform of a budding political group in Bulgaria called the Unified Roma Party and cognizant of Bulgaria's constitutional ban of ethnic and racial political parties, my mother invited a taraf, an ensemble of Lăutari Gypsies, to provide the musical entertainment for the evening. A former French opera singer, my mother held the quixotic view that all differences could be settled through artistic expression and that music was the great unifier, allowing divergent groups to come to a place of understanding. She believed the music of the Roma, an ethnic minority in Eastern Europe, would be a thought-provoking performance for our more politically-minded guests. Of course, settling upon such unconventional entertainment was made possible purely through the ignorance of my father, who remained blissfully unaware of my mother's potentially contentious plan until the party was well underway.

With the full course dinner complete and digestifs flowing, our guests made their way to the Grand Hall, a stunningly unique, just-shy-of-round ballroom with a glass domed ceiling and glittering French cut crystal and gilt bronze chandeliers. Essentially a room of glass, the distinctive shape and transparency of the Grand Hall always awed guests. Tonight was no exception. The iridescent glow of the nearly full moon reflected off the rolling waves of the sea, sending a cascade of cool light into the ballroom.

I made my way through a set of floor-to-ceiling French doors and stepped onto a large, wraparound veranda of antique Iranian travertine to take in the breathtaking, panoramic view of the Black Sea. Positioned towards the northernmost end of the veranda and concealed amid the shadows of the night sky was the Gypsy taraf. Its sounds were like nothing I had ever experienced. A pan flute danced sprightly over a violin, piano, cimbalom, and other instruments that were foreign to me. Almost immediately, I knew this music was dissimilar to the Bulgarian Roma folk songs I heard years ago on the streets of Sofia. Without thinking, I moved closer to the seemingly erratic, yet captivating melody.

Peering around an enormous zinc footed urn, I made out what appeared to be a young woman, the only female member of the group. Her diminutive frame held no instrument. She swayed softly to the music. Slowly, she stepped forward and lifted her chin, revealing a large set of onyx eyes. I attempted to absorb every aspect of her countenance, afraid she would disappear into the moonlight like an apparition. While her face was a beacon, the rest of her body was covered almost entirely by simple, conservative garb. It added to her appeal. I wondered what delicate mysteries could be found beneath her layers. Then, like a dream, the unearthly creature began to sing revealing an astonishingly deep contralto voice. I listened in amazement to the strange, hypnotic music and became engrossed in the tiny Gypsy's performance. It was as if I was drowning and soaring simultaneously. My heart was filled with so much emotion that I could neither move nor breathe nor think of anything but the enchanting enigma before me.

I hadn't realized how long I'd been watching her until a hoarse voice pulled me from my vortex. Philippe Roubert, the highest ranking member of the MFF, spoke out of the side of his mouth as he toasted the foot of his cigar.

"Amalie certainly has interesting taste in music, René. From the look on your face, I'd wager you agree?"

"Ah, Mr. Roubert. Sorry, you startled me." I felt my cheeks color a little under the aging politician's stare.

"Can't seem to take your eyes off that Gypsy, eh?"

"No, no…" I lied.

Turning my head to glimpse into the ballroom, I realized the guests were concentrating more on their cocktails than the taraf. Feeling somewhat embarrassed to have been caught ogling the girl, I blathered on.

"I was just now considering this evening's musical entertainment. Strange choice, even for my mother. But fascinating, non? These musicians are Gypsies—er, Roma, I suppose I should say. As you can probably tell, my mother has taken a particular interest in their cause."

Roubert responded with a snort.

"What say you about the proposed Roma political party?" I continued, attempting to make polite conversation. "I believe their cause is the catalyst behind this display."

Realizing that such an important political leader could already have a set stance on the issue of Roma inclusion, I stopped short of sharing my own thoughts on the matter.

"I will speak plainly, René. It's important that men like us educate ourselves on the matter of Gypsy migration to Western Europe. You may not realize this now, but containing the Gypsy population to the East is absolutely vital to France's national security." Roubert's sun-spotted hand motioned me to come closer. "A push is on the horizon for Western Europe's forced acceptance of these people. Consider what's happened here in Bulgaria already. First, they wanted us to call them 'Roma' as if we could forget the true nature of their origination and the facts about their kind.

Now they want to form a political party. It's happening in Bulgaria, Romania, Hungary, and Poland. I believe their leaders seek to take advantage of Eastern Europe's current instability by gaining political power."

I meant no disrespect to Roubert, who was nearly the same age as my father, when I chuckled gently at his genuine alarm of such seemingly harmless people. Most Gypsies had little money, education, or influence.

"Mr. Roubert, surely you can't be serious. Roma people, by and large, are disinterested in politics and generally don't possess the means, or even the mind, to get involved."

"Well, hear this. It's well-established that with Gypsies come disease and poverty, and with disease and poverty comes crime. I've also read reports that Gypsies are the perpetrators of growing attacks on our wealthier citizens, tradesmen, and tourists. In fact, there's a very important initiative that the Assembly will most likely vote on this fall, which aims to protect the French citizenry from these very people. Mark my words, the Gypsies will soon seek to enter our country and bankrupt the La Sécurité Sociale."

Roubert's revelation as to the nature and objectives of the Roma surprised me. Looking into the face of the lovely young talent with whom I was already in love, I simply couldn't believe the words of the esteemed politician.

"Certainly, Mr. Roubert, your fears cannot be founded. Observe this band of musicians—do you not hear their talent or feel their passion for their craft? With all due respect, perhaps you're mistaken? Allow me to conduct some independent research or inquiry into the subject of Roma migration to persuade you otherwise."

Roubert remained unmoved by my attempt to alter his pronouncement.

"These musicians look well enough, but I caution you, René. Don't allow your fancy for that Gypsy girl to twist your intellect. Our party's primary objective is to fortify France's national security and protect our country from every known and potential attack, including those to our nation's health and economic prosperity. If you wish to excel within the party, you must be on board with all of our platforms. I'm sure you understand."

"Yes, of course," I replied eagerly.

Roubert turned from me in the obvious direction of my mother who stood arm in arm with Mrs. Charlotte Post, wife of the American Ambassador to Bulgaria, Theodore Marshall Post.

No one could overlook my mother, Amalie, who effortlessly maintained her statuesque beauty over the years. The sequins on her crimson colored Armani Privé gown caught the glow of the chandeliers. Roubert looked her up and down at least twice exuding more than mere admiration. My mother, on the other hand, was completely oblivious to Roubert's attentions. She and Mrs. Post were all smiles, laughing blithely at the apparent expense of Ambassador Post who, in good humor, rolled his eyes at the pair and shook his head.

The obvious longing in Roubert's expression disgusted me. I loudly cleared my throat.

"René, you must know by now that I've always believed Amalie to be one of the most beautiful women I've ever known. It does her character credit to sympathize with the pitiable lives of lesser people. But seriously speaking, her interests in regards to this matter have been…misguided, I think."

Frustrated with Roubert's opinion and his particular attentions towards my mother, I scowled.

"Cheer up, René." Roubert patted me roughly on the back. "All this will ultimately make no difference. The Gypsies will fight to organize themselves but they will go nowhere. We should have this problem solved before it becomes any real concern for you. Am I right?"

Roubert winked at me and I understood his implication. For some time, he and my father shared hopes for my quick rise in France's political sphere. In fact, when Roubert became cognizant of my intent to return to Paris after Yale, he offered to mentor me.

The reminder of my bright political future and Roubert's offer pulled me from my gloomy state.

"Thank you for the compliment, sir. And what you say is quite true. The Bulgarian Constitution is clear concerning its prohibition of political parties based on ethnicity. The Roma party cannot succeed."

Apparently pleased by my response, Roubert's thin lips slowly curled into what could only be described as a devious smirk, not at all the type of amiable smile one shares with a friend.

"Let's chat when you return to Paris. I want to talk with you about my alma mater. Plus, I have a project you might help me with. It would be of great importance to me, as well as the Party."

Before I could respond, an irritating, demanding voice interrupted us.

"My darling, what is this conversation? Have you both been charmed by this Gypsy girl?"

We turned simultaneously and fell into grandiose bows as Philippe Roubert's round and very red-faced wife approached us. A famously social butterfly with the keenest of ears, sharpest of tongues, and most insatiable taste for gossip, Hillarie Bonaparte Roubert topped Europe's A-list of society. She also held the distinction of being a direct descendant of Napoleon Bonaparte, daughter of his youngest brother's only legitimate son.

"No, my dear, we were merely admiring this small girl's robust voice."

"Indeed, a truly unique sound." Mrs. Roubert's dismissive tone did not match her flattering words. After looking back at the girl with utter distaste, she turned towards me with an amused expression.

"René, the raison d'être behind your mother's pursuits always seems to go right over my head! But then again, musicians can be so eccentric. It seems like only yesterday when I hired Amalie to sing at Coco Chanel's seventy-fifth birthday party. But that's already, what—over thirty years ago! One year before she met your father. I dare say, she will forever be an avant-garde, don't you agree, Philippe?"

I didn't hear Roubert's response. His wife's condescending characterization of my mother pissed me off, but I stopped short of administering a well-deserved tongue lashing. To argue with a woman as powerful as Mrs. Roubert at my parents' party would surely end badly.

"Philippe, my heart, I have a headache," she whispered breathlessly, dramatically touching the back of her hand to her forehead. "Be a darling and come with me. I need more champagne."

"Tout de suite, ma chere."

Roubert offered his arm to his spouse. As the pair walked away, Roubert turned to peer back at me over Hillarie's dyed blonde curls that were stacked like little sausages on top of her head.

"René, remember to call me about that project I have for you when you return to Paris."

"Absolument, Mr. Roubert. Upon my word, I will not forget."

Chapter Three

"Hey, Princess! Didn't you know your throne is way over there?"

A hefty teen with a pierced tongue and protruding jaw pointed to the student bathrooms, which were nothing more than a row of glorified port-o-potties. The group of students clamoring around the lunch table looked back at the object of the boy's ridicule, who scowled while staring disdainfully at the thick line of black dirt that encircled the nail of the boy's index finger.

"Ew."

"What's your problem, Princess?"

"You really should wash your hands. They're disgusting. Oh, and you smell," she said, staring daggers at his friends. "I don't understand how anyone with a nose could possibly sit anywhere near you."

"Aw, come on, Princess, I'll make it up to you. Here, lemme clean your seat off for ya." The boy wiped his mouth with the back of his hand, flashed his tongue ring, and curled his lips into a devilish grin. His friends howled.

"You filthy pig! Nobody wants that, especially from you. Now if you'll excuse me, I'll leave you to your trough."

In a fairly dramatic gesture, she flipped her chestnut mane and walked off.

"That chick is such a bitch!" he exclaimed. "Hey Vadoma, maybe we should call you Queen Bitch instead?"

To her fellow classmates, Sofi Vadoma, a tall girl just shy of sixteen with piercing eyes, pink cheeks, and porcelain skin, seemed to originate from another planet. Somewhat standoffish and inexplicably mannered for a teenager from a poor, Roma village, she was an easy target for bored adolescents and likewise for teachers disgruntled by their less-than-ideal work assignments. After enduring the unpleasantries of her classmates, the ineptitude of her instructors, and the invariable odor of the segregated Gypsy school for the past decade, Sofi had learned how to tune out the rest of the world.

On the inside, though, she maintained a firm grasp of the reality of her unfortunate situation. Exceedingly intelligent and self-aware, Sofi's more contrived airs distinguished her from her peers. Not only that, she wanted to prove to the outside world that she was not a stereotype; that not all Gypsies are imbeciles and thieves. Her seeming pretentiousness made her the befuddlement of her peers and neighbors. What was, perhaps, even more perplexing to the people of Dobrai, a tight-knit Roma community outside the rural Bulgarian town of Tervel, was that the one person in her life who they felt should have been most bothered by her behavior never seemed to care. On the contrary, Nadja Vadoma, Sofi's young, single mother who was quite the outcast herself, was amused by her oddball of a daughter.

"Listen, Princess, I'll save some room for dessert in case you change your mind."

"Is that idiot still talking?" She rolled her eyes, sick to death of her ugly surroundings and lame classmates. "I loathe this place."

Sofi searched the field for an open table without success. She noticed a small group of teachers chatting under a canopy at one of the larger tables near the back wall of the school. Deciding to chance it, she cautiously approached the least easily annoyed instructor of the group.

"Excuse me, Mr. Zhadonsk?"

"What do you want, Sofi?"

"May I please go inside to eat? I can't find a place to sit."

Mr. Zhadonsk, a fairly attractive yet worn-looking young man, gave an exasperated sigh and peered at Sofi over his black wire frames. He knew that Sofi Vadoma was the only student in the entire school who would even think to make such a request.

"Sofi, you know we don't take our lunches inside until the cold weather comes. You'll just have to eat outside like everyone else."

"Yes, but—"

"Yes, but what?" he asked impatiently.

"Well, there's nowhere to sit. It was raining earlier today so the ground is wet. Plus, you can smell the excrement from the bathrooms once you're out in the field and it's unappetizing. Could I please go inside?"

In six years of instructing underprivileged students, the last three of which were spent at the Gypsy school, Mr. Zhadonsk had never come across a student as astonishingly articulate, or infuriatingly fastidious, as Sofi. He stared at her incredulously.

"Well, couldn't I just sit here with you?" she continued. "I'll eat quickly and I promise I won't say a word." In an attempt to convince her teacher, Sofi flashed her most brilliant smile and motioned to the empty seat.

Though somewhat annoyed by Sofi's persistence, he could not help but be entertained by her antics. He thought about letting her sit with him, but with the other teachers in easy earshot, he knew it was best to get rid of the girl before she found herself in any real trouble.

"Sorry, Sofi, but that's out of the question. The faster you learn your place in life, the easier things will be for you. Now, I don't want to hear another word. Go join the others."

Sofi conceded, standing quietly as she considered where to go next. Anton Sazov, one of the school's most intimidating and least tolerant instructors, stared at her hard, misinterpreting her silence for obstinance. In a single bound, he was in her face.

"Listen, Vadoma," he snarled, "take your food and your little attitude and get back out there, or I swear to God, I'll take my belt over your stinking Gypsy backside. Do you hear me?"

Sofi's eyes widened. She had an encounter with Sazov once before, so she knew this was no idle threat.

"Yes, Mr. Sazov. I'm sorry for any trouble."

"I don't want you to be sorry. I want you to get the hell out of here!"

To drive his point home, he smacked her lunch tray so hard that it broke in half and crashed on the ground. Cold mutton goulash oozed across the macadam. Her milk carton rolled into a corner. She stooped down to clean up the spill, but as she reached for the carton, Sazov stomped on it.

Incensed by his ridiculous tantrum, Sofi slowly pulled a crocheted handkerchief from her pocket and deliberately wiped her face. She could feel her classmates staring but she did not care. Her onyx eyes narrowed and she spoke clearly in Romani, the native Roma tongue. Unable to understand and fearful that Sofi had placed a curse on him, Sazov took an involuntary step back.

"Blasted Gypsy tricks," he mumbled, embarrassed. Like many non-Roma, he held the mistaken belief that the Roma had evil powers and could cast spells.

"Just pick up your crap and get out of here, Vadoma. Don't make me say it again or you'll be sorry!"

Sofi did not want one of her hands to suffer the same fate as the milk carton, so she stopped short of mouthing the words "miserable school," and instead picked herself up, dumped her broken tray in the trash, and strode towards the opposite end of the field. After distancing herself from the others, she looked up at the school's rear exterior wall and read the words that were etched into the gray stone:

The Tervel School for Children of Inferior Intellect and Ability Est. 1948

"'Inferior intellect my foot," she said. "Am I the only one who knows we don't belong here?"

Chapter Four

The Tervel School for Children of Inferior Intellect and Ability was established fifty years ago as an institution for the mentally disabled. Over time, and due to prevailing prejudice throughout Europe that Gypsies are genetically inferior, villages of Roma children were sent to schools like Tervel to separate them from the gadjé, a Romani slang word for non-Roma, or outsider. School officials classified these children as either mentally inferior or socially deviant. Over time, the Dobrich Province developed a protocol of placing Roma children in the Tervel school while non-Roma Bulgarian children who possessed actual learning disabilities were placed in special classrooms in mainstream schools. In the end, the Tervel School became known as the town's "Gypsy school," a segregated school for children of Roma parents.

Everybody knew that the objective of the Gypsy school was not to educate the Roma youth. Rather, it existed solely to keep the Province in compliance with a federal mandate that required all children under the age of sixteen to attend school. Thus, much of the school day was devoted to the all-important subjects of lunch, recess, and physical education. These classes consisted of sending the students outdoors in warmer weather and cramming them into the small, run-down gymnasium in the winter months. Only some students could complete basic math. Even fewer could read.

Overcrowded and in desperate need of repair, the Tervel School housed students of all grade levels from the Roma community of Dobrai. Principally a primary facility, the curriculum also included a declining secondary program for the small number of Roma teens who managed to stay in school. Non-Roma teenagers attended either Tervel Secondary, a comprehensive preparatory school for students who aimed to pursue higher education, or Tervel Vocational School for those who wished to learn a trade. Roma students were not permitted to attend the either mainstream school unless their parents completed a complicated written application. Of course, school administrators knew it was nearly impossible for most parents to even begin the application process due to rampant illiteracy among the Roma. Most Gypsy families emphasized family life, holding marriage and raising children as the golden standard.

Two years ago, Nadja Vadoma was the first Roma parent to successfully complete the application, which should have permitted Sofi's enrollment in Tervel Secondary. When Nadja went to the school to register Sofi for classes, she was physically removed from the building after school security falsely accused her of stealing textbooks. She was labeled a safety threat and was banned from school property indefinitely. The disappointment and embarrassment Sofi felt that day for her poor Mama stayed with her ever since.

She often wondered what her life would be like if things had turned out differently.

"Hey! What does this say?"

Not wanting to awaken from her daydream, which was infinitely better than yet another lunch period of unfriendly faces, bad smells, and chilly drizzle, Sofi ignored the familiar, high-pitched voice.

"Earth to Sofi! Hey, what gives?"

Frowning, Sofi looked to either side, then down. The shining face of her only comrade smiled back.

"Avelina, what are you doing down there? Your mom's gonna kill you if you ruin your skirt in that mud."

"There aren't enough lunch tables at this dump and I didn't want to eat standing up for, like, the billionth day in a row. So I made a little island for myself. See?"

Petite like a pixie, fourteen-year-old Avelina was expertly perched on two overturned lunch trays. Sofi could not help but be secretly impressed by her incredible balance and obvious creativity.

"Yes, I can see that, but what are you doing? Are you...*reading*?"

"Well, I'm trying. That's why I need your help. You know I'm no good at this."

"No good at what? What are you hiding over there?"

Avelina excitedly pointed to a thick fashion magazine filled with hundreds of glossy pages, which she had hidden underneath her bag. Sofi grinned intently at the sight of it, her eyes devouring the images of haute couture. However, her smile swiftly turned into a pout of disapproval.

"So where'd you get it?" she asked point-blank.

"What do you mean?" Avelina responded with mock innocence.

"I know you don't have the money for that, Avelina. Who'd you rip off?"

"Don't be so loud! Just listen. On my way to school, I saw this rich-looking gadjo and his girlfriend, who were clearly lost. Must have been on their way to Varna for vacation or something. Anyhow, they needed directions but didn't want to drag their crap along with them while they asked around. So, I offered to watch their stuff. This just happened to fall out of the lady's bag."

"You must really think I'm a moron if you expect me to believe that."

"No, for real! It fell out of her bag. I was gonna give it back, but I didn't remember until they were already gone. Who cares, anyway. It's just a magazine."

Sofi could have pressed but she knew that pulling the truth from Avelina would be more difficult than a tooth extraction.

"Geez, Sofi," Avelina continued, reading Sofi's expression, "I know you don't believe me, but you don't have to act so high and mighty. Those gadjé were grateful to me for watching their bags, so they gave me this." She proudly pulled ten euros out of the magazine. "How about that? I didn't even ask them for it. And so what about the stupid magazine! It's not like I took something important. Bet they figured I'd steal something from them anyway if they didn't gimme some money. You know those people think we're all a bunch of pickpockets."

"Well, aren't *you*, Avelina?"

"Whatever, Miss Perfect, it's only when I need something. Or really want something. It's not my fault, you know. It's the gadjé that keep us down. I mean, just look at this shit-hole they call a school! Besides, it doesn't matter if I'm a pickpocket or not. It's perception. They think I am, therefore I am. That sounded pretty smart, huh?"

Sofi nodded. She always admired Avelina for her quick wit. It was one of her most endearing traits, though she also managed to drive Sofi crazy with her less-than-bright ideas.

"Yeah, I know. You're probably right, but I'll never understand it. I've never taken anything from anybody. Neither has my mother. The gadjé can be so unreasonable."

Avelina rolled her eyes hard and sarcastically flicked her wrist at her Sofi. "Oh, I know. They are just oh-so unreasonable. Stealing is beneath me, and my perfect Mama, too."

"Whatever! Stop making fun of me," Sofi snipped as she gave her friend an exaggerated side-eye. "But you know, you're wrong about one thing. This isn't just some stupid magazine. It's *Almanak*. So I suppose I don't care how you got it!"

The girls shared an impish smile and simultaneously reached for the mag, but Sofi snatched it away before Avelina could even come close.

"Sofi, I can't see! Come sit by me. Look, you can have my spot."

"Ha, you've gotta be kidding. I'm not sitting anywhere near that soggy ground. We'll have to go somewhere else."

"You know this is why you have such a hard time here. You're so fussy."

"I don't care. I'll never compromise my standards."

"Ha, alright, Princess Sofi. Where ya wanna go?"

Recalling Sazov's harsh treatment the day before, Sofi easily persuaded Avelina to sneak into the building. She was willing to risk punishment for dry land and the opportunity to fully enjoy the certain delights waiting for them in the pages of Bulgaria's top fashion magazine. And, since the teachers rarely counted attendance, she was almost positive they would be safe.

After a quick scan of the empty rooms, the girls nestled under a folding table covered by a long tablecloth, which was strategically positioned to cover a gaping hole in the wall. While the two poured over each page, completely absorbed, they soon forgot about their dingy surroundings.

With half of the magazine still unexplored, Sofi's concentration was interrupted by the click of heels on the hard linoleum. The sound grew louder and louder.

"Avelina, I think somebody's coming. Stay quiet."

"But lunch isn't over yet—"

"Shhhhhhh, Avelina!"

Two figures engrossed in quick conversation entered the room. They were so preoccupied that they paid little attention to the classroom and thus did not observe the two girls hiding in the back.

"Shut the door, Chancellor, if you please."

Afraid to peek out, Sofi could only see a pair of large pumps attached to a set of heavy legs. When she mustered the courage to steal a better look, she discovered that the legs belonged to the superintendent of Dobrich Province schools, Chancellor Zlatomira Minzova, an unusually tall and robust middle-aged woman. With her stood a portly man with a red face who reeked of self-importance. He crossed his hairy arms tightly in front of him causing his forearms to bulge while anxiously pacing the width of the chalkboard. Sofi noticed a prominent vein on the left side his neck that throbbed so forcefully she was sure it would burst under the tension of his tomato face.

"Those UN pricks will be here next month and you know what that means for us. We don't have the funding, or time for that matter, to make this place presentable before their visit," he hissed.

Chancellor Minzova rubbed her temples and sighed loudly. While the man continued to pace, her pink cheeks blazed and her large chest heaved deeply.

"What do you want *me* to do about it, Mayor Georgiev? I can't make the school disappear. And I certainly can't build a brand new one in five weeks."

"Shut it down then!" the Mayor roared.

"Mayor, please! Lower your voice." Her deep-set eyes darted around as she spoke. "Too many students are enrolled in this school to close it down completely. The aid workers will take notice if all of the Gypsy kids are hanging around in the middle of the day. You know they'll march straight to Dobrai to interview the parents. That'll cause bigger problems for us than an overcrowded school. I'm sure we can find someone to fix to the septic system before their visit."

Mayor Georgiev responded with a snort.

"I simply don't see an alternative, Mayor. Besides, we won't be the only region included in UNICEF's report."

Mayor Georgiev turned to glare at Chancellor Minzova. "I don't want Tervel mentioned in that report, period. Do you hear me? And why the hell are they coming *here*?"

"How am I supposed to know? But they're going to be here soon, like it or not. You've got to cut me some slack —I'm in a real bind. I can't allocate funding away from the mainstream schools to make the necessary repairs. But we won't get future funding if this place doesn't pass muster. I realize this is less than ideal but what do you want me to do?"

"It's your job to fix this!"

"Actually, it's not. And for your information, this isn't my fault. I wanted to integrate the schools years ago, remember? If you would have listened to me then, we wouldn't be in this situation now."

"That will never happen as long as I'm in office. I've got my own plan so listen up. We're closing the Gypsy school in three weeks."

"No way. That's not an option."

"Oh, yes it is. We're closing this school. You can either like it or lump it."

"You'd better watch your tone. I don't work for you, Mayor. Let's not forget, the Province appointed me to my position. You, on the other hand, have to answer to the people of this little town." She moved towards the Mayor and pointed a large finger down at his chest. "Your time as Mayor will be up much sooner than you think if you don't check yourself. So don't push me."

Mayor Georgiev rolled his eyes and turned from the Chancellor.

"Okay, you've made your point," he conceded. "Let's just calm down. I have a solution."

"Yeah, right."

"Really, I do. Just hear me out. Like I said before, we'll close this hellhole in three weeks. Between now and then, the municipality will clear out the old Kraptevich building that's closer to town. You know where it is?"

"Yes, of course."

"We'll move the Tervel school's equipment and supplies there immediately thereafter. There's no gymnasium in that building, but I'm sure we can make it work. At least the plumbing functions properly. The kindergarten to eighth grade students can easily fit into that space. Some classrooms may be tight, but it won't be obviously overcrowded as it is here. And there won't be that sewage issue. The parents won't care. They never do. For the few who might complain, we can simply explain that a better building is worth a longer walk to school."

"Sounds like it could work, but what about the high school?"

"Shut it down completely. We have nowhere to put them and I don't want any of them mouthing off to those UN know-it-alls. Most of these Gypsies could care less about education, but they still won't pass up an opportunity to make us look like idiots. I don't want them causing trouble when they speak to the aid workers. I just want those people to make their findings and go back to Geneva. If we work together on this, I think we can avoid any real problems with that report."

Chancellor Minzova stared at the Mayor dubiously as she processed his plan.

"It's a good idea…but risky. Can't we just place the high school students in the vocational school until the UN workers leave? We can assign them to a special classroom so they don't mix with the others. There's only about twenty or so of them, maybe less. They won't take up much space."

"If we put these dirty maggots in school with our kids you're going to hear it from the parents. Plus, who knows how long those UN pests will hang around? It could be three days or three weeks. We can't put the Gypsies in a separate classroom for more than a few days before people start to talk. Besides, that's been tried in Bistrets and Severnyak. Do you remember? Those schools were forced to integrate last year after the Department of Education got hammered in last year's UNICEF report."

"Yes, I remember that."

"So, here's the bottom line. I don't want our children in close contact with Gypsy scum, especially at school. They get enough exposure to those characters on the street, and now they're all over the TV. Besides, I have to think about reelection next year. How will I explain to the people of this town that even more of their property taxes were wasted on Gypsies who don't pay a dime, don't work, but continually dip into the pot?"

"I understand, believe me. I'm just not sure how you want me to pull this off. I can't just send them all home!"

"Do whatever must be done. You only have a couple dozen high school students left in this school, if that. Expel those you can. There are plenty of screw ups just wasting space who can be cut for bad grades, poor attendance, behavioral issues—you know what I mean. Encourage the other slackers to quit on their own and we can fudge the books on the rest. Only a handful really care to be here, anyway. When it's all said and done, two teachers will be left without classes, but they can be reassigned. Or maybe you can use them at Kraptevich."

"I agree with you, Mayor. I just want UNICEF to get here already, finish their report, and leave us in peace. Hopefully they'll focus on Sofia. Thousands of Gypsies are crawling around there. Why pick on our rural villages?"

"The UN thinks they own Europe. But we'll make it past this so long as you're completely dedicated to the plan. We have no time to waste. But don't think for one second that I won't bring you down with me if Tervel is highlighted in their report."

"Don't threaten me, Mayor. As I told you before, I've got the upper hand. But I assure you, I'm fully on board with this scheme of yours. I think this will be the perfect solution for our mutual problem."

"Good. And one other thing. Use Sazov as much as you can. He'll be a great help to you when it comes time to start expelling students. Remember, the school needs to be cleared out in no less than three weeks time. We'll move the elementary students the following Monday."

When the administrators finally left, Avelina popped out from under the desk and jumped in the air. This was the best news of her life. It was not long, however, before she realized that she was the only participant in her impromptu celebration. Sofi, still huddled under the table, burst into a torrent of angry tears. The news came as a complete shock that jolted her like an electrical current, not to mention the extreme hurt after hearing them spit such vitriol for her people.

Avelina stared at her tear-stained face in complete confusion. In all the years they had been friends, she never saw her cry, even when she was being harassed by some of the school's cruelest students and teachers.

"Seriously, Sofi? I thought you hated this place!"

What Avelina said was true. Sofi detested the school. The years of mental, and sometimes physical abuse from the teachers, the constant stench of the crowded hallways, and the relentless taunts of her classmates made school absolutely agonizing. Still, she never once imagined that she would be denied an education altogether, albeit a second-rate one. Although she was proud to be a Gypsy, she took great satisfaction in the fact that she could read, write, and speak similarly to the gadjé. For years, she held onto the hope that she would one day attend mainstream school, if even for just one year. On top of all that, the Mayor's description of Roma children as "dirty maggots" injured her deeply. Perhaps worst of all was that she knew she was absolutely powerless to change her own situation, let alone that of her people.

"How can I bear this life forever?"

"Come on, Sofi, what the hell's the matter with you? Stop being such a weirdo. Isn't this what you wanted all along, to get out of this dump? You know this place sucks. It sucks!"

Sofi watched expressionlessly as Avelina cavorted, oblivious to the future ramifications of the scheme they just witnessed. She realized that Avelina, like most of her peers, could care less about what the gadjé had to say. In fact, most would continue to do everything in their power to keep from being like them. Certainly, Avelina and the others were the first to complain each time they were kicked out of a shop for suspected shoplifting, though most had a penchant for stealing. They would not give a second thought to smart-mouthing the police, or loitering in the town square until late at the night. It was as if they wore their stereotype like a badge of honor. How could it be so far beyond their com-prehension to recognize the links between the discrimination they faced, the education that was denied to them, and the poverty in which they all lived?

Sofi shrugged, accepting that her only friend would never understand her sadness. She pulled herself out from under the desk, wiped her tears from her thick, black lashes, and decided to save them for the walk home. She knew her mother, who was also an outsider in the eyes of their own people, would understand. She always did.

Chapter Five

Since the school offered zero extracurricular activities and few opportunities for jobs existed in town, the majority of Sofi's classmates left school each day and strolled to nearby Tervel to meet friends who had already dropped out. In what had become an afternoon ritual of sorts, the Roma teens of Dobrai congregated in the main square to hang out, smoke clove cigarettes, and listen to new music, especially by DJ Gip-C, a Czech-Romani rapper whose hip-hop style and unique sound spread quickly throughout Eastern Europe. His lyrics were particularly relevant to the neighborhood youth. He rapped in Romani and oftentimes spoke to hardships their community endured.

The habitual crowd of Gypsy kids certainly did not go unnoticed by the townspeople or local authorities. In response, Tervel's town council passed an anti-loitering ordinance to dissuade them from their usual antics, but it was to little avail. Regardless of the month, day, weather or season, Tervel's police invariably made their presence known towards the end of each weekday evening, ultimately disbanding the group of young people as a sort of finale to their otherwise uneventful day.

Sofi was one of the few Roma teens in the village who chose not to join in. On this day, however, her mother requested that she stop by Tervel's outdoor market on her way home. As Sofi strode down the main intersection, she caught sight of three officers making their way towards the twenty young people that gathered in the square moments earlier. Not wishing to be mistakenly associated with the raucous group, she instinctually straightened her shoulders and maintained her steady pace, but it was already too late. She inadvertently made split-second eye contact with Boiko Dragovich, a former classmate whose arrest record was as long as her life wish list. Directly beside him stood none other than Avelina. She was nearly hidden by the rowdy crew of mostly young men. She bopped up and down with a childish grin on her face and seemed not to notice when Boiko purposely tripped one of the officers.

Sofi watched Boiko's interaction with the police from the corner of her eye. They roughly patted him down while he hurled insults, insisting that he had the right to be there just like everyone else. Boiko was in his twenties, but Sofi remembered him from his days at the Gypsy school. Back then, he looked out for her; shielded her from the incessant taunts of her classmates. She thought he was the most decent person in the world, but something changed just before he dropped out. He had become cold with an obvious and deep-seeded hatred of the gadjé. Since then, every interaction she had with him had been unpleasant, even hostile. He either commented on her light complexion, her behavior or, as he saw it, her love of all things gadjé.

While being searched by the police, Boiko fixed his eyes on her. She turned her head quickly and tried to look away, but it was no use. He shouted at her in Romani.

"Hey, Princess Sofi! Be a good little girl and come help me out. Oh wait, I forgot. You think you're a gadjé!"

The teens gathered around Boiko burst into hysterics. Their laughter, though genuine, carried a hint of resentment. Sofi could feel it.

"Look at her. She even looks like one. Pale as a ghost! And probably dead inside too, just like them."

Sofi was hurt and embarrassed but she refused to let it show. Pretending not to care, she flipped her hair and walked away as pretentiously—and quickly—as possible, never looking back.

Each afternoon, Nadja Vadoma waited for her daughter's return home from school with ardent anticipation. With no friends or job to speak of, she was quite lonely each day. While Sofi was in school, she tried to keep busy with cooking, gardening, and reading, but the cool December weather ushered in feelings of dread. Soon, she would feel trapped by the cold and suffocated by the seclusion.

Sofi's afternoon homecoming was always the best part of Nadja's day. She could not help but dote on her daughter, who always had a dramatic story of woe or injustice to share. A keen observer of Sofi's persnickety moods and prim manner, she knew that the treatment Sofi endured each day at school was especially difficult. Though it pained Nadja to think that her own decisions caused her daughter to suffer, she often found her child's inherited standoffishness to be somewhat comical. She knew that despite Sofi's distain for the majority of her peers, it was nonetheless innate to her as a Gypsy to desire inclusion and acceptance.

Behind Sofi's strong façade was a perceptive, budding egalitarian. She had secret dreams of a better, more fulfilling life. The years of loneliness and ostracism affected her more deeply than she would ever care to admit. It was for that reason that Nadja resolved many years ago that she could never burden Sofi with details about the past, regardless of her own longing for acceptance. Instead, she always greeted Sofi with a happy face, a warm hug, and a sympathetic ear.

Despite her past decisions, which caused so much heartache many years ago, Nadja took great joy in the happy consequence of her mistakes; the creation of a fine and very loving young woman who touched her heart and gave her every reason to live. Nadja could not deny the insurmountable delight and satisfaction she felt each time Sofi's lovely countenance burst into a smile upon seeing her beloved Mama.

The Vadoma homestead was the last dwelling in Tervel's tiny Roma village of Dobrai. Nestled on a mid-sized parcel of land at the northern foot of the Balkan Mountains, their tiny brick house stood alone, down a private lane surrounded by tall evergreens that provided an impenetrable screen from their closest neighbors. They were totally isolated from the small cement apartments and random trailer units that lined the main road. Nadja liked it that way.

Beyond the fence, a long gravel drive led to a set of steps and a small cement stoop. Their lush yard was covered with clusters of white Bulgarian Gentianella blooms that looked like little stars in the grass. To the left of the stoop, a large barrel filled with rainwater provided a week's worth of water for the household. Thick knots of yellow roses that Nadja artfully pruned and cultivated throughout the Dobrich Province's many warm months grew under the picture window, though the flowers were beginning to fade in the colder weather. A gifted gardener, Nadja took pride in her ability to graft the roses so that three varieties grew from a single bush. It was an art she learned from her grandfather many years ago.

A wave of relief washed over Sofi when she unlatched the gate of the wooden fence that led to her warm, little house. Hurrying along the gravel drive, she grinned at the sight of her mother's silhouette, which lingered at the picture window.

When Sofi arrived, she immediately removed her boots and carefully placed them next to the entry. With Nadja still standing at the window, she darted to the washroom to scrub her hands, then rushed back to the front room to greet her tiny mother with a big bear hug and a kiss.

Since Roma students were rarely given homework, Nadja encouraged Sofi to read after school as a supplement to the lacking elements of her formal education. Unlike many Roma in Dobrai, Nadja could read and write quite well and somehow managed to keep a small library of classic literature in the home. She made careful efforts to instruct Sofi according to the way she, herself, had learned. Nadja's reading and writing abilities, combined with the fact that she ostensibly segregated herself from the Roma community, added to the suspicions the villagers felt towards the them since Nadja first came to Dobrai with her infant daughter over fifteen years years ago. At first, it was an insurmountable struggle for young Nadja to be separated from her peers. Over time, though, she began to appreciate the freedom that sometimes came with solitude.

What Nadja did have in common with the majority of the region's adult Roma population was that she, too, was chronically unemployed. Before Sofi started elementary school, Nadja had the good fortune to obtain a well-paying job. She was caretaker of a large, nearby vacation home owned by a wealthy Canadian huntsman who found the region's game of red deer, mouflon, jackals and wild boars to be particularly varied and challenging. Each spring, Aidan Laporte visited the Dobrich Province and stayed at his Bulgarian escape throughout the height of hunting season. His wife, Minerva, joined him for about half that time. Laporte and Minerva could not have cared less that Nadja was a Gypsy, even after the townspeople warned Minerva that Nadja was sure to seduce her husband, rob them, and bring disease to the household. Finding their new Bulgarian neighbors to be very ridiculous, indeed, and unnecessarily suspicious of such a tiny, unassuming young woman, the Laporte's treated Nadja and little Sofi kindly and kept Nadja in their employ for many years.

Before Sofi reached middle school, the local economy fell into a steep decline and many doubted that the municipality could sustain itself without a request for additional funding from the federal government. At that time, jobs were scarce for many in the region, so community business leaders met with the Mayor of Tervel to develop a solution to stimulate the local market. In what turned out to be a brilliant economic plan, Tervel began to advertise its towns as popular hunting destinations for overseas adventure seekers.

The local Chamber of Commerce approached international hunting agencies and negotiated lucrative deals that involved large-scale marketing campaigns of the region's wildlife, forests, and mountains to the hunting agencies' foreign clientele. Soon, the region became known as Eastern Europe's most exciting and plentiful playground. Scores of overseas hunters flocked to the area in search of adventure. Most of the American, Canadian, and British huntsman were willing to pay hefty sums for the opportunity to track and kill exotic game without the same pesky restrictions they encountered back home, such as quotas on the number of kills per hunter or fines for the use of certain firearms.

As the economy of the town stabilized, Aidan Laporte, the original hunter of Tervel, grew frustrated with sharp increases in local hunting license fees and the crowds of overseas adventurers who encroached upon his once-private hunting destination. Laporte had taken great pains over the years to keep his Bulgarian hunting excursions a secret from his fellow hunters back home, so when a Canadian hunting rival set up camp less than five miles from Laporte's Bulgarian escape, he decided to sell his property and relocate to an isolated region of Russia.

The Laporte's residence was sold to an affluent Swiss family in need of a vacation home. Once they learned that a "dirty Gypsy" served as its caretaker, they banished Nadja and Sofi from their property and refused to allow them to set foot on the premises, even to gather their personal belongings. They hired a team of maids to strip every square inch of furnishings and ordered that the items be bleached or burned. Not only that, the family took great care in notifying all the wealthy families in Tervel to be wary of a small, young woman with a daughter seeking employment as a maid or property caretaker. They also warned that although the two did not necessary have the look of the Roma, Nadja Vadoma and her daughter were, to be sure, Gypsies.

Even though the discrimination she suffered at the hands of the Swiss family was certainly cruel, Nadja did not mourn the loss of her job for long. Despite the fact that Laporte and his family treated Nadja kindly and paid her quite well, caring for a gadjé's home was no easy task. Like many of the non-Roma families Nadja encountered in the past, she found the Laporte's eating and hygiene habits to be unclean. The worst part for her, though a great favorite of Sofi's, was the family dog, Ranger, a Catahoula Leopard Hound that was granted access to every room of the main house. Years later, when Nadja thought back to the humiliating way in which she was removed from her position, she could not understand how the Bulgarian family could tolerate the leftover smell of the large hound, yet found her own, human remnants so intolerable.

Nadja shivered as she remembered Ranger running through the kitchen each night while she prepared the Laporte's supper. Tonight, she prepared their evening meal in the Roma way—by going to the washroom to scrub her hands and face before returning to the kitchen to wash the fish. Sofi watched in silence, noting the way her mother was mindful to use one set of utensils for the fish and a separate set for the vegetables. While Nadja, admittedly, did not adhere to all of the old-style Roma traditions, there were two areas in which she would not allow compromise: food preparation and cleanliness.

As Sofi observed Nadja's careful progression, she wondered how her gadjé teachers and the townspeople could believe her kind to be so filthy. On the contrary, cleanliness was of utmost importance to Roma families, and most go through great pains to avoid physical dirt, as well as moral defilement.

"Mama, I need to tell you something. Something happened at school."

Nadja looked up from her work and studied Sofi's face. She could see she was troubled.

"You know you can always talk to me."

Though Nadja had secrets of her own, she did not want Sofi to grow up in the same sort of closed household that she did, where subjects apart from work and the weather were simply not discussed. She thus tried to keep an open door policy with her daughter when it came to all topics but one—family history.

"So tell me, Sofi, what's going on?"

"It's such bad news, Mama. I found out that my school is shutting down."

"Shutting down? No…"

"Some aid workers are coming for an inspection or something. The Chancellor and the Mayor know that the building's in bad shape, so they plan to move the younger kids to the Kraptevich Building across town and close the high school. I don't think I'll be able to finish school, Mama!"

"How'd you find out about this?

"Well…" Sofi bit her lip. She searched for the right words to explain that she had eavesdropped on their conversation.

"Sofi," her mother commanded, "I want to know how you found out about this."

"Don't get mad, Mama."

"Just tell me, then I'll decide if you're in trouble."

"Well, I accidentally overheard them talking," she blurted out. "Avelina and I snuck into the school during lunch because it was so muddy outside. We were hiding in a classroom. When they walked in, we stayed quiet because we didn't want to get into trouble, so I heard the whole conversation. I bet they're gonna make an announcement on Monday."

"You're sure they're not planning to send the rest of you to the gadjé high school?"

"Nope. Definitely not."

While the news came as an unpleasant surprise to Nadja, she was not shocked. She read in the newspaper that some Roma schools were being shut down for preference of separate Gypsy classrooms within mainstream schools. The paper called it a pathway to desegregation. Nadja had her doubts and questioned the true motivations behind the changes.

"Sofi, I know you're upset, especially since we can't get you into the regular high school. Of course, that's what I've always wanted for you...but, the powers that be didn't take to the idea of our kind mixing with their students. I'm not sure what else we can do about it, but your lessons here at home will continue."

"I learn more here than I do at school, anyway."

"No doubt you're right about that. But actually, come to think of it, there's someone I can speak with. It'll have to wait until next week, though. There's not much more I can say for now, honey."

Sofi was sure that her mother would not be able to fix the situation. Though she placed her mother on a pedestal, she knew that a problem like this was far beyond her control.

"It's okay, Mama. I just wanted to tell you what I heard. I'm sure the neighborhood will be buzzing about it next week." Sofi paused as she remembered her friend's happy reaction to the news. "Avelina was with me when I overheard all this. She's glad the school's closing—thrilled, actually. I think everyone else will be, too."

"Of course they will be, and can you blame them? We all know what that place is like. I hate that you've had to endure it for so long. But you've been raised to value education, even the second-rate one you receive."

"Yeah, I know. I just wish…" Sofi shrugged dejectedly. "Oh, you know what I wish, Mama."

Nadja's eyes darkened and she looked at her sweet daughter's sad face very intently. "I promise you, Sofi, you will have a better life someday. And I swear, I'm going to get you into a real school. So chin up and let *me* do the worrying for now."

Saturday passed without further mention of the school's closing. By Sunday morning, Sofi awoke feeling much better, though the conversation she inadvertently overheard remained in the back of her mind. Sitting up in her snug cot, she gazed through her bedroom window and out across the bright green meadow at the foot of the nearby mountains. In the early morning light, the field looked like a rippling sea. The wind cut through the tall blades like a serpent while low clouds hung from the deep blue and golden sky, casting shadows on the grass. It was not long before Nadja ordered her out of bed.

"Time to get ready for church."

It was a cool morning, so Sofi hurried out of her short, white nightgown and layered a thick cream-colored sweater over a long, flowered dress. She pulled her hair into a messy topknot and slipped on her boots. Because both she and her mother planned to receive Communion, they abstained from breakfast and instead left their house hastily, not wanting to be late.

Five minutes into their thirty minute walk and Sofi could already hear her belly complaining. She groaned, anticipating the way she would inevitably feel in about an hour —clammy, dizzy, and distracted. This year, it had become increasingly difficult for her to skip a meal. On at least three occasions in the past several months, she had to sit down during church services and one time, she even fainted.

Last summer, Sofi grew a full eight inches. Now, nearly a foot taller than Nadja, the two shared the same lissome builds and piercing dark eyes, though Nadja's skin tone was considerably darker than Sofi's peaches and cream complexion. Nadja explained to Sofi that she felt so weak because of the growth spurt, but that it would soon pass. Sofi could not wait for that day.

Thirty minutes later, as they sprinted up the steep steps of Saints Cyril and Methodius Bulgarian Orthodox Church, Sofi felt that familiar, unpleasant sensation coming on and wished that she hadn't dressed so warmly. She tugged at the neckline of her dress to let some cold air in and tried to catch up to Nadja who was, by now, far ahead. Despite her mother's tiny stature, Sofi always struggled to keep up with her quick, steady pace.

Originally constructed in 1867, the church was completely rebuilt in 1922 after it was destroyed by fire in 1918. A pair of Carpatho-Russian architects, who sought refuge in Bulgaria at the height of the Russian Civil War, began working to restore the church a year after the blaze. Known for their interesting interpretations of the Ternopil Cruciform style, the architects reconstructed the temple in under three years. Since then, Saints Cyril and Methodius stood as a unique display of the understated wooden church architecture typically found in Eastern Slavic nations, a sharp contrast to the Byzantine Revival style of many Bulgarian churches.

The tall, almost boat-like structure, with its white-washed wooden shingles and narrow windows, sat picturesquely atop an emerald knoll overlooking a large pond and surrounded on all sides by expansive fields. The still water perfectly reflected the gleaming gold of the heavy three-bar crosses attached to the church's bright blue cupolas. Some thirty Scandinavian swans floated in the pond, resting before the last leg of their journey to Varna's hot springs, their winter migration destination.

Church was the only place other than school where Sofi interacted with gadjé. Here, she felt at home and was treated kindly by Father Viktor and his wife, Popadia Elena, though she could not help but get distracted during the latter part of the lengthy service. Lately, she had trouble concentrating and was, instead, preoccupied with her ravenousness.

This day ended up being one of those Sundays Sofi dreaded. Halfway into the service, she felt her head begin to swim.

"Sofi, dear," Nadja whispered in her ear, "you look like you're going to pass out. Go sit down over there."

Nadja pointed to one of the little benches that lined the perimeter of the church.

Sofi walked over and attempted to sit down gracefully, but instead, she plopped down between two very old ladies who took little notice of her. Through her fog, she managed to focus on their weathered hands and watched them count the knots on their black prayer ropes. When she could no longer concentrate on the women's prayers she bent her neck, closed her eyes, and absorbed the ethereal sounds of the chanters who lifted their voices to Heaven in perfect four-part harmony.

Let us, who mystically represent the Cherubim, sing the thrice-holy hymn to the life-creating Trinity...

When Sofi opened her eyes, the world was clear again. Standing up slowly, she gazed at the small children that freely teetered around the church, their angelic faces exuding wonderment as they pointed to the brightly colored icons and gleaming beeswax candles. She noticed that a particularly active toddler grew more and more fidgety with each passing moment. The little girl waddled out of the eyesight of her mother, Lyubov, and began to shake a tall stand covered in candles. Sofi instinctually rushed over and gently scooped her up. The girl giggled loudly and played with the knot of Sofi's white headscarf.

Finally realizing that her daughter had wandered off, Lyubov looked around nervously before catching sight of Sofi, the young Gypsy who always attended Sunday services with her childlike mother. She pushed past the crowd of worshippers, who stood like well-trained soldiers, and rushed to meet Sofi just beyond the first row of the faithful.

"I think this bundle belongs to you," Sofi whispered lightly as she carefully placed the little girl into Lyubov's outstretched arms. "She nearly toppled the candle stand! But don't worry. I reached her just in time."

Lyubov wrapped her arms protectively around the small child and looked up at Sofi's sweet face with genuine surprise. She never exchanged words with Sofi before and was taken aback by her gentility.

"Thanks. Sofi, right?" she said tentatively.

Sofi nodded.

"Thank you very much, Sofi. You're a good girl." With that, Lyubov was gone and Sofi was left to stare blankly at the group of women beside her who, in unison, solemnly bowed at the waist towards the altar. Sofi thought she detected a tenor of embarrassment on the part of Lyubov, but with her hasty departure, she could not be sure.

"Sofi, what were you doing over there?" Nadja hissed.

Sofi was looked down at her tiny mother, who was suddenly at her side.

"Come with me this minute. And pay attention!"

On the walk home from church, Sofi was unusually quiet. She considered her encounter with Lyubov and tried to ascertain at which point in life human being develop prejudices towards one another.

We're not born with these feelings, that's for sure. That little girl wasn't afraid of me at all, and neither are the other gadjé kids. I

wonder why the adults make such unreasonable judgments about us?
God gave us the ability to reason, so how can it be that some of us are
so unreasonable? Some Roma steal, it's true—but some gadjé steal, too!

"Did you say something, honey?"

Sofi looked over at her mother, but simply shrugged
her shoulders.

"Are you upset with me because I reprimanded you
earlier? You know I just want you to be a good girl and do
what you're supposed to do. It's very important that you be-
have yourself in church. You're nearly grown up!"

"I know. You're right about that, Mama. And I'm
sorry that I got distracted. But just now, I just thinking about
something else, that's all."

"What's up?"

"Well, I was just wondering why the gadjé despise us
so much."

"Come now, Sofi, you're being overly dramatic…"

"I know. I didn't mean that. Of course, I know not
all of them hate us. At church everybody is pretty nice, or
okay, at least. But even they seem to be afraid, or uncertain—I don't know, maybe both. They act like we could hurt
them somehow. I just can't understand it."

"Did something happen?"

"No, no. But before you came over to tell me to pay
attention, the youngest daughter of that lady, Lyubov, almost
knocked over a candle stand. She could've been hurt. I saw
what she was doing, so I just picked her up—no big deal.
Anyways, when I brought her back, Lyubov seemed so unsure about me. Then, after I said something to her, she
seemed very surprised. She gave me such a weird look, like
she expected me to breathe fire instead of speak. I know I

overanalyze these things all the time, Mama. And I know that what the gadjé think shouldn't matter to me. They live in their world and we live in ours. But, I can't help but believe in my soul that it's wrong, all wrong. We can't go through our entire lives without interacting with them! And how are we supposed to change their mind about us if we never have the opportunity to show them who we really are?"

"Why do you expect more, Sofi? We are infinitely blessed. We should be thankful to God for all things—the good and the bad. Our struggles help us grow closer to Him. I know deep inside, you believe this. So what are you *really* trying to say?" Nadja gently challenged her daughter. "Do you believe that you are somehow entitled to more than anyone else?"

"I'm no better than anyone else...I guess. I mean, no one deserves to have a better life at the expense of another. But the gadjé have so much *more* than us. Doesn't the injustice of it all make you angry? To want to fight? To demand equality?"

Nadja could not help but smirk at her dissident daughter. Of course, she wanted more for Sofi and wished that she could give her daughter the answers she so desperately desired. At the same time, she did not want to reveal so much as to encourage Sofi to act in some way that would only hurt her in the end.

"Sofi, I realize this is very hard for you. Believe me, I know from experience. It can be confusing to feel like you're the only person you know who wonders about the outside world. And, I know you feel that life can be very unfair. You're right. It is. We have the power to change only some situations. Others we cannot and should not change. The same goes for people. With patience and perseverance, you might be able to change a person's opinion about a certain thing. But it's nearly impossible to change deep-seeded prejudices that developed over hundreds of years. You're curious about the gadjé, I know. Funny, I think some of them are equally as perplexed about you as you are about them." Nadja paused to wink at her daughter. "But believe me when I tell you that pushing yourself into their world is *not* a good thing. It will only end in disappointment. You're so young and full of life! Focus on being you. Glorify God in all that you do. Concentrate on learning as much as you can. Master the things you love to do. Find joy in the life that has been given to you! The outside world will hold nothing but pain for you, Sofi, if you try to force yourself into it."

There was no break in Nadja's kind expression as she spoke, though Sofi thought she saw something flicker in her mother's black eyes.

Despite Nadja's tender advice, Sofi was left unsatisfied. Dozens of questions consumed her. She was sick to death of always wondering why she didn't seem to fit in anywhere; why she was always the outcast.

"Mama, there's so much I want to see, and so much I want to know. I want to keep going to school—to college, even. What's out there for me? I feel like I have no future." Sofi kicked her foot, pummeling a large stone across the dirt path.

"In time, more doors will open to you. But you must be patient and wait for His timing. Not yours. All will fall into place eventually. I promise."

"Are you happy, Mama, or do you wish that your life had been...different?"

The soft beginnings of a wistful smile spread over Nadja's face as a flood of memories passed through her mind. Not wanting Sofi to see her expression, Nadja turned her head and looked out at the deep green fields and azure sky.

"I'm happy to have *you*, my dear. You're the greatest blessing in my life—my joy! And because of you, I wouldn't have changed a thing."

Chapter Six

The beginning of the end of the Gypsy high school soon came to pass, and the first phase of the transition was implemented rather painlessly. As Sofi predicted, the teachers wasted no time announcing that the school would relocate to the Kraptevich Building. Written notice was sent to the parents explaining the reasons for the move and the projected timeline. Since most parents could not read, the letter served no actual purpose. Sofi wondered if anyone really cared much at all. Apart from a few complaints about a longer walk to school, most of her peers gave little thought to the big changes ahead of them.

Sofi and Nadja, one the other hand, read the letter together that week. The intentional omissions were glaring. The note simply indicated that the sewer problem could not be remedied and the move to the new facility would benefit the entire student body since it was larger, newer, and could accommodate the students more comfortably. There was no mention about the UNICEF visit and no hint of the high school's permanent closure.

The letter did, however, contain an interesting caveat for the secondary students. The Chancellor made it perfectly clear that if less than half of the high schoolers showed up for classes at the new building, all secondary classes would be canceled indefinitely. The letter cited a new school district regulation giving administrators the option to cancel lessons if a class size was comprised of less than eight students. The letter went on to indicate that the inability to fill a classroom to capacity would be a gross waste of space and staff—resources that the Dobrich Province simply could not spare.

During week two of the transition, the next phase of Chancellor Minzova's scheme was aggressively put into play. The first expulsions came after lunch period on Monday. While the older students waited to file back into the building, Sazov casually approached three of the largest, most virile high school boys. No one could hear the words exchanged, but something triggered the boys to react quite violently. One even screamed that he would kill Sazov, and it took several teachers to hold them back. Nearly everyone who witnessed the altercation believed that Sazov was attacked without cause, so the boys were arrested and charged with assault. Of course, Sofi knew better. This was just one of the underhanded methods the teachers would utilize to swiftly rid the school of its high school students.

The Chancellor executed her plans as inconspicuously as possible. Through her staff, she carefully employed techniques to provoke the most testosterone-filled students into expulsion and break the confidence of the least scholastically-inclined students by giving them the option of dropping out or suffering the embarrassment of repeating the same grade the following year.

Perhaps the most morally reprehensible method was one designed by Sazov himself, which targeted the girls.

Since Roma families traditionally adhere to strict rules for morality and hold chastity as the highest honor, he systematically targeted the quieter girls, cornering them in the hallways when they were alone to grope, harass, and intimidate them. His sickening behavior persisted all week. One by one, the girls stopped coming to school, unable to bear the shame and fearful of being maxrime, or defiled, which would mean exclusion from their community. By the end of the second week, nineteen high school students in all were either expelled or dropped out leaving just six secondary students in the entire school.

Included in the long list of dropouts was Avelina, but not because she fell victim to one of the administration's schemes. Rather, two weeks after the school relocation was announced, fourteen-year-old Avelina made an announcement of her own. She was engaged.

"You're getting *what*?"

"I'm so excited, aren't you? I'll be the youngest girl since Rada Merejan to get married. The whole neighborhood is talking about it. And guess what?" Avelina leaned into Sofi ear, though the volume of her blaring voice remained unchanged. "His family is paying mine the largest dowry this village has ever seen!"

Avelina giggled uncontrollably while Sofi stared expressionlessly at her friend. There was absolutely no way that she could share in Avelina's misguided excitement.

"What's the matter, Sofi? Jealous?"

"No! I'm not jealous."

"Well, what's your problem then?"

Sofi thought long and hard about what to say, but all she could do was stare at the ground. After what felt like a lifetime of silence, she managed to formulate a response, though it was not at all congratulatory in nature.

"You seriously want to get married, Avelina? I know school's closing soon, so there won't be much else to do, but marriage? That's kinda extreme."

Sofi heard about the Roma tradition of child marriage, but there had not been a bride in Dobrai as young as Avelina in all the years she could remember. Many Roma ceased to follow the illegal practice after police began crackdowns in most countries. Of course, it was still common for seventeen-year-old girls to wed similarly aged boys, but fourteen seemed young—too young.

"So who's the lucky guy?" she choked out sarcastically.

Avelina looked at Sofi with a very dreamy look. "Boiko Dragovich," she cooed, taking the greatest pleasure in uttering his name.

"Boiko!"

Sofi stared at her friend in complete disbelief. Not only was Boiko a decade older than Avelina, he was constantly in trouble with the law.

"Wasn't he arrested a few weeks ago?"

"Oh, that. It was nothing. He got released the next day."

"Well, how did his family get the dowry money?"

"I'm not sure, exactly. I think Boiko's dad and uncles went to the casinos in Varna last month to bet on the football games. Mr. Dragovich won big at the Desperado. He knew that Boiko was interested, so he gave him exactly what he wanted— me!" Avelina told the engagement story so nonchalantly that it made Sofi even more uncomfortable.

"You know," she continued, "at first my parents said no. My dad was pissed, actually. Then they said we could get married, but we'd have to wait a couple years. But when Mr. Dragovich told my dad about the dowry he was ready to pay, my parents couldn't say no."

Oddly to Sofi, Avelina seemed to have no qualms admitting to the fact that the Dragovich family essentially paid for her as though they were buying a horse. Surely, Avelina was worth the price. She was very young, so no doubt a virgin, and quite beautiful with her bronzed skin and shiny black curls.

"So, you're happy about it, I see. But I didn't know that you even liked Boiko." Sofi could not recall Avelina ever mentioning an interest in the aspiring criminal.

"Oh yeah, we've been hanging out a lot. He's super cute and really built, too." Avelina raised her eyebrows at Sofi and winked.

"Avelina!"

"So what? I can say whatever I want now. He's my fiancé—" The imp stopped short when she caught Sofi's shocked expression. "Listen, Princess Sofi, you need to relax and get over yourself. I'm getting married! Just be happy for me and stop being bitter. It's not my fault that I'm your only friend. Oh yeah, that reminds me. We're not gonna be able to see each other very much after next week, so you better be nice to me while you still can."

"What do you mean by that?'" Sofi's intonation revealed her growing irritation with Avelina's blissful ignorance and obvious naiveté about the situation. "What's after next week?"

"The wedding, duh! On Saturday, I'll be Mrs. Boiko Dragovich."

Sofi wasn't sure if she could handle any more surprises. Between the school's closing, witnessing the underhanded tactics of the instructors, and Avelina's impending nuptials to one of the town's most notorious troublemakers, she felt like her world had been turned upside down. That was not to mention that the engagement of her only friend forced her to deal with the realization that she, too, would soon be expected to marry if she ever wanted a chance to be accepted by her fellow Roma.

The last day of school came and went quickly and uneventfully. When classes were dismissed for the last time, Sofi gathered her things and trekked home slowly and sullenly. Her typically arrow-straight posture was weighed down with teenage stress. While she longed to be in the comforting arms of her mother, she could not seem to force her feet to quicken their pace. She trudged home all alone with her gloomy thoughts as her only companion.

Chapter Seven

Nadja's dark eyes zeroed in on the black Mercedes Benz that crept down the driveway. It came to a stop just a few yards from the front door. A lean man with salt and pepper hair wearing a smart wool suit and black driving cap emerged.

Unprepared, though not surprised to see the familiar face, Nadja hastily placed her tea glass into her bronzed podstakannik. She threw a thick sheepskin cardigan over her shoulders and met the man before he reached the front steps.

"Haven't seen you in a while. I was beginning to think she finally decided to leave us in peace."

The man's gentle face did not offer a retort to Nadja's fueled remarks. Instead, he smiled kindly and bowed.

"It's a pleasure to see you again, Nadja. You look well," he replied in Bulgarian, though his accent was distinctly French.

While Nadja knew that the infinitely patient gadjo was personally guilty of no faults against her, she could not help but regard him with subtle animosity. Her hostility was not intended for him, but rather for the family with which he was associated. This man was a stark reminder of the pain of years past. It was impossible for Nadja to push those memories aside for the sake of etiquette.

"Believe it or not, I'm actually glad you're here," she said. "I've been meaning to speak with you for some time about my daughter. She's the reason for this visit, isn't she?"

The gadjo nodded, then looked cautiously to either side.

"Nadja, I would be happy to discuss Sofi with you. But before that, perhaps we should go indoors where we won't run the risk of being overheard? Unless you're comfortable talking here in the open."

Nadja scanned the perimeter of her property. She spotted a group of older men hovering at the edge of the lane. They peered curiously through the trees at the Mercedes, an unusual vehicle of choice or affordability for anyone who lived in Dobrai.

"I suppose you're right, but I think it would be best if we talk out here. The last thing that Sofi and I need right now is for everyone to think I'm entertaining some rich gadjo inside my home. I can only imagine what they already think of me…"

Nadja shuddered involuntarily. She remembered the rumors that spread throughout the neighborhood so many years ago after the man came to call on her and little Sofi for the first time. With that in mind, she led him to the side yard, which was completely enveloped by a dense wall of tall evergreens.

"We're out of sight now. I'm sure of it. No one will hear us unless they walk right up to the house, which nobody ever does."

The man respectfully stood a few paces away from Nadja and gave her his full attention.

"I've been giving this a lot of thought and I think it's time for us to move. You probably haven't heard the news, but Sofi's school is scheduled to close any day now. There's no other school in the area that will accept her as a student, and you know it's important to both of us that she continues her education. Now, neither of us have any prospects here." Nadja crossed her arms behind her back and began to pace. "If we stay, Sofi will be expected to marry in the next year or so, and I am very much opposed to that. You've got to agree that your Madame can't protect Sofi from growing up. And I can't exclude her from all of our traditions…that is, so long as we're here."

"You've done a fine job raising Sofi thus far. And of course, you're safe here."

"But we're completely cut off from our community. One day, I'll be gone and Sofi will not have the support of our people because I've had to—to separate us from our tribe for so long. She'll be completely alone. Doesn't she realize, or even care, how hard it is for us to feel so isolated?"

"Of course Madame cares."

"But not enough to do something about it."

"We both wish to keep you *safe*. That said, consider what you're proposing very carefully. Obviously, we can't physically restrain you from leaving. But, I must caution you. If you decide to go, you risk placing yourself—and Sofi—in harm's way. I'm not entirely sure that Madame can protect you in France as she can here. I assume that's where you'll go?"

The gadjo gave Nadja a knowing look. She ignored it.

"Nadja, there are forces at work in that country that simply don't exist here. You don't want to bring any unnecessary attention to yourselves, especially since you've been able to live for so long without being detected."

Nadja did not agree with the gadjo's assessment, preferring instead to believe that time caused people to forget the past.

"It doesn't matter anymore," she growled. "I can't live my life in fear any longer. Sofi deserves more and I believe she needs answers, too. She's— she's so unhappy."

Nadja's determination grew fierce. She thought about the years of suffering her precious child endured; suffering that could have been prevented if she had been accepted and loved.

"Sofi might actually have a chance for a good future if we leave this place! At least she can be properly educated and I can find a decent job. Don't think I don't know. France has programs in place to help people like us."

"That's true to some extent, but there are many who will try to exploit you."

"Please, no one's going to recognize us. Sofi is nearly a grown woman. Who would ever suspect us, or even care who we are? Besides, we'll live far beneath anyone's radar to become a target. To the outside world, we'll just be two more lowly Gypsies in Paris. That's all."

The gadjo fell silent and looked thoughtfully at Nadja. Though he knew her to be an intelligent and selfless woman, she was still rather young and quite naïve about the outside world, having lived in seclusion for over half of her life. He figured that a gentle reminder of the potential dangers associated with such a drastic move would convince her to act in the best interest her daughter.

"Please try to think about this rationally. We don't know who else has been watching you over the years. It's not worth the risk, can't you see? Even if you can manage to live in anonymity, life will be very different. Much more difficult."

"It can't get much worse than this."

"I urge you to reconsider. Madame feels it's best to stay here where you're safe and protected. However, if you decide you must go, it's imperative that you tell me beforehand so we can make some sort of…arrangements."

Nadja looked away as though she did not hear him.

"Nadja Vadoma," he reiterated firmly, "do not leave without notifying us first. We must be kept abreast of your plans and where you will be."

Sensing it would be a mistake to press the issue any further, he turned the conversation to the purpose of his visit.

"I actually drove out here because Madame has been meaning to give something to you to give to Sofi. It's quite special."

He slid his hand into the breast pocket of his black wool jacket and revealed a blue box with gold trim, which he handed to Nadja.

"Open it."

Nadja took the box in her tiny hands and lifted the lid. Inside was a unique and evidently expensive oval-shaped pendant attached to a gold rope chain.

"This has been in the family for some time. If you look very carefully, it opens there—on the right."

Nadja studied the heavy gold and sapphire pendant carefully. The ornate piece depicted a detailed coat of arms. A golden dragon holding a large cerulean sapphire orb twisted its body around a powerful lion wearing a crown comprised of a dozen small cerulean sapphires. An intricately bejeweled Greek cross separated the two animals. As Nadja looked even closer at the fascinating piece, she noticed that the orb was actually the top of a clasp, which also served as a handle of sorts. With her small, deft fingers, she pulled the pendant open to reveal a secret locket, which she would have never noticed if he had not pointed it out. Inside, the locket contained a scroll of neatly rolled parchment paper tied with a satin ribbon that matched the blue of the locket's sapphires.

She looked at the gadjo with a quizzical expression. He nodded his head encouragingly. She opened the scroll and found a few lines of text, apparently written in French, as the letters used were clearly different than the Cyrillic letters of the Bulgarian alphabet.

"What's this all about?"

"Madame directed me to give the locket to you to give to Sofi for her sixteenth birthday. But she doesn't know about the scroll inside. That is courtesy of me. If the time ever comes when you need to tell Sofi the truth, tell her to open the locket."

"Sofi never needs to know."

"If God wills it, it will happen. Neither you nor Madame nor anyone else will be able to prevent it. You know that over the years, I have not been completely supportive of this—this *arrangement*. I don't like to keep secrets from the master. However, as time has passed, I've come to terms with the fact that it isn't my place to get further involved. By including this information, I simply thought that if a time should ever come in Sofi's life that she needs him, she would at least have a clue to help her along her way. The writing there on the parchment is the name and address of someone who can one day be of aid to Sofi. Someone she can trust. But you must realize that Sofi will not know that the locket opens unless you tell her. It's a secret locket by design. Therefore, it is up to you to decide when and if you want to tell her."

"I'm not giving this to her. What am I supposed to say when she asks me how I got it? No. Tell your precious Madame that I won't allow it. I'm not prepared to deal with this."

"You don't have to lie to Sofi, if that's what you're concerned about. If she asks, which she will, just tell her the truth. It's a family heirloom that you've been saving for her sixteenth birthday. She'll be excited to have a piece of jewelry so she won't dig too deep into your answer. It's rightfully hers, Nadja," he said, raising an eyebrow. "Take it."

"Fine."

Nadja placed the locket back in the box and stuffed it in the pocket of her cardigan. "Sofi deserves to have something valuable that's hers. And like you said, it may be useful to her later. She can always sell it."

Before the man could respond he saw a tall, slender female figure in the distance. As she walked up the drive, he realized that it was Sofi home from school. She was deep in thought, so she took no notice of him.

"Ah, there she is! My, she grows taller each time I see her, though I'm not surprised. But by the looks of her, I'd wager she's had a bad day. I shall leave you." He bowed at the waist and tipped his wool cap. "You know how to reach me, Nadja. Au revoir."

He turned gracefully, strode across the yard, and slid into the car.

As the Mercedes sped away, Sofi looked up just in time to watch the elegant vehicle coast by. Wondering why he had come to call, Sofi turned and met the gaze of her mother, who stood motionless amongst the evergreens.

While Nadja appeared to be calm, Sofi thought she saw a hint of tension in her mother's usually smooth brow. Upon closer inspection, it was clear that Nadja was very tense, indeed. A crease tore across the otherwise perfect smoothness of her forehead.

Sofi's concern for her mother pushed her own worries about Avelina's sudden engagement out of her head completely. Her thoughts overflowed with questions about what transpired between her mother and the man in the Mercedes.

Though she never had direct contact with the gadjo who left the property in such a hurry, Sofi knew that he was not a stranger. Years ago, Nadja told Sofi that the man was a French associate of Mr. Laporte's who visited the region periodically throughout the year to scout the availability of certain wildlife that might be of particular interest to hunters. Nadja explained that when Laporte and his wife quit their residence for good, they asked the man to check on the Vadoma's whenever his business brought him to Tervel. At the time, that explanation seemed entirely plausible so she never felt a need to question her mother about the man or his motives. However, the gadjo had not been around for some time, so Sofi wondered what business could have prompted his return. She hoped it had something to do with possible employment for Nadja or the return of the Laporte's to Tervel, though she could not help but feel a sneaking suspicious that they had been arguing.

"What was that all about?" she demanded.

"Nothing. Besides, you shouldn't speak to me in that tone. I'm your mother."

"Mama, something happened," she pressed. "Didn't you tell me that gadjo is an associate of Mr. Laporte? Is Mr. Laporte coming back? Did he find a job for you?"

"No, the Laporte's aren't returning to Tervel."

"Well, what was the man doing here, then? What did he want?"

Nadja had enough of Sofi's questions. She looked at her daughter with such intensity that Sofi was sure her mother's black eyes would burn a hole through her skull.

"All you need to know is that we won't be seeing that gadjo anymore, or anyone else in this wretched village. I've decided we're leaving. We're going to France."

Chapter Eight

Standing at the expansive north windows of the Golden Room, René Arnauld Stefan Hartenau-Hesse surveyed the Winter Gardens. In the few spare moments of solitude he stole from his schedule each day, the President of the French Republic could usually be found here, collecting his thoughts.

Today was a particularly splendid December morning in La Ville Lumièr. The cool azure of the morning sky against the lush green of the Winter Garden's perfectly manicured lawns made for a scrumptious visual feast. Relishing the silence, René's well-built body relaxed and the tension in his temples softened. He focused on the amusing dance of a tiny Blue Tit that was perched atop an orbicular marble fountain. The bird's mate, nestled in one of the intricately trimmed evergreen topiaries that lined the garden's perimeter, jutted out to join her companion.

Élysée Palace was a lively and spectacularly luxurious complex situated near the busy store-lined streets of the Champs-Élysée. Before being designated as the official residence of the French President in 1873, Élysée Palace housed and hosted a long list of prominent historical figures. In the

1750's, King Louis XV's chief mistress, Madame de Pompadour, notoriously called the Palace home until her demise in 1764. Later, it housed both Napoleon Bonaparte and Joséphine de Beauharnais, though separately, as well as guests like Tsar Alexander of Russia and The Duke of Wellington.

While his immediate predecessor fancied the presidential apartments, René preferred to spend as many weekends as possible either at his family's centuries-old estate in nearby Versailles or the official Presidential retreat, Fort de Brégançon. Élysée Palace was hardly quiet enough for René, an intensely private individual who became even more protective of his personal life after the tragic death of his daughter, Rosamonde, just three years ago.

At the time, René was unsure if he and his wife could handle the rigors of the campaign season on top of their intense grief for the loss of their only child. He devastated the French citizenry when he announced his intention to remove his name from the Presidential ballot. No one could convince René to change his mind, not even his one-time mentor, Philippe Roubert, former head of René's political party, Mouvement pour la France Fortifié. Thus, it had appeared by all accounts that the long-awaited frontrunner in the 2007 Presidential elections would withdraw from politics indefinitely.

Unable to accept that their most favored candidate for the most powerful position in France had voluntarily pulled out of the elections due to such sorrowful circumstances, hundreds of thousands of French citizens took to the streets of Paris to show their support of the Hartenau-Hesse family. Their overwhelming display of support

touched the broken heart of First Lady Viviane. She ultimately convinced René to quit his family estate, return to
Paris, and reaffix his name to the ballot. She told René that
Rosamonde would not have wanted her father to abandon
his political aspirations, but rather serve the people of the
country he loved so dearly.

In the end, the young and wildly popular René
Hartenau-Hesse, former Minister of the French Interior and
highest ranking member of the MFF, won the French Presidential elections in a record setting landslide, defeating his
nearest opponent, Jean-Barthélemy Bordieu of the Parti So-
cialiste by over thirty percentage points. Just forty-three at
the time of his inauguration, René also held the distinction
of being France's youngest President since Louis Napoleon
Bonaparte.

The sound of a dozen quick footsteps and noisy
chatter broke René from his fleeting moments of mental
relaxation. He turned around to glance at an ornate clock
that was situated amongst a myriad of other gilded objects,
including two tall candelabras, which flanked either side of
the mantle. They cast a dazzling reflection on the enormous
beveled mirror that dwarfed the fireplace below.

Known for his proclivity for punctuality and strict
adherence to what could most aptly be described as ritualis-
tic scheduling, President Hartenau-Hesse rose at five to welcome each day with an hour of calisthenics with his personal
trainer, a former captain of the French Army. Before le petit
dejeuner with Viviane, René retired to the Presidential suite
to shower and dress. Fastidious in his appearance and aware
that the public took great interest in the fashion choices of
both the President and First Lady, René selected his clothing

with great precision. His usual selection was a well-fitted Hugo Boss suit that became his signature look over the years.

Despite the fact that Hugo Boss cut suits to the perfect proportions of René's imposing frame, his choice initially drew disapproval from the French Fashion Federation, which was shocked by the President's preference for the German fashion house. However, after America's Esquire Magazine named President Hartenau-Hesse "world's best-dressed man of 2007," criticisms of René's style sense cooled significantly.

Once France's Head of State was carefully outfitted, meticulously coifed, and sufficiently nourished, he began his descent to the opulent Golden Room to steal thirty minutes of reflection before delving into his daily briefing and subsequent meeting of the Ministers.

Six men in smart dark suits and bright silk ties filed into the Golden Room like a well-trained brigade ready for battle.

"Seven-forty on the dot," René said approvingly.

"Good morning, Mr. President!" the men said, greeting him in unison. They gathered around a French neoclassical sofa at the edge of the President's office.

"Good morning, gentlemen, and please be seated," René smoothly instructed. "I'll be with you momentarily."

The aides settled in, shuffling their stacks of papers. René looked to the only aide who remained standing and signaled him towards the north facing window. Without a moment's pause, the olive-skinned young man of twenty-six crossed the expansive room to meet his boss of over a decade.

"Yes, Mr. President."

"Isaiah, before we begin, I ask that you run through today's briefing as swiftly as possible," René instructed quietly, not wishing to be overheard.

"Of course, Mr. President. I can get us through the briefing in thirty minutes. I trust that will leave you with sufficient time."

"Yes, Isaiah, that'll do nicely."

"Did I miss something on the agenda?"

"No, no. I've got a matter of particular importance that I must be addressed before the meeting of the Ministers. Your presence is vital."

"Will anyone else be joining us?"

"Yes."

"Okay. May I ask *who* will be joining us?" Isaiah said with a smile, "or is it a surprise?"

"Well….it's Roubert. He insisted we meet."

"Roubert," Isaiah repeated flatly as he tried to keep a straight face.

"Isaiah, this is a delicate matter that I'd like to explore more thoroughly before bringing it to the attention of the Ministers. Roubert has spent many years on this issue, so I want to hear what he has to say."

"Understood. I'll be sure to be on my best behavior," Isaiah promised unenthusiastically with a half smirk. "But you know he irritates me."

René returned the grin, but said nothing. He had Roubert to thank for his quick rise in French politics.

"One more thing. After the briefing, ask Amié to pull the report. You know, the one you showed me last week."

Isaiah nodded, already anticipating the President's request. "Not to worry, Mr. President. I brought it with me."

René smiled at Isaiah and patted him on the shoulder, then turned his attention to the other aides who were by now in the throws of a spirited discussion about a controversial health care plan proposed by America's President-elect.

"Alright, everyone, let's get started."

Isaiah Becerra was the only child of Sephardic Jews with deep roots in Andalusia. His father, David, was an innovative landscape lighting designer from Granada who moved his family to France in the early 1980's after he was commissioned to oversee the "City of Lights Project," a multimillion dollar initiative that spanned over a decade and sought to bring nighttime illumination to over three hundred of Lyon's most historic buildings and monuments.

Blessed with a gifted mind and an IQ of 154, Isaiah received his baccalaureate at age twelve and enrolled in René's alma mater, Pantheon-Assas, soon thereafter. His academic achievements and youthful presence made him a well-known figure, not only amongst the university's faculty but throughout France's intellectual enclaves. Isaiah soon rose to the top of his class, notably graduating with an advanced degree in Political Philosophy at just sixteen years old.

Upon graduation, he served as a consultant with the MFF. It was not long before the young aide gained René's trust and admiration for his sound mind, solid morals, and critical thinking abilities. Soon, René requested that Isaiah be assigned to his political campaign for député of the French National Assembly. At the ripe age of nineteen, Isaiah was named as René's top political strategist, becoming a permanent fixture throughout René's ascent through politics.

Over the years, the two political standouts developed a strong friendship, which was strengthened after the death of Rosamonde. With the exceptions of his wife, Viviane, and Absolon, his family's most trusted servant who looked after René's mother, Amalie, at the family's estate in Bulgaria, there was no one that René trusted more than Isaiah.

After René was briefed on the most pressing matters of the day, the aides were dismissed, leaving Isaiah and René with some time before Philippe Roubert's arrival.

"René, how are you doing today?" Isaiah asked carefully.

"Ah, Isaiah, it's been a difficult week," René confessed. "It's hard to believe that tomorrow is already three years since the accident." He stared out the window, twisting a large gold and sapphire ring of his family crest.

"You know, it's strange," he continued. "With each year that goes by, it becomes more and more difficult to remember the sound of her little voice. I find myself wondering what she would look like today. How she would have flourished. She seems to drift farther from me each year." René shook his head and looked down. "I was always a selfish and obstinate sort of person, but all that changed when Rosamonde was born. She was our miracle."

Isaiah nodded, thinking back to the numerous miscarriages Viviane suffered before becoming pregnant with Rosamonde.

"I remember the day Rosamonde was born," Isaiah said. "It was a sunny and cold morning, much like today.

When I got to the hospital and saw you looking down at her, I knew you'd changed."

"That's for sure…"

"Rosamonde did you a world of good, René." Isaiah chuckled and patted him on the back.

"You're right, Isaiah. I was never the same after she came into our lives. I think Viviane liked it that way."

"Well, look what the poor woman had to work with before!" Isaiah joked. "You used to be such a bastard."

"Don't I know it. My wife is a saint! Thank God for her. And thank you for taking the time to remember my daughter with me. I think everyone else here is too afraid to even utter her name—like I'll jump down their throats if they even mention her."

"You're an intimidating fellow, sir."

"Oh, come on, Isaiah. I'm not that bad."

"No….not *that* bad."

The two men shared a laugh, though it was peppered with melancholy.

"I know that the pain will always be there—it's simply unnatural to outlive your child—but I can't pretend that she never existed. Talking about her makes me remember the good times. I don't ever want to forget that."

"Of course, René. You know everyone loved her. I think of her all the time. She'll never be forgotten. I can promise you that."

They were awkwardly interrupted by the nervous voice of René's receptionist, Amié, as it ripped through the speaker system.

"Excusez-moi, Mr. President. Monsieur Roubert is here to see you now. I asked him to wait, but he's walking down the hallway this very minute. I'm so sorry."

"That's fine, thank you, Amié."

René was accustomed to his uptight old mentor, who had become more irritable ever since his wife, Hillarie, passed away several years ago.

"Oh, Amié, don't forget. This is a closed-door meeting so we mustn't be disturbed unless it's absolutely necessary."

"Of course, Mr. President."

René turned his attention back to his trusted friend.

"Isaiah, would you please open the doors for Roubert? You know they're too heavy for him."

René could already picture Roubert cursing loudly while struggling with the substantial floor to ceiling doors.

Isaiah begrudgingly rose from his comfortable seat, trudged over to the heavy gilded doors of the Golden Room, and pushed them open at the very same time Roubert reached them.

With his permanently bent posture and perpetually crotchety attitude, Philippe Roubert appeared to be even older than his biological age of eighty-two. However, despite his deteriorating health and weak exterior, no one, not even Isaiah, could deny that Roubert's mind was as sharp as ever. His ability to analyze policy trends and perceive emerging national security concerns remained as polished as it did nearly thirty years ago when he sought the French presidency but lost to Socialist candidate Claude Bensimon.

Without so much as acknowledging Isaiah's presence, the considerably aged and crag-faced Roubert petulantly shuffled into the office, beating his cane against the marble floor.

"Ah, René! We need to talk."

Roubert's once strong voice had become low and very hoarse after suffering from chronic laryngitis, a condition he developed in his advanced age from fifty years of habitual cigar smoking. Consequently, each time Roubert attempted to raise his voice, which was quite often depending on the topic of discussion, the invariable result was a maladroit shriek and an inhuman-like gurgle followed by the uncomfortable pause that Roubert took to collect himself before proceeding with his rant of the day.

"I see your people were benevolent enough to fit the old man into your schedule. You will soon understand why this could not wait, I assure you."

With that, the elderly statesman hobbled to the nearest armchair and plopped down, breathless.

Isaiah could not help but stare incredulously as Roubert opened his left breast pocket and nonchalantly pulled out a Romeo y Julieta cigar, Winston Churchill's favorite, which had clearly been extinguished only a few minutes prior. After relighting the tip and taking in several deep puffs, Roubert tilted his head and gazed at the carcinogen with the deepest admiration, his lips curling into a satisfied grin.

It was not before until an uncontrollable, hacking, and very disgusting cough from deep within his chest interrupted his ecstasy. When the sputtering finally subsided, Roubert wiped his mouth with his unoccupied hand and motioned to Isaiah, who stood gaping at the irony and complete idiocy of the entire scene.

"You! Get me some wine." Roubert waved his hand irritably at Isaiah, who responded with an exaggerated eye roll.

"Really, sir, it's nine in the morning. Amié can bring you some tea, or perhaps juice, instead."

Isaiah turned his back to Roubert and looked imploringly to the ceiling, already exasperated with the antics of the cantankerous politician. René, on the other hand, smiled broadly, barely holding in a guffaw. It was a good thing that the old man's cataract surgery had been rescheduled for next month or else Roubert would have observed Isaiah's animated reaction.

"Fine, I don't care. Just bring me something and make it snappy." Remembering his companion, the cigar, Roubert took another long puff and held it in his mouth for what seemed to be an eternity before shouting out again.

"Hey you, Spaniard! Come back over here. You're supposed to be an aide, right? Well, start aiding your President. We have an important matter to discuss."

Chapter Nine

Philippe Roubert carelessly brushed little mounds of cigar ash that gathered on his Burberry dress shirt onto the silk rug. After straightening his sport jacket to the best of his ability, he strained to reach for his African rosewood cane and nearly fell out of his seat.

Seeing that his old mentor was clearly struggling, René picked it up easily and placed it on top of the glass coffee table. After acknowledging his protégé turned President with a quick nod, Roubert placed his feet squarely on the floor and adjusted himself to a somewhat more upright position.

In preparation for his well-rehearsed speech, Roubert puffed rhythmically on the same Cuban cigar that precipitated his bronchial attack minutes earlier. He slowly savored each inhalation, allowing the tobacco-filled smoke to seep into his mouth and nostrils. Isaiah stirred in his seat impatiently and looked at his watch.

"We only have thirty minutes before our next meeting, Mr. Roubert," Isaiah reminded.

"Fine," Roubert sneered, giving his young counterpart a condescending look. "I'm ready to begin."

"Then, sir, if you please."

"As I indicted in September's report, an imminent national security risk is upon us. We're not talking about Al-Qaeda or another emerging Islamic extremist group, although we're aware that they've got sleeper cells here in France. But of course, that's a topic for another discussion.

Mr. President, the danger I intend to bring to your attention originates from a different source—one that I've tracked for many years and long before you entered politics. Twenty years ago, when the threat first presented itself, I was confident that it would be resolved quickly and that it wouldn't even come close to infiltrating our borders. But I was wrong. Today, we see that the threat has grown.

In the nineties, we observed a slow yet steady increase in the numbers of undocumented individuals from Eastern Europe and northern Africa who descended upon our country in droves and began to set up makeshift camps outside our major cities. Not so coincidentally, during this same period of time, increased numbers of Islamists left the Middle East to take up residence in France. The result has been a marked societal shift; Islam is now the second most practiced religion here in France, preceded only by Catholicism. There have since been numerous attempts by these new residents to change the fabric of our culture. Under your leadership, Mr. President, France made powerful moves to fight this infiltration. Your words, actions, and policies have sent a clear message both here and abroad that France is a nation historically rooted in Western values. And, despite the fact that outsiders are accepted here, they cannot and will not change our way of life."

René thought back to the anxiety he felt just before his first globally reported press conference that occurred shortly after he entered office. During that speech, he welcomed Muslims to France as new residents of the European Union but warned them not to provoke the general public with ideologically-rooted demands that could impinge upon traditional French society. Following his speech, René made a somewhat controversial decision to push what became known as "anti-burqa legislation," which prohibited women from completely covering their faces in public and in pictures used on state-issued identification cards. While hotly debated amongst international human rights organizations as well as the leaders of EU member states, French citizens widely supported the measure.

"Though many member states, like France, are becoming more Eurocentric, others have forgotten what it means to protect what is uniquely theirs," Roubert continued. "Fortunately, nationalism is certainly alive and well in France. It is what the people want and it is what our country needs in order to remain safe and secure."

"So what are you getting at here, Roubert?" Isaiah interjected. "I know you didn't call this meeting to give us a history lesson. Thus far, you've presented us with no new information."

"I believe you came here today to present an addendum to September's report, isn't that right?" René gently tried to move Roubert along. "We've been waiting anxiously for this information."

"Thank you, René. And just as a warning to your impatient aide here, I must provide you with a short explanation of some recent history from one of our neighboring member states so you can draw the necessary correlation between our mutual problems. I'm sure we've not yet run short on time?"

"We still have plenty of time. I've instructed Amié as to the confidential nature of this meeting so we shan't be interrupted. If you please, Mr. Roubert. Go on."

"Thank you, Mr. President." Roubert nodded deeply to René, then looked at Isaiah triumphantly. Isaiah met his gaze with a deep frown, which Roubert ignored.

"Of course, you are both aware of the tendentious, yet effective, policy that Italy adopted last year to combat their problems with border jumpers. For his entire term, Prime Minister Puccilli has been hit from nearly every direction with hundreds of thousands of undocumented, unidentified migrants. First, they came from Africa and nearly sank Sicily, though the Africans proved to be ambitious and eventually contributed positively to the Italian economy. But more recently, the Italians were forced to deal with a different sort of immigrant—the Gypsy. These nomads flocked to Italy for no other purpose but to reap the benefits of their social welfare programs. Last year, the official number of Gypsies who entered Italy was 175,000, and that only accounts for those that the Italian government could document. It nearly bankrupted the country! So, what did Puccilli do?"

"Italy revised its immigration laws, of course," Isaiah said, jumping in to answer Roubert's intended rhetorical question. "Some critics argued that their new laws were created as a direct response to their growing Roma population. But the Italians managed to amend the law in such a way that didn't blatantly target them. I believe they accomplished this by utilizing their already existing criminal code to strengthen their deportation policies. For example, everybody knows the Roma use their children for panhandling and petty thefts—the revised code calls for severe penalties for adults who force children to commit crimes. Incidentally, I believe that Finland is considering a similar measure."

Isaiah paused dramatically and looked to René. "However, I already know where Roubert's going with this. I believe it would be premature to compare our situation with that of Italy. Our Roma population is far fewer. We have the situation under control. In fact, Roubert's September report substantiates that."

"You bring me precisely to my point, Mr. *Becerra.*" Roubert exaggerated the Spanish pronunciation of Isaiah's last name, annoyed that his loquacious flow was interrupted. "We've got the same problems, and I can prove that you are quite mistaken as to the scope and scale."

As if out of thin air, Roubert produced a thick, bound report and waved it at Isaiah. "The numbers are in and they are staggering. Truly staggering! According to these projections, the number of Gypsies that are settling into camps outside of Paris, Marseilles, and Lyon will reach the 150,000 mark in less than six months if we don't act. And that's not all. They are going to bankrupt us faster than anyone could have ever anticipated."

René and Isaiah looked at Roubert quizzically.

"See for yourself."

Roubert politely handed a copy of the report to René and threw another across the coffee table in Isaiah's general direction.

"Page seventeen, si vous plait. The numbers are quite astounding, non? Keep in mind that these figures are based on the number of people we can actually account for. Undoubtedly, there's thousands more that fly under our radar."

"These statistics are troubling," René remarked.

"If you turn to the next page, you can see how many taxpayer dollars are being spent to feed, clothe, and hospitalize them, particularly their offspring. The Gypsies are targeting France because they can show up here and seamlessly enroll into our social programs. Many of the Gypsies we interviewed said that they came here for their children to be educated—a noble reason but unfairly burdensome for our citizens. They're also working without permits. If the costs continue at this rate, it's going to cause a significant dent in our surplus, which we need to maintain since so many of the other member states are carrying such high deficits. Not only that, we are in the midst of a worldwide economic crisis. Europe won't come out of this unscathed. Take for example the Greeks—those fools. They are about to completely tank any year now, mark my words. The Irish will follow. And then what is the EU going to do? Borrow from China like the Americans do? Bah! René, I hope your aide here knows better than to think that France is immune to this impending economic catastrophe."

"Mr. Roubert, I'm sure you remember that Mr. Becerra has a particular expertise in political economics. He and his team have been tracking the American real estate market and investment climate for some time. We believe Wall Street will tank any day now. So yes, it's vital that our surplus be maintained."

"I'm relieved to hear that we're all on the same page," Roubert replied. Aware that the kicker of his presentation was coming soon, he forged on.

"These Gypsies bring other problems with them. Let's turn to page forty. You've already read in September's report that the Gypsies live in makeshift camps on land owned by the federal government. These camps are a breeding ground for countless crimes, not to mention disease. As you can see, crimes in and around Paris committed by Roma have increased by over 140 percent from late 2007 to present. And it's not just muggings and pickpocketing. We learned last month that one of the world's most wanted heroin smugglers and human traffickers, Arthit Domaphong, leader of Thailand's Green Dragon Triad Gang, entered France through Charles de Gaulle, completely undetected. He was accompanied by fifteen Thai prostitutes. After the girls were dropped at one of the clubs here in Paris, he rented a car and visited a large Gypsy camp outside of Grenoble. We believe he stayed approximately three days and ultimately returned to the Golden Triangle by way of Italy with several Romanian Gypsy women."

René stared at the addendum, obviously angry. "How did you learn of this? I've never seen any of this in the DGSE reports."

"The Direction Générale de la Sécurité Extérieure is not going to be helpful with this matter. Their concern lies with security threats from the Middle East. If you recall, I initially provided September's report to DGSE, but Director Salazar dismissed it, which is why I then brought it directly to you," Roubert reminded. "But listen, René, you know I've tracked these Gypsies for decades and I warned you about them for years. Don't think that I haven't noticed your seemingly continuous resistance to my guidance on this matter. Of course, I understand why…"

Roubert glanced at Isaiah in an effort to determine the extent of his knowledge about René's past. Judging from the unchanged expression on the young man's face, Roubert ascertained that he was still in the dark.

"After our last meeting, I got the impression that it was going to take some more convincing for you to be on board with my policy recommendations. So, I commissioned private American security contractors to observe all of the dealings inside some of the major Gypsy camps around Paris. I know what's happening out there. This report provides you with reliable numbers on how many of those people are coming in and not leaving. I can assure you, René, we've only touched the tip of the iceberg with September's report. The rest is detailed in this addendum."

"We've got limited time here, Roubert, so let's get to it then, shall we? Isaiah had quite enough of Roubert's rhetoric.

"I thought you'd never ask, Becerra." Roubert winked at Isaiah, which infuriated the younger of the two.

"It's time to face the facts. Among other things, this addendum provides evidence of terrorist cells living amongst the Roma. Blending in with the Gypsies enables them up to set up shop without attracting attention. These Gypsies are so stupid, easily fooled into thinking that any dark-skinned wanderer who speaks Romani is one of their own. It's the perfect scheme—terrorists using ignorant nomads to harbor them and help disguise their vicious plans. On top of that, we've documented rampant disease throughout these communities and three times the births per Roma woman as compared to our own French citizens. We are open to a public health crisis if we don't act soon. And, since the Gypsies refuse to go to the hospital unless it is an absolute necessity, the costs to treat them are very high."

"That's a lot to take in."

"Perhaps most telling, Mr. President, is that the French people have simply had enough. Gypsies don't assimilate to the country in which they live. They will have a major hand in our ruin! These populations have ways of life that vastly differ from our society and conflict with our ideals. The citizens we've canvassed are afraid to walk down the street for fear of being accosted by Gypsy children who pull at their pockets, Gypsy teenagers who mug them, and worse! We've got to get a handle on this now. The sooner the better. Now's the time for France to endorse strong criminal and immigration crackdowns. René, your administration must send a message to the Roma, just as you did to the Islamists, that our country will not tolerate their behavior. France will not bend over and allow them to overrun our nation! You have the precedence of Italy's recently enacted legislation, the overwhelming support of the public, and soon, you will have the backing of the National Assembly. I can promise you that."

"So what exactly do you propose?"

"First, get the police to systematically raid and dismantle the camps and ship these people back to where they came from. This problem should not be ours to handle. Romania and Bulgaria need to take responsibility, since most of these Gypsies originate from their nations. The reason why these populations come here in the first place is because their home countries lack the necessary programs to feed and educate them. The social welfare model under President Bensimon opened the door to this. But we know that the French public is beginning to resist the once-popular Socialist model. Consider how they completely rejected Bordeiu."

Roubert snickered as he thought back to the day his protégé annihilated his Socialist opponent in the general election, receiving an unprecedented seventy percent of the vote.

"Roubert, the will of the French people is imperative, of course," René said, "but we must look at this from a legal standpoint and be ready for widespread opposition. Now that Bulgaria and Romania are part of the European Union, nationals of those countries, including the Roma, are free to travel throughout the EU and stay here in France for three continuous months before they're required to show the purpose for their presence. For that reason, we can't simply burst into the camps and send them home."

"These people are highly transient and move from camp to camp. More and more infiltrate our borders every day. By nature and culture they do not make ties with the outside world. Again, I must impress upon you that they refuse to assimilate to the nation in which they live. It is imperative that we move on this quickly," Roubert warned.

"I understand your sense of urgency, but now that Bulgaria and Romania are part of the bloc, these same individuals cannot be prevented from returning here in the future. They are free to turn around and come back again."

"Mr. President is exactly correct, of course," Isaiah interjected. "On top of that, we can't categorically target the Roma population. It will be in violation of the free movement of persons, which is a guaranteed, fundamental right of the Treaties of the European Union."

"Do you think I've not thought of that?" Roubert responded agitatedly. "Here's what I propose. Present this to the Assembly as a multifaceted approach to combat rampant crime, curb illegal immigration, and preserve national security. We must protect our citizens from the street crimes they face on a day to day basis from these Gypsies. We must also ensure that people who come from Eastern bloc states are properly documented to both live and work here. Most importantly, we have evidence that Islamic terrorists have tested Gypsy camps to use as hideouts to prepare for their attacks. There's enough evidence in that report to support a policy proposal from a national security position alone!"

"Similar arguments have been made by other member states," Isaiah conceded. "Even the Americans share similar concerns in their dealings with Mexican and Central American immigrant influx. Of course, Finland, Italy, and Switzerland have already acted on this matter with success. But we cannot present the legislation in a way that targets the Roma."

"Exactly, Becerra. No doubt those countries will support us, which will bolster our position in the Assembly. Mr. President, we must be strong in showing this population, and the rest of the EU, that France will not be Eastern Europe's doormat."

"Mr. Roubert, you've made a persuasive argument. I'd like to conduct some additional research of my own, but I can promise you that Mr. Becerra and I will review this addendum in great detail and we will be in touch with you very soon. I appreciate your efforts regarding this matter."

René extended his hand to Roubert, who shook it gruffly, then used it to help himself from the armchair.

"I've told you before and I'll tell you again—nothing is more important than the security of our nation. It's what our party stands for, René. It's part of who I am."

"I understand. Thank you for your service, Mr. Roubert. And please give us an update on your health next week. Your procedure is Tuesday, right?"

Roubert grimaced as he thought of his impending cataract procedure. "Yes, yes. I'll be back on my feet in no time. These doctors today are so damn cocky. They tell me I'll be better by week's end, but we'll just have to see about that." Roubert continued to grumble while he gathered his things. "Keep up the good work, Mr. President. And give my regards to your mother and Viviane."

René and Isaiah watched as Roubert turned his back to them and loudly shuffled out of the office, banging his wooden cane against the marble floor and yelling some sort of complaint down the hall to Amié.

"Roubert has a point, but I don't trust him, René. Never did."

"I know, Isaiah, but in twenty years, he's never once led me astray."

"Whatever you say, Mr. President," Isaiah said, shrugging his shoulders. "Well, if your administration was to implement a closed immigration policy, now would be the appropriate time. However, I'm not convinced that Roubert's plan will comply with the Directive on the Free Movement of EU citizens. That's already been in place for five years, for goodness sake."

"Is that your only objection?"

"This subject...it doesn't sit well with me, René. To be sure, it will be popular with many of the people, but not amongst the EU as a whole, and certainly not with those in the human rights community. We'll get killed in the press."

"Isaiah, if we decide to proceed with Roubert's proposal to mirror Italy's so-called 'expulsion laws,' we must be prepared for a challenge from the European Commission. It's imperative that we prepare our arguments ahead of time to illustrate that the laws are, indeed, in compliance with established European Union law. Apart from that, I don't see a problem. Our primary concern is the French citizenry. The international human rights community has got to take a back seat."

René could already envision a complete piece of brilliant legislation that dazzled the people of France. The opinions of international media outlets were the least of his concerns.

"Isaiah, I want your team to draft a proposal for the MFF assembly members along with a timeline for projected ratification. We'll also need to make sure that the Minister of Immigration and Nationalism is on board with this. Make sure they're clear that it must be framed as a immigration policy to curb crime and potential terror attacks and not a plan aimed specifically at any one group. Again, try to use Italy's recently enacted legislation as precedence. And see if we can't pull Ms. Cotillion in on this for the more technical legal aspects. She's a great resource."

Isaiah usually enjoyed teaming with Marie Cotillion, an Élysée Palace attorney and the Administration's resident expert on immigration law, but he was not looking forward to working on this particular initiative, which was apparently to begin sooner than he originally thought.

"Isaiah, we must also be ready for Granger," René continued. "He won't take this lying down. You know he's a Socialist wolf disguised in conservative clothing."

Isaiah was all-too-familiar with Edouard Granger's opposition to just about every initiative of President Hartenau-Hesse. The Minister of Foreign Affairs was a remnant of the previous administration. Just two years ago, he did a terrific job convincing René that he would be loyal to the MFF despite any past differences. At the time, Granger assured René that as a 'slightly left-leaning centrist,' his presence as a key member of René's cabinet would serve a shining example of cooperation for the National Assembly and Senate, who were, at the time, in the throws of divisive political gridlock.

Almost immediately after René took office, Granger's true intentions were made apparent. Again and again, he thwarted the more conservative, nationalistic policies of René's administration and questioned every measure initiated by the President himself, regardless of the nature of the proposal or where it sat on the political spectrum. Moreover, Isaiah suspected Granger of leaking certain information about René's past relationship with an American Oscar-winning actress to the media in an effort to damage René's reputation. Fortunately it backfired, making René more popular than ever.

While his actions were not enough to block René's policy reforms completely, Granger's constant opposition certainly caused a lot of controversy amongst the Ministers. René had plans to replace Granger should he win reelection in 2012, but that was three years away. Some of René's advisors, including Isaiah, counseled him to enlist the help of the Prime Minister in order to remove Granger before the end of René's five year term. René resisted this advice.

"Of course, sir, I'm always mindful of Granger. But, if I may, Mr. President, I still believe that your decision to keep him in your Cabinet is overly cautious. Your approval ratings are some of the highest in the history of the French Presidency. I don't believe they would falter with the ousting of Granger."

"Isaiah, I understand your position and I realize that at first blush, it would appear to be the easiest solution for us all. However, while I accept that no President will be able to please every citizen of France in every aspect of his presidency, I still wish to keep the people as satisfied as possible. The Socialist Party is still strong. I don't want them coming down on us. It'll cost us later down the road."

"In that case, I'll prepare a separate statement for Granger. And, if you're positive that you wish to proceed in the manner Roubert suggested, I can make the necessary calls this evening; although, if may be best to slow this down. I, for one, would like to read the addendum in greater detail and conduct some independent research of my own, as you suggested to Roubert not ten minutes ago. We've got to substantiate his findings. I still have doubts."

"Alright, Isaiah, I agree. I'm moving too quickly. Contact Ms. Cotillion and perform your due diligence. I'd like a full report next week when Viviane and I return from Lyon. Then we can decide *if* we will present this to the Ministers."

"Very good, sir."

Isaiah was relieved. He hoped to prove to the President that a small subset of a politically powerless ethnic minority was not as ominous a national security threat as Roubert would wish them to believe.

Chapter Ten

LYON, FRANCE

The First Lady of the French Republic stepped into the brisk night air to admire the splendor of Place des Terreaux. The bright amber lights of the cheerfully lit square filtered through the long, private balcony's ornately carved stone railings, filling the sumptuous hotel suite with a soft, luminescent glow. Positioned in the very heart of Lyon's Pres-qu'ile and overlooking the expansive Place des Terreaux, the four thousand square foot penthouse presidential suite of the Royal Renaissance Hotel was the perfect location for President Hartenau-Hesse and First Lady Viviane to take in Lyon's annual Festival of Lights.

Standing on the chilly balcony, Viviane paid little attention to the tall frame of her constant companion, an intimidatingly built secret security agent named Marcel who quietly followed her, then disappeared into the shadows. She listened to the confident, booming voice of her husband, the President. His welcoming address was followed by the loud cheers of thousands that gathered in Lyon to witness one of the most spectacular and famous lighting display in all of Europe.

With René presently occupied in the square below and no one else nearby except for the silent and ever-present Marcel, she allowed her thoughts to drift away to one of the happiest times of her life that took place on this very balcony; her final trip to Lyon with her daughter.

The Festival of Lights had always been the Hartenau-Hesse family's favorite event of the year. Each December and without fail, the trio visited Lyon on the night of France's commemoration of the Immaculate Conception of the Virgin Mary to take in the dream-like light displays of the Festival, which showcased Lyon's most fascinating and detailed sculptures, fountains, historic buildings and neighborhoods.

Painstakingly planned and systematically timed lighting installations could be found throughout the city, particularly in and around the town's two main squares, Place des Terreaux and Place Bellecour. Tonight, the President and First Lady had the best view in town for one of the most exciting and highly anticipated light shows in the country. The display would be centered on La Fontaine Bartholdi, a famous stone fountain crafted by famed French sculptor Frédéric-Auguste Bartholdi shortly after he designed the Statue of Liberty for the United States.

Rosamonde loved the beauty and wonder of the lights more than anyone. Each year, she could be found standing on her toes, wrapped warmly in her favorite, furry pink blanket and peering over the balcony's edge to look the crowds of people who excitedly gathered in the middle of the square. Instead of focusing on the light show, Viviane would marvel at how the warm glow of the illuminated square formed a golden halo around her daughter's chestnut curls.

After Rosamonde's death, Viviane could not bring herself to attend the Festival. She feared that partaking in their once treasured family tradition without her little angel would bring too much pain for her to bear. When the mayor of Lyon received word about the tragic death of the President-elect's young daughter, the city decreed that it would dedicate one of its spectacular light displays to Rosamonde each year. Of course, in light of such a moving and meaningful gesture, Viviane could not be kept away. She soon realized that this was a way to honor Rosamonde and preserve her memory. This year, the light display at La Fontaine Bartholdi was named "La Hommage de la Petite Fleur, Rosamonde."

Viviane's greatest comfort through her grief was the companionship and love of her husband, whom she had known literally all her life. The two were playmates from birth because their mothers were best friends.

A meek child, Viviane idolized René, her polar opposite. Confident and outgoing, he was her friend and protector who frequently stood up for her against the bullies she encountered at their private primary school in Paris. As they entered adolescence, Viviane's admiration for René turned into a crush, but she was too shy to ever reveal her feelings. Silently she suffered as René dated other classmates yet came to her for girlfriend advice.

Throughout their school years, she remained his steady confidant in matters of the heart and listened to him patiently as he vented the frustrations he felt towards his father as he was pushed into politics. After baccalaureate,

René remained in Paris to study at Assas while Viviane left for Switzerland to study international relations at the prestigious University of Geneva, where she developed a strong interest in humanitarian causes.

Upon graduation, she accepted an internship position with the International Committee of the Red Cross at their Geneva headquarters. While there, she authored an important and widely-circulated report on the hurdles faced by women in areas of armed conflict, which she ultimately presented to the United Nations Security Council in the spring of 1992. At the same time, René was overseas completing his LL.M. at Yale University Law School.

With thousands of miles separating the two and plenty of work aspirations to keep them thoroughly occupied, Viviane and René did not see or speak to each other for some time. It was not until Christmas Eve 1994 when the pair reunited. Viviane had recently accepted a position as a member of the Paris delegation of the Red Cross working to integrate international humanitarian law into national legislation. René had just finished the last leg of his academic career, a final year of study in Paris before his jump into politics. Both eager, ambitious, and ready to take on the problems of the world, they had much to discuss.

René was instantly drawn to the passion and vigor of his once shy and somewhat awkward childhood friend. He also longed for companionship after suffering from a love affair gone wrong two years prior. After spending nearly every day together, they married the following year, each at the age of thirty.

Three years later, they tried for a baby, but ran into great difficulty. Viviane suffered four miscarriages in two years. Eventually, they learned that she would likely be unable to carry a child to term due to complications of a bicornuate uterus. After giving up hope, the couple was shocked when Viviane became pregnant in 1999 and was able to carry the child for eight of the nine months of pregnancy. Thus, after years of heartbreak and disappointment, René and Viviane finally welcomed their tiny miracle into the world on January 1, 2000.

With René's steady rise in politics, the Hartenau-Hesse family soon became one of the most popular political families in France. Rosamonde, a precocious child with curly dark hair, blue-gray eyes and round, pink cheeks was a favorite among the French. Photographs of the young politician's seemingly perfect child and his willowy, chic, and intellectual wife began to appear in magazines and newspapers across Europe. It was not long before politicians, pundits, and the European public proclaimed the young Hartenau-Hesse family, led by the dynamic and striking René, as France's next "First Family." They were often likened to John F. Kennedy Jr. and Jacquelyn.

"Life was truly perfect," Viviane whispered.

She gazed down at the exquisitely lit Place des Terreaux and marveled at its beauty, the same beauty that once kept her daughter captivated for hours. Golden and amber lights danced off the water of La Fontaine Bartholdi while a bluish green glow radiated up to the very tops of the historic Hotel de Ville de Lyon and the Museum of Fine Arts. Higher in the distance, the narrow, sloping streets of La Croix-Rousse Hill were transformed into a brilliant maze of lights and merriment.

The sounds of heels on marble broke Viviane's bittersweet reminiscing. She easily recognized the familiar rhythm of the strides.

René soon appeared and made his way towards his wife. He wrapped his long arms around her narrow waist and greeted her with a kiss.

"Hello, my love."

Though Viviane responded with a smile, René could immediately sense that she had been thinking about Rosamonde.

Instead of questioning his wife or attempting to console her, he knew it was best to maintain a happy and positive mood. He pretended not to notice her sadness and instead attempted to turn her focus to the present.

"Where is your coat, silly wife? It's very chilly outside. I think I see a little icicle on your nose." He squeezed Viviane tighter and teasingly rubbed his warm face over her icy cold one.

It was only with René's mention of the cold that Viviane felt the December air pass through her silk shirt and trousers, causing little goose bumps to appear across her exposed collarbone. She shivered involuntarily. René grinned, kissed her neck, and encouraged her to go inside.

"Let's have a glass of Clicquot. We still have a few minutes until the light show begins, and the lead engineer promised it's going to be spectacular. Then we can get you bundled up properly before we come back out here to watch. I know you didn't bring that fur along as a pet." René's eyes drifted to a luxurious gray chinchilla coat that was strewn across a chaise.

Viviane's countenance was full of love as she looked up at her husband, who tried so hard to please her.

"Of course, my dear, that sounds like a wonderful idea. And you're right. I was crazy to come out here in just this." Viviane looked down at her champagne colored silk pants suit and shrugged her shoulders. "Whatever was I thinking?"

The two laughed blithely while looking into each other's faces, then walked arm in arm through the French doors. They took a comfortable seat on the Louis XVI sofa positioned in front of a glorious double-sided fireplace in the center of the room. Viviane kicked off her Louboutin heels and rubbed her feet back and forth on the rich Savonnerie rug beneath her.

"Ah, René, I'm really enjoying our time here in Lyon."

"So am I. Things will be so hectic when we get back."

Viviane nodded. After being married to a career politician for thirteen years, she knew that the days immediately preceding Parliamentary recesses were frantically busy.

"But remember, darling, Christmas will be here before we know it."

"It can't come soon enough. And now, on top of everything else we've got going on, I have to get a handle on an issue Roubert brought to my attention."

"Roubert? Really, René, hasn't he retired?"

"You'd think he'd hang it up by now, but no."

"That's a surprise to me. The last time I saw him, he was in terrible shape. He could barely speak three sentences before breaking into a coughing fit! I suggested he see a doctor…though I distinctly remember he was none too pleased with my unsolicited advice. But that's typical Roubert, am I right?"

"He definitely prefers to be the advisor and not the advisee," René responded, chuckling lightly. "You would not believe how hard it was for me to convince him to see that ophthalmologist. The man could not see past his own hand! But yes, my dear, you are absolutely right. Physically, he is weak. His mind, on the other hand, is still quite strong. Perhaps sharper than ever. You would not believe the report he presented last week."

"Report? Should I even ask?"

"Ha—do you really want to know?"

"That bad?"

"Oh yes."

René shook his head. The mere thought of the information contained in Roubert's report caused his temples to throb.

"So Roubert and his people managed to obtain intelligence that the DGSE didn't even have. Reports of human trafficking, drug smuggling, and the spread of disease in and around those horrible Gypsy camps throughout Paris."

"Are you quite serious? How did he manage to get his hands on that information?"

Viviane took a breath before answering her own question. "He's got people watching the camps, I'm sure of it. He's always been obsessed with those people. It's incredibly odd. I could never understand it. René, you must have some idea why he feels so strongly about them?"

René sighed deeply and took a large swig of champagne.

"I can't be sure. Many years ago, he cautioned me in no uncertain terms about the ways and predilections of the Roma people. He's never once been able to convince me to come on board with his line of thinking, but I must admit that his last report was persuasive and...unsettling. He outlined a somewhat extreme policy recommendation. Under normal circumstances I would've dismissed it. But in light of the information I received, I've got to consider his position seriously. Isaiah is working with Marie Cotillion on the specifics now."

"Well, well, well...what's this really about, I wonder?" Viviane was part annoyed, part intrigued as to what could possibly be contained in Roubert's report. "With Roubert's involvement I can only assume it has something to do with national security, which is obviously vital. But what can be so threatening about the Roma that would cause you to consider a course of action you would otherwise reject?"

"He presented us with credible information that the growing Roma population here in France is a national security threat."

"You mean to say that the Gypsies are joining terrorist groups? If so, that's absurd."

"No, nothing like that, Viviane. It's more a series of occurrences and trends among the Roma people that, when combined, put great pressure on our society, the economy, national security, heck, even public health. It's not any calculated actions on the part of the Roma. Let's just say it has more to do with the unintended effects their culture has placed upon our French society."

"I don't understand, René."

"I didn't either. That is, until we received Roubert's last report. It's quite alarming. But I really don't want to talk about this now. I'm sure we'll be sick to death of discussing this in the next few weeks."

"Roubert's pushing his agenda hard, huh?"

"Doesn't he always?"

"He never takes a break."

"I should cut him some slack, though. Frankly, given what I've read, I don't blame him this time. Bottom line is that if his information checks out, we'll be moving some controversial legislation through the Parliament after the New Year. So get ready."

"Well, don't let him try to strong arm you into anything you don't feel complete conviction about. Roubert has his own agenda. And he's a shrewd politician, to be sure. But you know I share Isaiah's reservations about him."

"Thank you, my dear, and believe me, I understand your concerns. But, Roubert's report cannot be ignored. This issue will be one of my top priorities for the next few weeks. Probably months."

"Very well, René. Of course, if there's anything I can help with…"

"Darling, remember, you've got to prepare for your trip to Senegal."

Viviane smiled broadly when she thought about returning to Africa. She felt a strong connection to the Continent ever since her first visit to Kenya during her internship with the Red Cross. Though it pained her each time she and René were apart, which was rather frequent since he became

President, she was nonetheless very much looking forward to her upcoming visit to the Republic of Senegal.

During what was sure to be a whirlwind tour, Viviane was to first meet with Senegalese National Assembly leaders in Dakar to discuss proposed anti-human trafficking legislation. If passed, the legislation would serve as a model for other African nations hoping to implement similar laws and restrictions. She was then to preside over an event sponsored by the Red Cross to recognize the great success Senegal made over the past decade to contain and prevent the spread of AIDS and HIV in their nation. The First Lady's tour was to conclude in grand fashion with a state dinner honoring female Senegalese human rights leaders who worked to free child laborers and sex slaves.

"You will be greatly missed, my dear, but you have very important work to do. And just think. When you return, Christmas will be here and I'll hopefully have a handle on this issue with Roubert and the Roma. Then we can take off for Versailles and have a few days of peace."

A smirk slowly crept across René's face as he thought about the upcoming holiday season.

"You know, I'm actually looking forward to seeing your mother."

"Oh really? Is that because Amalie will also be with us?"

Viviane knew that her husband always got a kick out of watching the two former French opera singers gossip, giggle, and argue about the most meaningless matters.

"Yes, indeed. Mother will fly from Varna with Absolon in one week's time. Thank goodness she changed her mind."

"Changed her mind? I didn't realize she may have had other plans."

"For some reason, Mother was reticent about bringing Absolon this year. I couldn't imagine why. He's been our most trusted servant since I was a child. He's practically family."

René hated the idea of excluding Absolon from the Hartenau-Hesse Christmas festivities.

"It actually took quite a bit of persuasion on my part to finally convince Mother that Absolon must come. He could never be left behind. I told Mother there was absolutely no way I would ever acquiescence to leaving Absolon all alone in Bulgaria for the holidays."

"I wonder what could have been the issue? Perhaps they had a disagreement? Or maybe he had somewhere to go this year?" Viviane offered with a wink.

"I just can't see that happening. Absolon is nothing but courteous and kind. I have never seen him lose his temper or raise his voice to anyone, let alone my parents. And there's no way that he's dating someone. Something else happened...now that I think of it, not long ago Mother mentioned being worried about something happening in Varna while she was away. She wanted Absolon to stay at Aytos Manor to keep an eye on things. She sounded very worried. Perhaps there was a problem with some of the help, or with the grounds?"

"Well, whatever it is, it has been resolved—or at least put on hold. And you were able to convince Amalie to bring Absolon, so we will all be together for the holiday. He will never be left out, René. You know he is a favorite of mine, as well." Viviane always enjoyed the company the good-natured man who faithfully served the Hartenau-Hesse family for the past thirty years.

"René, can you imagine what Christmas Eve dinner will be like with our mothers together?" Viviane chuckled as she envisioned the scene.

"I can just picture the two of them."

René and Viviane smirked as they anticipated their mothers—best friends for fifty years—dripping in jewels, the necklines of their Christmas Eve gowns plunging past their wrinkled décolletages as they put on airs for their guests.

The comical picture soon evaporated and the warm glow of the steady fire was replaced with a brilliant emerald light. With a barely audibly squeal of excitement, Viviane hopped to her feet and slipped on her shoes while René strode across the expansive room to grab her chinchilla coat.

"This should keep you warm, my love. Now, let's go watch the show for our girl."

René winked at his wife and they shared a smile. They walked together onto the beautiful stone balcony, which was already flooded with a dazzling display of gem-colored lights.

Chapter Eleven

"Oh my God."

Sofi dropped her satchels onto the cold, dusty track and stood motionless, mouth gaping, at the sight of the dingy trailer unit. Based upon the directions in her hand, it appeared as though this was to be their new home.

With its discolored and peeling siding, dented metal door, and scratched fiberglass windows, the trailer was truly a depressing and disappointing sight. It was not at all what she envisioned when her mother told her they would be making a new home in France. Rusted train tracks littered with trash ran across a hill directly behind the trailer. Beyond the tracks, a concrete structure covered in colorful graffiti surrounded an enormous garbage heap.

Sofi looked up and down the path at their neighbors' homes. Most were either broken-down trailers or shacks pieced together with random roofing materials, wood, and metal. Fortunately, these places appeared to have heat. Sofi watched steam rise from a makeshift chimney on the tarp-covered roof of one of the nearby dwellings. Without thinking, her fingers found their way to the beautiful gold and cerulean sapphire pendant that dangled from her long neck. She grasped it tightly, closed her eyes, and made a wish that she was back in Bulgaria and the scene in front of her was a dream.

Just one month ago, her mother excitedly suggested that with her school permanently closed, now would be as good a time as any to start fresh in a new completely new place. Uncertain about the true reasoning behind Nadja's quickly hatched idea and shocked by the suddenness of the news, Sofi initially refused to discuss the matter at all. After a few days of avoiding the topic altogether, she became willing to at least talk about a potential move but could not hide her skepticism. She was not at all thrilled with the thought of leaving their comfortable little home, or traipsing clear across Europe to a place they knew nothing about to live among people who were foreign to them. Of course, she was aware that the prospect of traveling should have been a naturally pleasing and exciting occurrence for her, since Roma are usually constant, happy travelers. Still, Sofi did not have a good feeling about her mother's scheme from the very beginning and she vociferously encouraged her to reconsider.

In the weeks that followed, Nadja managed to make the move appear more propitious. She explained that unlike the segregated Gypsy school, France's public schools allow French and Roma students to study together and that more opportunities for work would be available. After two weeks of promises and persuasion, Sofi eventually acquiesced to the plan, though she remained uncomfortable with the uncertainty of it all. Consequently, in the weeks leading up to the day they were to leave Dobrai, Sofi used her time to learn French words and phrases. She also purchased a map and used it to study the layout of Paris and the outlying regions of the city where she and her mother were to make their home. Fortunately, due to her ability to learn quickly and remember facts, figures, and photos nearly verbatim, she made quick progress. She soon developed a working, albeit basic grasp of the French language, and she looked forward to practicing her newly acquired skills.

A few families in Dobrai caught wind of Nadja's plan and viewed it as a prime opportunity for the village to finally rid themselves of the two loners they distrusted so much. They agreed to help Nadja with the move by providing her with information about their family members who left Bulgaria for France. They settled in a Roma community called the South Commune, located just outside of Paris proper near Choisy-le-Roi and very close to the railway and Périphérique de I'lle de France, one of Paris' busiest highways. One of Nadja's neighbors put her in touch with his cousin, Marko Lubvic, who lived in the South Commune with his young wife for over a year. Like other Gypsies, Marko left Bulgaria after hearing about opportunities for work in Western Europe. He applied for a European Union work visa, which was granted. At first, he planned to go to France, work hard for three months, and return to Bulgaria. However, after her found a steady position as a janitor with the Transilien Transport at the Reseau Express Regional's Villeneuve-Prairie train station, he decided to overstay the visa and had been living and working in France illegally ever since. When Nadja asked how he was able to keep his job with an expired visa, she was told that it was not a problem because French officials checked his visa once in all the time he was there, which was when he initially entered the country.

Nadja was not completely convinced by the explanation. When she spoke with Marko by phone, he gave her every assurance that others in the South Commune did not have visas at all. Indeed, Nadja did not have a visa and she certainly did not have the time to sit around and wait for one, especially if they were to leave before the man in the Mercedes and his employer could stop them.

On the phone, Marko seemed excited at the prospect of new neighbors. He promised to secure a comfortable and clean home for them for a sum of five hundred leva. Though initially skeptical about wiring money to a person with whom she had no previous dealings, Nadja ultimately decided to take a chance and send it. She had a secret savings account, which she kept for this very purpose—her escape from Bulgaria.

To Sofi, her mother's decisions, especially trusting other people, appeared highly uncharacteristic. Nadja was typically reserved, overly cautious, and even reclusive. In light of her mother's strange behavior, Sofi could not help but worry that there was some underlying reason to explain her apparent desperation to leave Bulgaria.

A week before embarking on their journey to Paris by way of a thirty-two hour train ride with seven rail changes, Nadja was calm and seemingly happy. She came into Sofi's roommate at the stroke of midnight to present her with a special gift—a large, stunning sapphire and gold necklace that depicted a very interesting and ostensibly ancient coat of arms. Sofi marveled at the sparking blue orb, which was held in the clawed hand of a powerful dragon. She could not believe that her mother would give her something so extravagant.

Sofi thought back to the loving way in which her mother placed the beautiful jewelry around her neck and the look on her face as she beamed with pride when she stood back to admire her daughter.

"This is a very special family heirloom. With your sixteenth birthday upon us and this new chapter in our lives just beginning, I thought now would be a fitting time for you to have it. When you look at this, always remember that you, too, are special—unlike anyone else in the entire world."

Memories of the touching moment she shared with her mother just days ago momentarily spared Sofi from the depressing sight before her. When she opened her eyes, the scene struck her like a slap in the face. Forlorn-looking Roma women and children from various regions of Bulgaria and Romania aimlessly meandered past her and down the dirt path. Several men with large bellies stood around smoking cigarettes.

Did all these people come to France with hopes for a better life?

"Mama, are you sure this is where Marko said he'd be? This place is nothing like the neighborhood you described."

"I'm not sure, dear. This is not at all what I expected. But Marko promised he would be here. We must have written down the directions incorrectly." Nadja's voice was steady, but she nervously twisted her hands.

"Let's get out of here."

Sofi and Nadja turned their backs to the trailer and began to walk away, but a surprisingly jovial voice boomed from behind causing them to stop dead in their tracks. They turned to find that the voice belonged to a jovial, round-faced man in a bright red Che Guevara t-shirt, a too-tight puffy coat, and skinny jeans. He was all smiles as he approached the two women with outstretched arms.

"Welcome to the South Commune! You must be Nadja. I am so happy that you have found your way. And this lovely young girl must be your daughter. I am Marko Lubvic and welcome—welcome to our little village!"

To Sofi, Marko's enthusiasm was exceedingly strange. His remarks seemed a more appropriate welcome to the Magic Kingdom than a Gypsy shantytown. She stared at him in disbelief.

"I know what you're thinking, young lady. This place doesn't look like much, but you will soon see that we are all very happy here," Marko continued cheerily. "Besides, most of us have it much better here than we did back home. So turn those frowns upside down while I show you around."

For a heavyset man, Marko seemed sprightly as he all but skipped down the lane while blathering about superfluous details as if he was selling a piece of real estate.

"As you know, the South Commune is centrally located near a major train station, which is where I work. We are also within walking distance to Lycée Aalis, which is where you will attend school, I presume," Marko said, motioning to Sofi. "And, for your convenience, we have a hotel, grocery store, bus route, and restaurants all within one and one half kilometers. Lots of opportunities to find work!"

Taken aback by the stark contrast of their bleak surrounding with the amusing and amiable Marko, neither Nadja nor Sofi were able to speak. Marko seemed oblivious to their shock and visible awkwardness. Instead, he merrily droned on about various neighbors, local points of interest, and the trouble he had securing the trailer that was to be their new home.

"Across the lane, you will find the Popazov family. They have a new baby who was born here in France at an actual hospital. So, he has a birth certificate. That little boy is set for life! Next to you lives Luluja Hlutev, but we all call her Lulu." Marko's voice dropped to a loud whisper, though no one else was in earshot. "Lulu is a little cuckoo."

He crossed his eyes and made a tweeting sound. Sofi could not help but find him humorous.

"She's really crazy?"

"Well, she's very weird. She won't tell anyone where she came from or how she got here, even though she's been living in that trailer for damn near six months. But, she's one of us. And, I am willing to bet that she's from Varna, but I couldn't prove it if I had to. She keeps to herself most of the time and hardly leaves her house, but you'll see her staring out of her window in the middle of the night. She also makes some very smelly dishes, but I don't know how she gets her food because she never goes to the market, at least from what I can see. Don't be scared though. She's harmless."

Marko continued to speak as he hoisted their bags over his shoulders and carried them into the trailer, dropping them in a heap on the floor of the tiny sitting room. He reached for a bandana that was stuffed inside the back pocket of his too-small trousers and wiped his forehead with it. Though it was mid-January, he had worked up a noticeable sweat from carrying their bags. Beads of moisture poured from his brow as though he had been doused with a pitcher of water.

"So, this is it. Like I said, I had trouble finding a place for you, but this trailer freed up after the family that lived here before you left for Grenoble two weeks ago. I guess the husband got a job as a day laborer at some factory there. So, off they went, and he brought the *whole* family with him."

"Whole family? What do you mean?"

"Well, I thought he'd leave the wife and kids here for a little while until he got settled in. But they all left together. Husband, wife, and six kids under the age of eight. That's a risk if you ask me. Who knows how long his job is gonna last!"

Sofi turned from Marko and looked around the small trailer. Though tidy, it was going to be a tight fit. She could not fathom how two people, let alone eight, could cram into what appeared to be no more than three hundred square feet of space.

"So where do you and your family live, Marko?" asked Nadja.

"We have a trailer there at the end of the path. We started off in a smaller one when we first came here, but upgraded quickly. The best part about being here is that you will be able to save any money you make, since we don't have to pay rent. See that dump site over there?" Marko pointed to the nearby junkyard Sofi saw earlier. "We pulled our trailer from that. Others pull scraps of metal and tarps to make roofs and porches. You can find all kinds of treasures in there!"

"Really?" Nadja said politely.

"Oh yeah. Because of that, I am able to send one hundred and fifty euros a month to my mother in Bulgaria, which is far more than any of my siblings can," Marko continued, smiling. "You will see. Everyone here is friendly enough, and the gadjé don't seem to bother us too much. We are pretty much left alone here to do as we please."

Nadja and Marko continued to chat but Sofi could no longer keep up. This was a nightmare. She felt drained. Marko was the first to notice.

"Ah, I can see that you are both worn out from the long train ride. You probably want to unpack and get settled in. But, please, come to my house for dinner tonight. We would love to welcome you into the neighborhood officially, and you can meet my wife. I believe that she is just a few years older than you, Sofi. I have a feeling that the two of you will have much to talk about."

Sofi's eyes widened as she pictured the thirty-something Marko with such a young wife. Her thoughts could not help but go to Avelina.

"Thank you for your kindness, Marko," Nadja interjected quickly. "We look forward to meeting your wife later this evening." Though her voice was kind, Sofi could tell that her mother was out of her comfort zone.

"See you tonight, ladies. We are so happy to have you both here!"

Nadja subtly ushered the jolly man towards the trailer's metal door. Hastily closing the door behind him, she turned to face her daughter with a pleading look.

"Sofi, I am so sorry! I had no idea that we would come to live in such a place." The words came quickly, almost out of control. "I cannot believe that this is what I paid five hundred leva for. How stupid I was! We cannot live in a place like this. We should just leave. Yes, we will leave as soon as we can. This was such a bad idea!"

Nadja put her head in small hands and began to sob, angry at herself for bringing her precious daughter such a long way to a place she knew nothing about. As the tears fell, she could hear the gadjo's gentle warning about leaving Bulgaria ringing in her ears.

"Dammit, Absolon!"

"What did you say, Mama?" Sofi got up and put her arm around her little mother.

Realizing she had said too much, Nadja wiped the tears from her face and stood straight up.

"Forget it, just forget it," Nadja said hurriedly as she smoothed out the wrinkles in her skirt and brushed back her long, black hair with her fingers. "Don't worry about what I said, okay Sofi? Let's rest for a while. Then we can figure out what to do."

Nadja grabbed her bags and neatly arranged them beside the orange and brown plaid couch that was pushed against the back wall of the trailer. After laying her coat and scarf on a nearby chair, she went to the sink to wash her hands and found that there was no running water. Looking down, she noticed a large bucket on the floor by the kitchen sink.

"Don't use that, Sofi," she warned. "We will have to boil the water."

Seeing her mother fight to push back her fear and disappointment in an attempt to make the seemingly bleak situation better, Sofi felt sorry for her poor Mama. She decided that she would follow her mother's example and do her part to improve their situation. As long as they were together, they could get through anything.

"You know, Mama, this place might not be so bad. True, this trailer is pretty small and…well, it's really crappy. But we didn't come here for a fancy home. We came here for opportunity. Once I enroll in school and you find a job, I think that things will get a lot better. We have to start somewhere. Besides, if the others here are as friendly as Marko, I think we'll really enjoy ourselves. Could you imagine us having friends?"

They looked at each other with identical expressions and broke out into genuine laughs.

"You know, Sofi, you may be right. Let's give this place a week and see how it goes. It might not be so bad. And if it is, we will find a way to go back home."

Chapter Twelve

Sofi watched the cool glow from the nearly full moon cascade off the ceiling of her tiny bedroom area, an unobtrusively placed closet just off the trailer's small eat-in kitchen. Her ankles and feet, which she had wrapped in a fleece blanket to keep warm, hung off the edge of her little cot, skimming the wall. Though the space was incredibly cramped, Sofi was relieved to have a little piece of privacy.

Exhausted, but unable to sleep, she studied the intricate details of her new locket while thinking back to the entertaining dinner they enjoyed at Marko's trailer earlier that evening. Both she and Nadja were unaccustomed to being guests. They never received an invitation to dine anywhere other than the Laporte's, which was many years ago, so they certainly did not expect the warm welcome they received.

Marko was right about his wife being near to her age. In fact, Sofi remembered Anka well. She attended the Gypsy school over four years ago when Sofi was in sixth grade and Anka was in ninth. Even back then, Anka seemed much older than Sofi, a late bloomer. Even now, nineteen-year-old Anka had more in common with Nadja than Sofi. Still, she was kind and amusing, just like her husband. In fact, watching them interact was like a comedy. It was as if they had been married for forty years.

Over dinner, Anka told Nadja and Sofi the story of how she and Marko met, calling it love at first sight. She explained that they were married just over one year ago. They were a mismatched couple both in terms of age and appearance. Marko was short and round with tight clothes and slicked back hair. Anka was thin and bohemian with the look of a traditional Roma. What the two shared were their outgoing personalities and warm, welcoming demeanors. It was abundantly clear that they loved each other very much.

Marko explained that after he obtained his work permit, he felt confident that he could find work in France, so the two left Bulgaria shortly after their late fall wedding. They learned about the newly established South Commune from Marko's childhood friend who was one of the camp's founders. When the newlyweds arrived, they were pleased to find that it was so closely situated to the Villeneuve-Prairie train station.

Sofi wondered how anyone could be impressed with this place. It was nothing more than a shantytown. Marko, though, insisted that his living conditions were much worse back home, and that Sofi and Nadja were lucky to have lived in the countryside.

The brilliance of the locket's cerulean sapphires shone in the moonlight, turning Sofi's thoughts away from the Lubvic's. She was captivated by the way in which the bright blue gems caught the moon's iridescent glow and she turned the locket from side to side as she watched the nighttime rays bounce off the stones' many facets.

Settling deeper into the covers, she took a deep breath and sighed, finding surprising comfort in the tiny cot. Shortly after drifting off, Sofi awoke to a loud sizzle that sounded like a rattlesnake. She sat up straight, then quickly turned around, knelt on the cot, and looked out the small window.

Aided by the moon, Sofi saw a person she could only assume was Luluja Hlutev, the crazy woman Marko warned her about. She was dressed in many layers of black and silver fabric and she paced across the width of her trailer while sprinkling some sort of powder along the edges of her dwelling. With each dusting, she hissed loudly and looked to the moon, whispering words to the sky.

What in the world is she doing out there?

Initially frightened by the sight of the strange woman partaking in what appeared to be a nonsensical ritual, Sofi hid under the covers. She thought back to Marko's explanation of Lulu's odd—yet harmless—behavior, and laughed at her own uneasiness. The situation could be much worse. Thank goodness Lulu was just poking around her trailer and not cooking up some far-wafting and foul-smelling brew.

No wonder people think we're a bunch of thieves and fortunetellers. It's people like this who give Roma a bad name.

Sofi peeked out again, unable to take her eyes off the woman's antics. After Lulu finished sprinkling the powder, she lit a long tapered candle and touched its flame to the places where she poured the substance. When the orange flame united with the white powder, it caused a spark, then transformed into an unnatural azure blaze. The blue fire quickly encircled Lulu's trailer, which alarmed Sofi. Before

Sofi could call for help, the fire extinguished itself. Then, Lulu calmly blew out the candle and casually went back inside as if nothing had happened.

Completely perplexed, and still somewhat disturbed, by what she had seen, Sofi could not sleep. She decided that in the morning, she would muster the courage to go next door and introduce herself to the peculiar lady with the funny name.

Sofi did not rise until nearly eleven the next day. With the long journey and the stress of the previous day, Nadja figured that she would not disturb her growing daughter from the rest she needed. When Sofi finally drew back the long curtain that separated her little space from the kitchen eating area, she was surprised to see that Nadja had already prepared a warm and delicious brunch. She distinctly remembered that yesterday, not even a slice of bread could be found in the cupboards. In fact, she was disappointed to have gone to bed hungry.

"Mama, where did you get all this food?"

"I walked to the market this morning. It's almost a straight shot and only about two kilometers away, just as Marko said. I was there and back in less than an hour. I also poked around outside before I left and wouldn't you know that I found a metal pushcart on the roof of the trailer. So, getting back was very easy. We should have had one of those in Dobrai. Anyways, it is much colder here in France than it is back home, so make sure you dress warmly. I brought some wool yarn with us. Shall I make you another set of mittens and a hat? Bright blue to match your new necklace. How does that sound?"

Sofi nodded enthusiastically as she scarfed down her scrambled eggs. She was glad that her mother seemed better this morning. Nadja was likewise pleased to see that her daughter's appetite was intact. As she watched Sofi devour the food, she could not help but notice the heavy pendant hanging from Sofi's neck. She knew she had better talk to Sofi about her present.

"Sofi, how do you like your new necklace."

"Mama, I absolutely love it! Thank you so much. I will treasure it always."

"Good, honey. You know, I think it is stunning on you and I never want you to take it off. Seriously, you should always wear it. However, we don't yet know the people here in the South Commune, or their situations. That said, I think that maybe you should wear it on the inside of your clothes from now on. These people appear to be very poor and I wouldn't want them to feel tempted to steal it. Plus, after being out in town earlier, I have the feeling that the gadjé here feel similarly to us as they do in Bulgaria, though they're not as obvious about it."

Sofi reached protectively to clasp the locket and held it tightly.

"You really think that someone would want to take it?"

"Yes."

Sofi considered her mother's wishes. She definitely did not want anything to happen to her only piece of jewelry. She knew it was very special—a family heirloom—so it made sense that her mother would want for her to guard it carefully.

"Well, I suppose you are right. It is so expensive-looking. And I know that it's important..." Sofi's voice trailed off as she looked down at the striking piece.

"Yes, exactly. It's *very* important. I also know you would be heartbroken if you lost it or if someone took it from you. And as I've often told you, the best way to avoid temptation is to avoid the occasion, right?"

Sofi smiled at her mother. She had heard that little piece of wisdom a million times before and she knew that Nadja was right. For as long as she could remember, she dutifully adhered to her mother's mantra, which had kept her out of trouble and harm's way her entire life.

"Okay, Mama, I'll keep it tucked in my shirt, as you said, and I promise to be very careful with it."

Sofi was not pleased about having to keep her beautiful new present a secret, but she understood her mother's concerns and realized that her points were valid. She crossed out a mental note she had made the night before about asking Marko if he knew anything about the coat of arms. She decided instead that she would have the opportunity to research it in the library once she started school.

After brunch, Anka stopped by to invite Nadja and Sofi to accompany her to one of the hotels that Marko mentioned previous evening, which was located near the busy central area in Choisy-le-Roi, just off the Avenue Victor Hugo. According to a few of Marko's coworkers at Villeneuve-Prairie, a European economy-style hotel chain called the Sherpus recently put out a call for applicants for a variety of positions, including maids. Before Christmas, the Sherpus completed a large renovation, which included the addition of two hundred rooms. With a greater occupancy to service, the hotel needed to fill open positions in a hurry before their grand reopening scheduled for next week. Anka assured Nadja that the Sherpus was a desirable place for the Roma to find work because the hotel was notorious for keeping rather lax employment records. Because neither Nadja nor Anka had valid European Union work visas, the Sherpus Hotel was the perfect place for them to find jobs.

Despite Nadja's obvious excitement about the interview, she worried about Sofi's safety. She decided that Sofi should stay behind while she and Anka ventured to the hotel. The arrangement suited Sofi just fine. She had little desire to stray far from the warm trailer on such a cold day. Besides, she had an interview of her own. She planned to pay a visit to their new neighbor, Luluja Hlutev.

Sofi felt butterflies in her stomach as she approached the front door of Lulu's large trailer. With no more six feet separating her from Lulu's porch, she decided it was too late to change her mind. Closing her eyes as if anticipating something dreadful, she knocked and waited for the witch-like woman to burst through the door and whisk her inside the trailer never to be seen again. However, nothing at all happened.

Puzzled, she thought back to Marko's description of Lulu. He said that she rarely left the house, not even for food. Perhaps today was one of those rare occasions? Curiosity outweighing her consternation, Sofi knocked again, this time louder and waited another minute. She turned around and began to retreat but stopped dead in her tracks when she heard a very raspy voice coming from within the trailer.

"Where are you going, Sofi?

Intimidated and a little frightened, Sofi turned around slowly. She was shocked by what she saw and could not help but stare.

The enigmatic Lulu was not at all what she expected. Before her stood a curvaceous and very attractive middle-aged woman. Her oval face was framed by curly hair so black that it almost looked blue. It reached all the way past her lower back and was completely devoid of even one strand of gray.

"You know who I am?" Sofi asked.

"I know who you are, but do *you* know who you are?" Lulu raised a perfectly shaped eyebrow, then broke out into a loud cackle when she saw Sofi's astonished look. "Don't be so shy, young lady. Come in! Since we're neighbors, we should get to know each other, don't you think?"

Lulu turned her back to Sofi and shuffled into her living room. Sofi followed tentatively.

At first glance, the trailer appeared to be clean, warm, and tastefully furnished. Immediately, Sofi felt somewhat silly and embarrassed. She expected Lulu's home would be some sort of witch's lair. Clearly, this bright and organized room was the complete opposite of the dark, cavernous space she expected.

"You have a nice place."

"Thank you, my dear. Now, before you sit down, you may wash your hands over there." Lulu pointed to a washbasin and a neatly stacked pile of hand towels on a pretty little table to the right of the front door.

After carefully washing her hands, Sofi took a seat on a beige love seat positioned across from a comfortable looking rocking chair where it looked as though Lulu has been occupied with some knitting. To the right of the rocking chair stood another small table with a gilded podstakannik sitting on top, much like the one her mother used to hold her tea glass.

"Your ways seem very similar to my mother's. Where do you come from?"

"Did Marko not tell you where he thinks I am from?"

"He said that no one in the South Commune knows much about you at all, and that you keep to yourself."

"Ha! I knew he would mention me. And since you haven't even asked me my name yet, I can only assume that you already think you know who I am."

Sofi did not know how to respond. She stirred a little but kept eye contact with the increasingly interesting Luluja.

"You don't have to answer that, Sofi. Marko means no harm. But I'm quite certain that he, along with the others here, are suspicious of me—and for good reason! You should know better than anyone that it is not natural for Roma people to separate themselves from one another. In fact, it's the cruelest punishment for Roma to be shunned by their community."

"Yes, I know." Sofi said quietly. She lived her whole life in awkward separation from her neighbors and classmates. "But how do you know who I am and about my life? Are you from Varna as Marko suspects?"

"I can see why Marko believes that, but no. I do not come from your region, or Bulgaria even, though I've been to Varna many times. My family settled in a small village on the southernmost part of Ukraine's western border, outside of Matros'ka. It is very close to Romania, where most of our people live. We are Lăutari."

"Lăutari?"

"Yes, of course, Lăutari. We are Roma elite! How have you never heard of us?"

"Well, I don't know…" Sofi's cheeks flushed.

"We are extremely talented musicians. Others are well educated because of the opportunities that have come along with our music. I can't believe your mother never told you about us."

"I'm not sure what you mean. This all sounds very unfamiliar to me," Sofi answered.

"That's very strange."

"Why do you say that?"

"Well, about forty years ago, when I was just a girl, a small group from our village decided to leave Matros'ka. They traveled south, following the Black Sea coast through Romania and into Bulgaria. In the end, they settled outside the coastal town of Varna because of the temperate climate and many opportunities for work. So that's the connection. Sound familiar?"

"Not really, Lulu. That's very interesting, but I've never heard that story before. But then again, I don't know anyone from Varna. Tervel, the town closest to our village, is over an hour and a half away from Varna by car. At least that's what I've heard."

"Unbelievable! Are you telling me that your mother never told you about your ancestors?"

Sofi looked at Lulu with a blank expression. "I don't know anything about my family. We have never talk about it. It's always just been the two of us—me and Mama."

Lulu sighed and looked down. "I'll stop then. There must be some reason why your mother didn't tell you about your family history."

"Lulu, wait. I've always wanted to know where we came from and why our lives were so different from our neighbors. I can't believe that we moved here to France and here you are! You must tell me. Please."

Lulu sat quietly for some time, studying Sofi.

"Very well then," she said. "You're a grown up sort of girl. I can only assume your mother came here so you won't have to marry soon. You can make your own decisions, so if you want to hear the story, I'll tell you."

Sofi sat up straight, bracing herself for the story she longed to hear for as long as she could remember.

"Do you remember that group of Lăutari I mentioned? The ones that left Matros'ka and settled in Bulgaria?"

Sofi nodded.

"Well, when they came upon Varna, they liked the region so much that they decided to stay. One of the members of that group was my Uncle Danya. He and his closest friend were talented violinists. They started a musical group that became popular amongst the gadjé elite in Varna and they had great success for over fifteen years. You see, many rich gadjé vacation around that area. They hired my uncle's Lăutari band to perform at their parties, especially in the summer months.

When I was a teenager, our family often traveled to Varna to visit my Uncle Danya. He and my father were very close, so it was difficult for them to be apart. My final visit to

Varna came just before my twentieth birthday. Before my wedding."

"That must be why Marko thought you were from his region. But how could he sense that connection? Could he have met you before?"

"Well, you're right to question it, Sofi, but, no. Marko and I had never met before I came to the South Commune. I believe that Marko is perceptive, despite his silly outward demeanor. He also likes to talk, so watch what you say to him. Anyway, he knows virtually nothing about me. I made sure of it." Lulu paused, turning her head sideways to look directly into Sofi's eyes. "But I know about *your* mother."

"I don't see how that's possible," Sofi answered somewhat indignantly given Lulu's tone. "We never lived in Varna, and I was born well after your final trip to Bulgaria. Besides, my mother is, no offense, much younger than you. I don't see the connection."

"Think again, Sofi. Your mother was born in Varna. That's where she's from."

Sofi's desire to learn more about her family vanished. Uncomfortable with where the conversation might be going, she stood up quickly and smoothed her skirt.

"Lulu, it was very nice to make your acquaintance, but I'd best be going. My mother will be home soon and I don't want her to worry about where I am."

Lulu watched Sofi walk to the door. As she lifted the handle to leave, Lulu called out.

"I'm surprised by you, Sofi. Not at all inquisitive, are we?"

"What do you mean?" Sofi could not help but to ask.

"You said yourself that you have been waiting all your life to hear about your family, but now you choose to leave. I'm surprised, that's all. Most people love juicy gossip and interesting stories."

"I don't like gossip, Lulu, and I take no pleasure in salacious stories. Such trivialities are beneath my interest, though I don't mean to judge those who enjoy such things." Sofi spoke confidently now. "Besides, I don't know you, Lulu, so there is no way for me to substantiate your story."

Sofi was sure that Lulu would be insulted by her comments, but her reaction was quite the opposite. She seemed genuinely amused.

"I've rarely heard one of our kind speak as you do. And what airs you have!" She looked at Sofi quizzically, as if she were putting together a puzzle. "Perhaps the rumors are true…" Lulu laughed loudly, slapped her thigh, and pointed at Sofi. "You are quite an interesting young woman. But you don't even know what I am going to tell you, so why are you so defensive?"

"I'm not sure I want to hear it anymore. As you said, my mother kept our family history a secret for a reason. It's probably for the best if I don't know."

Sensing Sofi's fierce loyalty to her mother, Lulu thought better than to tease her any longer.

"Forgive me, Sofi. It was wrong of me laugh at your confusion. I must admit that I am not a naturally kind person and I like to make a lot of jokes. But, I can see you that you love your mother very much and that you are a serious sort of girl. So I, too, will try to be serious."

Lulu made a very solemn face, which looked quite comical. Sofi could not help but laugh at the expression.

"Seriousness does not seem to suit you, Lulu," Sofi ribbed.

"Ah! Finally some humor! Good. Now let us be friends and I'll share something with you. A secret about me."

"A secret?" Sofi involuntarily took a step closer.

"Indeed. You see, the reason why none of our neighbors here know why I am here is because I, myself, can't explain what brought me to France. All I can say is that I had a dream, and in that dream a bright blue bird with sparkling sapphire eyes sang to me. In his song, he told me to come to Paris—that I would be needed for an important purpose. The dream seemed so real, and with my husband dead and no remaining family members nearby, I decided to follow the bird's advice. Six months ago, I left the Ukraine and traveled all the way here—to France. But imagine if I'd told that story to anyone. Then they'd really think that I am crazy! Not that I care, but still."

With each moment that passed, Sofi became more intrigued by this odd woman.

"You're very brave, Lulu, to come here all by yourself."

"I felt as though I had to do it," Lulu continued. "When I arrived in France, I asked around and was soon put in touch with Marko. He set me up here. Finally, after months of nothing, after waiting and waiting for something to happen, you and your mother showed up. As soon as I saw the two of you, I knew that it couldn't be coincidence. It must be the will of Devla."

Lulu's use of the old Romani word for God did not pass Sofi's notice.

"So please, Sofi, sit back down and visit with me for just a little while longer. We can chat about anything you'd like."

Sofi stood by the door and considered her options. She wanted to leave immediately and tell Nadja everything that had happened, but she had a feeling that her mother would not be open to a discussion. The only time they ever quarreled was when Sofi asked too many questions about their family or the past.

"Alright, Lulu. I can stay a little while longer." Sofi returned to her place on the love seat. "Please continue with your story about my family."

"Are you sure, dear?"

"Yes, I wanna know."

"Okay, young one. Earlier, you asked me how I know you. Well, I don't know you—not really, anyway. But, I knew your lovely mother many years ago when I was a teenager and she was a child. At the time of my final visit to Varna, your mother was about eight years old. Even though she is a grown woman now, I recognized her immediately when I saw the two of you arrive yesterday. She looks very much the same as she did back then."

Sofi could certainly understand that. At thirty-four, Nadja appeared to be much younger. Time did not seem to alter her appearance.

"Your mother was the youngest daughter of my Uncle Danya's best friend, Aza Vadoma and his wife Katarzyna. Aza was the brilliant musician I mentioned earlier—the one who started the taraf with my uncle."

Sofi's eyes widened. Her mother never once spoke about her parents, or any other members of their family for that matter.

"Nadja never told you about your grandparents?" Lulu asked, reading Sofi's expression. "I should have guessed based on what you said before. Well, I suppose it would be unfair to you if I stopped the story now. But I don't want to cause any trouble between you and your mother. I can pause here if you'd like."

"No, please go on. I'd like to hear what you have to say."

"As you wish." Lulu cleared her throat before continuing on. "Your mother was a very special child. From the time she was a very little girl, her father and my uncle groomed her to join the taraf as their lead vocalist. Nadja had an unbelievable voice that could rival any adult singer. It was full and deep—not childlike in the least. As you could probably imagine, her voice was especially ironic given your mother's tiny frame. A perfect juxtaposition. My Uncle Danya was sure that Nadja was going to be a star. You know there are some very famous Roma musicians, writers, and artists out there, by the way. Not all Roma live as we do..."

Lulu stopped to look around her trailer. She gave Sofi a knowing smile and continued on.

"Because your mother's singing ability was so unique, your grandfather wanted to share her talent with family and close friends only. He was a naturally cautious person and very protective of your mother. Above all, he distrusted the gadjé. He feared that if they recognized your mother's talent, someone would try to exploit her. He was adamant that they wait until she was married before offering her a position with the band. Uncle Danya didn't agree, but since Nadja wasn't his daughter, what could he do? As the years went by, he tried to persuade Aza to bring her to their more upscale events. Uncle Danya finally got his wish when your mother was about seventeen."

"Wow, I've never heard my mother sing. I wonder why she gave it up?"

"I'm sorry, but I couldn't say. She used to sing all the time. She loved it—we all did! In fact, my Uncle Danya wrote a letter to my father when your mother first joined the taraf because he was so excited. Soon after that, though, *nothing*. None of us knew what happened. Uncle Danya stopped writing to my father. My parents' visits to Bulgaria stopped. We only heard bits and pieces of information from our neighbors who continued to visit their own families in Varna, but who were unattached to the Vadomas."

"So you don't know anything else?"

"Like I said, after your mother joined the taraf, I heard very little else about her, or her parents for that matter. Uncle Danya withdrew from Roma society. We heard that Aza and Katarzyna banished your mother from Varna's Lăutari community after some scandal erupted. No one saw or heard from her ever again. Of course, there were rumors, but you already said that you are not one for gossip. Though, by the looks of you, the rumors may have been true…"

Lulu paused and looked as though she was calculating something in her head.

"How old are you, Sofi?"

"Sixteen."

Lulu raised her eyebrows and gave a surprised smile, but quickly caught herself and relaxed her expression.

Sofi was too engrossed in her own thoughts to notice. She could not understand how or why her mother could be banished from her own family. She could hear her heart beating in her ears. Her feelings soon turned to anger and confusion.

"That can't be right," Sofi fumed. "My mother banished? I can't believe it. Something else must have happened. My mother is a wonderful person, and up until we came here, she always followed the rules. I don't believe it!"

She wanted Lulu's account to be a fabrication, a retelling of vicious gossip. But in the pit of her stomach, Sofi knew that it sounded right somehow, minus the most important missing piece of the puzzle—why? Lulu's story certainly explained her mother's solitude all these years as well as their lack of connections, friends and family. It would also explain why Nadja kept to herself so much and why the Roma community in Dobrai did not trust them. Once a Gypsy is stained, it stays with him for life.

Sofi wondered what her mother could have possibly done to deserve ostracism, one of the worst punishments of all. And could she even be sure that this Lulu person was who she purported to be? Dozens of questions whirled through Sofi's head as she tried to wrap her mind around Lulu's version of her mother's alleged history. She felt guilty.

"I should go, Lulu. My mother will be back at any time."

"I didn't mean to upset you, Sofi. Honestly, I didn't realize how little you knew about your own family. I'm sorry it came from me. I understand if you never want to speak to me again."

"I don't like keeping secrets from my mother, Lulu. But I can't tell her what you told me. What am I supposed to do with this information?"

"You can talk with me. I know you must feel very alone at times. Perhaps this is the reason why I am meant to be here? To be of help to you."

Sofi thought about Lulu's dream and the story she shared. It was all too coincidental. Still, something inside of Sofi told her that Lulu was not a liar and she was definitely sane. Somehow, the story made sense. She could feel it in her gut.

Instead of judging the veracity of Lulu's story straight away, Sofi decided it best to sleep on it. She also knew that she needed a second interview with Lulu, and soon.

"I would like to speak with you again."

"Of course, Sofi. Come by whenever you'd like. You know I won't be anywhere but here."

"See you later then."

With that, Sofi was out the door and back in the dirt path. She was grateful for the slap of cold wind that whipped across her face, waking her up from what felt like a nightmare.

As she turned her head towards the direction of town, she saw her mother and Anka walking together. The sight was so strange to Sofi. Never in her life had she seen her mother walk with another person. It pleased her immensely to see it.

As Sofi watched her mother pass the Lubvic trailer and say goodbye to Anka, some of her agitation from her conversation with Lulu dissipated. When Nadja saw her in the distance, she raised her arm and waved happily. Sofi waved back.

I can't tell her, she decided. *Not yet, anyway.*

Nadja's pace quickened with each step she took towards Sofi. She was almost skipping but he time she reached her daughter.

"Oh Sofi, I have so much to tell you!" Nadja touched Sofi's cold, pink cheek with her small, gloved hand. "You'll never guess what happened."

"What, Mama?"

"I got a job."

Chapter Thirteen

"All those years of wishing for work back home. We come to France and in less than twenty-four hours, I have a job. What a country!"

Sofi watched Nadja bounce around the tiny kitchen and listened as she recounted all that transpired during her meeting with the hotel manager earlier that afternoon.

"When do you start, Mama?"

"Tuesday. At first, they wanted me to come on Monday for some sort of orientation with the rest of the new hires. But, I told Mr. Pervais, my manager, that I had to register you at school. I was afraid he would take back his job offer, but he said it was not a problem at all. In fact, he's having one of the maids train me tomorrow instead so I can officially begin work on Tuesday with everyone else. I cannot believe how accommodating he was! Friendly, too." Nadja shook her head in disbelief.

"So, I go back tomorrow morning to finish the rest of the paperwork, then they'll issue my identification card and master room key. In the afternoon, I'll train with a maid named Colette, then come home."

Nadja was so proud to have found work. She had not held a job since her time with the Laporte's over six years ago. And, while a hotel maid was certainly anything but a glamorous position, it was steady work with a decent paycheck and within easy walking distance to the South Commune.

"By next month, we'll be able to move out of this trailer and into a real apartment."

Armed with a job, Nadja felt powerful for the first time in a long time. She could not believe that they were able to leave Bulgaria undetected and settle into Paris, finally living their lives without the constant watchful eye of a certain woman and her minion.

She looked out the window and envisioned her daughter studying French at the kitchen table of a comfortable little apartment in Paris. Despite the warm welcome they received from Marko and Anka, Nadja had promised herself that their stay in the South Commune would be short. She knew what kind of neighborhood this was.

"You wouldn't believe it, Sofi. When I was in the market area, I noticed that some Roma here live amongst the gadjé."

"Well, I am very proud of you, Mama. Yesterday seemed pretty bleak. But just one day later and things are really looking up."

While Sofi's sentiment was optimistic, she delivered it in a rather robotic tone. Though she was truly happy for her mother, she could not help to think back to her conversation with Lulu earlier that day. On one hand, she was relieved to finally have answers to some of the questions she quietly held onto for most of her life. However, she also felt conflicted and was unable to shake a strong, underlying sense of guilt. She wished her mother did not have to endure the pain of the past all alone and at such a young age. A part of Sofi also wished that she had never gone to call on Lulu at all; that she could have remained blissfully unaware of the story behind her lack of family ties.

With a whirlwind of thoughts and mixed emotions swirling through her mind, Sofi turned her back from her mother and bit her lip. She was unaccustomed to keeping secrets from her mother, so as the evening progressed she found it increasingly difficult not to broach the subject or share her concerns and frustrations with the one person who was always there for her.

Certainly, Sofi's quiet mood did not go unnoticed. However, because Nadja was soaring high after a very productive and promising day, she misinterpreted her daughter's silence for boredom.

"Sofi, I'm sorry to have gone on and on about my new job. I didn't even realize that you must have been very lonely today, that maybe you feel as though there is nothing here in France for you? Would you like to come to the hotel with me tomorrow instead of staying here by yourself again?"

"No, Mama. I—I kept pretty busy today. I promise that I will find something to do tomorrow. I just feel a little homesick, I guess."

Nadja studied her daughter's expression and pinned her sullen mood on a combination of homesickness, tiredness from the journey, and maybe some hormones, as well.

"Try to cheer up, honey. When you start school next week, things are really going to improve for you. Think about how much you'll be able to learn!"

Sofi kept her head down and mindlessly twisted the chain of her necklace. She pressed her index finger down upon its blue sapphire orb, which made a temporary indentation in her finger.

"I've learned enough for today," she muttered.

"What did you say?"

"Nothing, Mama."

In an attempt to liven her daughter's spirits and lighten the mood, Nadja switched the subject.

"It was good of Marko to set this place up for us."

While it was not an ideal living situation, Nadja appreciated that Marko took the time to ensure that the trailer was furnished with all the basics and figured that part of her five hundred euros must have been used for that purpose.

"Yeah, Marko's cool. Anka, too."

"I guess that today must have been pretty uneventful for you, Sofi. What did you do?" Nadja tried to sound casual, asking the question without looking away from the pot of hot soup she was making.

"Oh, nothing much," she lied. "I took a nap and then walked around the area for a bit. It was so cold, though, so I stayed inside most of the day and studied my French dictionary."

Uncomfortable lying, Sofi continued to avoid eye contact with her mother. Instead, she buried her head in *Le Parisien*, which Nadja had brought home from the hotel.

"I'm looking forward to learning more about this country when I start school, although I'm a little nervous since I won't be able to communicate with anyone. I wonder what they do with students my age who don't speak fluent French?"

"I believe the school has a special class for students who come from other countries. But, I'm sure there will be other Roma students there to talk with, Sofi. There are actually many people living here in the South Commune—at least twelve families. I thought I saw some kids your age heading back from the school when I was walking up the lane earlier this afternoon. Either way, you are a strong and confident girl. You will be just fine."

With Sofi's naturally persnickety attitude towards her peers, Nadja felt sure that she would fit in more with the French student population than she did with the Roma, if, of course, they were willing to accept her.

"Will you be alright here alone while I'm at the hotel tomorrow, Sofi? I need to be there by ten, but I should be back later than two-thirty. Maybe we can explore the area together when I get back and have dinner with Marko and Anka?"

"That sounds fine, Mama. And don't worry about me. I'll find plenty of things to do."

That certainly was no lie. Sofi already had plans to call upon her new acquaintance in the morning.

In the few minutes of silence that followed, Nadja watched in amusement as Sofi studied the French newspaper, her soft face screwed into a funny little furrow as she attempted to make out the headlines on the front page.

"Why don't you read the headlines out loud? We can try to figure out what they say together."

Sofi looked up at her mother and finally smiled. She thought that it was a great idea and was thankful for a task that would distract her from Lulu and the story about Nadja's banishment.

"Okay, the first headline says, *La police française retient le suspect de terreur à Paris.*" Sofi spoke the French words slowly as she tried to make out their meaning.

"Something about the French police doing something with a terrorist in Paris. I don't know that word...*retient.*"

"I don't know that word, either, but I think I saw your French dictionary on the sofa. Why don't you look it up?"

Sofi grabbed the dictionary, brought it back to her place at the kitchen counter, and flipped through its pages.

"It means 'keeps or detains.' Okay, so the headline reads, 'French police detain terror suspect in Paris.'"

"Wow, you figured that out quickly, Sofi! You'll be speaking French in no time." Nadja was genuinely impressed, though not surprised by her daughter's ability to pick up the language. "Why don't we try another one?"

"Okay, this one says, *Président Hartenau-Hesse retourne aux Des Etas-Unis.* It's talking about the French President but I don't know any of these other words. From the picture here, it looks like the President is either going somewhere or just came back."

"Let me see that!"

Nadja's eyes flashed. She snatched the newspaper from Sofi's hands and stared at the headline.

"President Hartenau-Hesse?!"

Nadja scanned the front page first, then ripped through the other pages of the newspaper's first section, trying desperately to make out the articles.

"Mama, calm down! You're gonna tear the newspaper." Confused by Nadja's sudden outburst, Sofi tried to appease her. "Just give me a second to look it up in the dictionary, okay?"

Nadja hurried through the entire paper, then returned to the front page and gawked again at the headline and its accompanying picture of the French President and First Lady stepping off a plane.

"What's the matter, Mama? Something in the paper has upset you. Tell me what it is."

Nadja managed to compose herself almost as quickly as she had flown off the handle. She folded the paper carefully, laid it down, and went back to stirring the soup.

""I'm so sorry to worry you, Sofi. When you were reading that article, I happened to look around your shoulder and saw a headline on the front page about the kidnapping of a Roma girl in Paris. There."

Nadja pointed to a prominently placed story of a teenage Gitana who was taken from her family, apparently by another Roma family who wanted to avoid paying dowry.

"Reading that headline scared me, honey. Remember, we're from a small village where few incidents like that ever occur. But this is Paris. It's a major city of the world. Kidnappings, terrorism, who knows what else happens here. It makes me worry for you. We need to talk about how important it is for us to be careful here."

Sofi could see that her mother was visibly shaken. She got up from her stool and walked around the counter to stand beside her.

"It's okay, Mama. I promise I will be very careful. And Marko said that I don't have to walk very far to school. Maybe you can walk me to school on your way to work?"

Sofi chuckled a little as she pictured her tiny mother reaching to hold her hand as she crossed the street, as if she were a little girl.

"It will be *fine*, Mama."

"I don't know. Perhaps they were right. Maybe I made a mistake bringing you here?"

Nadja gave a defeated sigh and threw the wooden spoon in the sink. She looked up into the sweet face of her daughter, who had grown yet another inch over the past month, and gave her a little smile. "We're still giving it a few weeks?"

"Yes, Mama. We're in this together."

Sofi gave her mother a tight hug, and Nadja held on for a long time.

"I love you so much, Sofi, more than anything in this world. Everything I do and everything I've done is for you—to protect you and keep you safe. There isn't anything I wouldn't do for you."

"I know, Mama…"

Sofi hugged her mother again, bending down to bury her head in Nadja's shoulder. Nadja put her hand on her daughter's soft, chestnut hair and patted her head gently, laughing back tears.

"You're a good girl, Sofi. Now, sit back down and read me another headline."

Chapter Fourteen

As soon as Nadja's was out the door, Sofi hastily laced her well-worn boots and threw her crocheted cape around her shoulders. She had plans of her own today, which included a return visit to Luluja Hlutev.

Last night, Sofi heard little activity next door. However, a pungent odor of what smelled to be rotten eggs hit her nostrils around one in the morning. It awakened Sofi long enough for her to determine that the stench emanated from Lulu's kitchen. She wondered what sort of unearthly concoction Lulu could have been brewing at such a late hour.

She tapped lightly on the front door of Lulu's trailer, then quickly second-guessed her decision to call again on the strange woman. Before she could even think to turn back, Lulu appeared at the doorway with her hand on her hip. She was fresh-faced and draped in a colorful array of purple and green fabrics. Her unruly black curls cascaded down her shoulders.

"Good morning, young lady! I see I failed to scare you away yesterday." She winked and flashed a brilliant smile.

Sofi was a bit taken aback. Lulu was so charismatic, glamorous even; such an odd contrast to the bleak surroundings.

"I hope you don't mind. My mother started work today and I'm alone at home. So I thought I'd pop over. If you're busy I can come back later…"

"Nonsense! Please come in. I'm glad you're here. I can certainly use the company. I was about to make my special tea, but be forewarned, I'm not going to offer any to you. Your mother would not approve, of that I am sure. It's quite strong and can have some interesting and unwanted effects on certain individuals."

Lulu rubbed the palms of her hands together mischievously. From the rascally expression on her face, Sofi assumed that the tea's effects were more likely interesting than unwanted.

"Perhaps you'd like some warm milk with honey instead?"

Sofi nodded and smiled. She watched Lulu pour six spoonfuls of leaf tea into a saucepan of boiling water. Lulu ignored the strange mix for a good ten minutes while she prepared Sofi's warm milk and honey. After the leaves sunk to the bottom of the pan, she filtered them out and filled her tea glass with the bitter-smelling black liquid.

"What kind of tea is that, Lulu? I've never seen or smelled anything like it."

"It's chifir. Very strong, highly caffeinated. It's drunk in Russia and it's very popular underground. Especially in prisons." Lulu laughed deviously as she stirred the drug-like drink. "I started drinking it after my husband passed away. It helped numb the pain. Now I live for this stuff."

Maybe that tea is the reason why Marko thinks she's a little cuckoo, thought Sofi.

After a large swig of chifir, Lulu became quite animated, giddy even. Sofi, sensing Lulu's good mood, decided to ask her about the strange ritual she saw her perform two nights prior.

"So the other night, I saw you outside pacing around your trailer. It looked like you dusted some sort of powder around your house. Then, you lit the powder and it created a blue flame."

"You saw me!?" Lulu roared. "Should have figured somebody would. I was noisy enough."

"What were you doing?"

"Protecting my place from those damn suited gadjé that keep poking their noses around our camp!" Lulu's pupils were dilated at this point.

Sofi shuddered, remembering that Marko had mentioned in passing that a group of men visited the South Commune about a week ago. She also recalled her conversation with her mother the night before about Paris being an unsafe place.

"Do we need protection from them, Lulu? Are they dangerous?"

"I don't trust them and I suggest that if you see them, you steer clear away. I don't know why everyone else here seems to think it's perfectly normal to see a bunch of fancy gadjé nosing around a Roma camp. Do *you* think it's normal, Miss Sofi?"

"Um, no…I guess not. But Marko told me they're harmless."

"Marko doesn't know what he's talking about."

Lulu took another swig of tea, waved her hand in the air haphazardly, then held it still to examine it. After opening and closing her hand several times, she laughed and reached again for her podstakannik. Sofi wondered if it was possible to get high from tea.

"What was I saying?" Lulu continued. "Oh yes. I have a feeling that they are watching for something, or someone. They might be undercover police. Or, they could be planning to disband the camp and throw us all in jail. I can't think of any other reason for them to come here. Whatever they want, I can tell you that no good will come from interacting with them."

Sofi thought carefully about Lulu's warning. Surely, Paris was not like Dobrai, that was abundantly clear. Back home, she could traipse around the lush, green fields safely, alone, and as often as she pleased. Here, it seemed as though there were far more opportunities but less security.

Lulu saw Sofi's worry in her expression.

"Try not to worry, dear. Just be sure to heed my advice and you should be fine. If you ever see those men, turn and walk the other way. Just walk the other way...but don't run! That will arouse suspicion." Lulu waved her hand again in a drunkenly fashion.

"Perhaps I should go, Lulu. Like I said earlier, I didn't mean to disturb you."

"What are you talking about? You stay right there. Really, for such a young girl, you are very uptight. You need to learn how to relax. You're like...you're like a little prim princess sitting there. I know, you're *Princess Sofi!*"

Sofi could not help but roll her eyes. She had heard that one before.

"So that fire you lit around your house. You said that's supposed to protect you?" she said, attempting to change the subject. "How is that? And how did you turn that powder into a blue flame?"

"Ah! Well, that necessitates a story."

"Okay."

"Sofi, my dear, I've had quite a life with many ups and downs—exposure to a wide array of beliefs and cultures. My married life was not typical, at least for a Roma woman. I consider myself fortunate in that regard."

"What do you mean?"

"Years ago, while my husband was at University—"

"University?"

"Oh, don't look so surprised, young lady. My husband was a proud Rom, and an academic! While he was at University, I learned about...*witchcraft*. Not the fake stuff most of these gadjé think Gypsies do, but the real stuff. If anyone in my village ever found out about it, I would have been brought before the kris."

"What's the kris?"

"The Romani Court, of course. Anyway, what you saw the other night was a protection ritual. The purpose of the blue fire that encircled my trailer was to shield me from danger. There was a full moon that night. The fuller the moon, the greater the energy. That's why the flame blazed so brilliantly."

"So you're a witch?" Sofi could not believe their conversation could get any stranger.

"No, no. I'm no witch. I just like to dabble."

"How did you create the blue fire?" Sofi was intrigued, though she was beginning to think that Marko's assessment of Lulu might have merit.

"I simply soaked sawdust in copper chloride, then let it dry through. It's the copper that causes the flame to turn blue when lit."

Sofi was surprised that Lulu's response was so technical. She began to realize that Lulu was quite an unpredictable woman. One minute she seemed like a crazy lady while in the next breath she sounded like a scientist.

"As I mentioned before, Sofi, I had the opportunity to experience a wide array of interesting things throughout the earlier part of my life. It all happened after I met my husband."

"I thought life ended after marriage."

"Oh, not for me. That's when the adventure began."

"So how did you meet your husband?"

"While traveling back from Bulgaria with my family for the last time, a young man named Andrej joined our caravan. He wasn't Lăutari, but he came from a neighboring tribe. He was very young and extremely handsome. Our eyes locked each time I looked back at him during our journey. Anyway, he was supposed to continue north after stopping in our village, but he decided to stay. He wished to court me. Soon, Andrej asked my parents for permission to marry me. They agreed and the dowry was paid. Within two months, we were married.

In addition to his good looks, my Andrej was exceedingly intelligent, which was why my parents permitted me to marry outside my tribe. In fact, the year after our wedding, Andrej received a scholarship to study engineering and physics at Kiev Polytechnic Institute. We could not believe that he was actually accepted into the school, but being as smart and driven as he was, he impressed the admissions board. In fact, he was the first Roma to ever be admitted to the school. While he studied, I had the chance to meet all kinds of different people, mostly gadjé. Surprising, most of his classmates readily accepted us and were very kind."

"You lived among the gadjé? I've never heard of such a thing!"

"These days, it's commonplace. You may not realize it, but there are Roma lawyers, doctors, politicians, and professors throughout Europe. Most people just don't know—or care to know. They'd rather believe we all live like this."

"Did you like living in the outside world?"

"I must admit, I enjoyed living in Kiev. Even though I distrust many gadjé, they aren't all bad. In fact, after Andrej's first year of study, I became best friend with a non-Roma woman named Nina. She was the wife of one of Andrej's teaching assistants. Like me, Nina spent a lot of time alone since her husband was so busy with his research. Over time, she developed an interest in magic and the dark arts, but kept her hobby a secret from her husband—and everyone else for that matter. After we had already been friends for over a year, she finally told me about it. I was fascinated. At first, I think it was out of sheer boredom, but I gradually developed a genuine interest. So, while our husbands the scientists spent hours in the lab, the two of us conducted our own experiments. I was careful to keep my newly found hobby from Andrej, since I knew he would not have approved. But it was easy since he was typically so occupied by his work. I soon realized that in order for us to practice many of our spells and experiments, we needed knowledge of science and chemistry, so I started to ask Andrej all sort of scientific questions. He thought I simply wanted to learn more about his studies, so he gave me little chemistry lessons from time to time, which proved to be handy, indeed. He never once found out about all the spells and tricks I concocted with Nina, though."

"So how long did you live in Kiev? Did you ever return home to your family?"

"After graduation, Andrej accepted a research position at Odessa National Polytechnic University working under the direction of one of the country's top physicists. I was sad to leave Nina, but we couldn't pass up the opportunity. Andrej was a part of the research team for over eight years, two as team leader. They made great progress in the study of the physics of flow. One day, he was badly injured after an apparatus he used exploded during an experiment," Lulu sighed and shook her head. "He suffered severe burns on his hands and forearms and was hospitalized in Odessa for six months. He managed to heal somewhat, but never fully recovered. After the accident, Andrej tired easily and he was left with a lot of scar tissue, which prevented him from having full range of motion in his hands. Together, we decided to move back to Matros'ka to live among my families and our own Roma people, which is where we stayed until he passed away last year."

"Oh, how tragic!"

"In some respects, yes, life was tragic for Andrej. Here he was, the first of our people to be admitted into Kiev Polytechnic. He could have become one of Eastern Europe's leading physicists. But, alas, we spent the majority of our lives in our small, simple village as relative unknowns."

"Were you unhappy to move back home?"

"No, not unhappy. The life we made for ourselves after the accident was bittersweet. There was nothing we cherished more than being with family and among our own kind, but it was difficult to come to grips with the fact that Andrej would never reach his full potential."

"Did you ever tell him about your secret experiments?"

"No way! When we first moved back, I continued to study my craft but then gave most of it up. I got in too deep, you see. Tried to communicate with the dead."

"Oh."

Lulu traced the green and purple piping of one of her flowing pieces of fabric with her right index finger as she continued on with the story. "I know, I know…that was not a good thing. But, I am no scientist. In fact, I was the complete opposite of my husband. He was very logical and always searched for a scientific explanation to life's questions. I, on the other hand, have always been drawn to mystery—the unknown. To this day, I believe that there are things on this planet that extend far beyond our human comprehension. That's why I try to channel Earth's energy and project it onto myself and the things and people around me. But I also believe that if God wills something to happen, there is little we can do to stop it."

"My mother believes that, too—in the will of God, that is. I believe that."

"That's because you're a smart girl. Now let me share something with you about that blue flame. I've lately begun to feel unsafe here. I also know that there's an important purpose for my presence here. I can't explain it—it's just a feeling, maybe brought about by those gadjé who keep nosing around our camp. So last week, I decided to do something about it."

"What did you do?" Sofi nearly jumped out of her chair in anticipation.

"Years before my husband's accident, Nina and I studied the powerful and protective qualities of blue fire. I decided I would try to create it and harness its power. So, I asked Andrej a few questions about blue light, and he showed me a rather simple way to cast and create blue flames—by mixing a solution of copper chloride. You simply soak whatever you want to burn in the solution, let it dry, light it on fire, and poof!" Lulu raised her hands and jumped a little from her chair. "A blue flame is produced. So, as I told you before, the other night was a full moon. I wanted to take advantage of the heightened energy!"

Sofi chuckled. She found Lulu to be incredibly easy and engaging, yet extremely weird.

After chatting some more about the properties of blue light and the egg-like smell sulfur produces when burned—which explained the stench that emanated from Lulu's trailer the previous night—Sofi somehow found herself settling into comfortable conversation. The topic naturally progressed from Lulu's life to friendships and marriage and eventually to her own, conflicted feelings about Avelina's recent marriage to Boiko Dragovich, which weighed on her mind for over a month.

"I can't understand it, Lulu. She's only fourteen years old! Why would her parents allow her to get married?

My Mama would never agree to that. They could have waited a couple of years. And who knows? Maybe Avelina would've changed her mind if she had more time to mature and really think it over?" She shook her head, disappointed by the whole situation. "Boiko's such a troublemaker. I wouldn't be surprised if he found himself locked up sooner than later, especially with the way the police are always on his case."

Lulu listened sympathetically as Sofi laid out her feelings and frustrations. She realized Sofi could benefit from a truthful discussion about the reasons behind the Roma practice of child marriage, which she clearly did not hear at home.

"Sofi, your mother must have told you how important it is for our young ladies to remain pure."

"Well, yeah. Of course."

"Then you must try to understand that in the past, there were practical reasons for parents to marry off their very young daughters."

"Practical reasons?" Sofi's confusion was obvious.

"Oh yes. It's time for some real talk, young lady. Let me tell you a little bit about our history as a people."

Sofi's eyes widened. She leaned forward, hungry for information she longed to know for as long as she could remember.

"When our ancestors came to this Continent, European landowners enslaved us. Many of these landowners raped our young women and as a result, the girls became pregnant. Even those who didn't become pregnant were still considered unclean. This left the girls, and their babies, in a terrible position. Even though they committed no wrongdoing themselves, they were still viewed as dirty and unchaste. And, according to our laws, they had to undergo shudine, or banishment. The landowners also rejected them, so these girls were left completely alone."

"How cruel!"

"Yes, but as you know, the world can be a cruel place. I know that *you* are no stranger to misfortune."

Sofi looked down and gave a noncommittal shrug.

"Anyway, my dear," Lulu continued, "as a solution, Roma parents began to arrange marriages for their very young children to prevent them from being raped—and it worked. The landowners didn't view them as objects of desire anymore because they were no longer virgins. After five hundred years, child marriage became ingrained in our Roma culture. Today, we're free from institutionalized slavery, but we still suffer. Our problems are different now— mostly economic. So, the tradition of child marriage is still viewed by many as important. Why? Because it can be very profitable. Virginity is a commodity that some families essentially buy and sell...and for good money! Early betrothal preserves a girl's virginity. Early marriage protects young people from fornication. Roma girls can find themselves in pretty unfortunate situations if they don't wait for marriage, if you know what I mean."

"So you're saying that apart from the money, Avelina's parents only wanted what was best for her?" Sofi was unconvinced.

"You know your friend better than I do. What do you think would have happened if they said no to the offer? Would Avelina have just given up on Boiko, or would she have gotten herself into trouble? You can't be so naïve as to not comprehend what I mean by that."

Sofi sat quietly as she considered the choice her friend would have made had her parents not succumbed to the tempting dowry.

"Avelina's pretty headstrong, but I could tell that Boiko and his friends were a bad influence on her. I mean, she's my friend and all, so I don't mean to judge. But I know her. She probably would have found herself in trouble with him over time. Besides, he's a lot older."

"Exactly. You know, fornication is the major cause for shudine." She looked at Sofi and raised her eyebrow. "Avelina's parents likely wanted to protect her from the possibility of a love affair outside of marriage. If your friend became pregnant before the wedding, she'd be brought before the kris. If the kris found her guilty, she'd become an outcast—banished from your village. And of course, there's a financial aspect to all this, too. The kris would impose a fine on the girl's family."

"So how is a someone found guilty of fornication?"

"Well, the alleged fornicator is brought to the kris where they can argue their case to the krisnitori, or adjudicator. If the person is found guilty, she's usually sentenced to a period of banishment, depending on the severity of the offense."

"You said that my mother was banished from her village."

"Yes, I said that."

"Do you know why? Was she brought before the kris?"

"That I do not know, Sofi. I don't know the details. But as I told you before, I believe her banishment began sixteen years ago."

Sofi's stomach dropped. She realized the implication and pictured her tiny mother being brought before the Roma court with no one to help or defend her.

Sensing Sofi's mood, Lulu tried to change the subject. "What time is your mother due to come home, Sofi?"

"What?" Sofi was so immersed in her own thoughts that she did not hear Lulu's question.

"When will your mother return from work, dear?"

"Uh oh! Lulu, what time is it? She said she'd be back in the afternoon. I don't want her to worry…"

"It's okay, you're just next door."

"No, no. You don't understand. Last night, Mama got really upset by an article she saw in the newspaper. Something about a young Roma girl who was kidnapped. I never saw her so scared. I just don't want her to freak out if she comes back and can't find me."

"In that case, you'd better head home. Hard to believe you've been here for so long!"

"Yeah, time flies," Sofi muttered under her breath as she gathered her things. "Thanks for the talk, Lulu."

"Anytime, Princess Sofi."

After Sofi left, Lulu could not help but smile to herself, thinking that Europe's biggest surprise could be right under her very nose.

If the rumors are true, I'll need to keep an eye on that girl. I could be wrong, but she may need my help more than anyone.

Chapter Fifteen

"Julian, I want you to go back this afternoon. Bring the entire team. If what our fat informant says is true, a new family moved to the South Commune from Bulgaria just a few days ago—a young woman and her teenage daughter. I want to know who they are and where exactly in Bulgaria they came from."

"Sir, with all due respect, we've been making the rounds at every Gypsy enclave within a fifty mile radius of Paris for nearly two months now. We even have people stationed permanently at each of the major camps. We know exactly what's going on, and there's nothing new to report. They still live like dogs, and almost all of them have either overstayed their visas or never had one to begin with. They continue to breed like rabbits. A few of the women are turning tricks, but we haven't seen activity like we did when Domaphong trafficked those Gypsy girls to Thailand. Our presence on the ground is obviously working."

"I need to know more."

"We've given you all the intel we have. Most of these people are very cooperative, especially if given the right motivation. I don't see how two women from some dinky Bulgarian village will make any difference to President Harte-nau-Hesse for that policy he's pushing."

"It matters to me."

"But he's already got plenty of information to go on. And I think that whiz kid he works with finished his due diligence."

"I already told you, I want information on *every* Gypsy woman with a teenage child that comes to Paris from Bulgaria, do you hear me!?"

The voice on the other end of the line was very raspy, hoarse even, and it grew grainier and harsher with each loud, angry word. "You do as I say and ask no further questions. Remember, you work for me, not the President."

"Yes, sir."

"I am not paying you for half-assed information. You will go to the South Commune this evening and check on those women. I expect you to call me with a detailed report as soon as you're through. I don't want to hear back from you until it's finished and the information is confirmed." The voice paused for several uncomfortable seconds. "I hope I don't have to remind you that if I find out you've mentioned this to any of the President's people, especially that Spanish Jew puppet of his, you're dead. Understand?"

Julian could not wait until this job was through. He and his team of private military security officers were former members of the Belgian military who independently contracted themselves out to some of the best paying, and most clandestine, customers around the world. For the past six months, they had been keeping tabs on all the Gypsy camps located in Paris proper's southern half extending all the way down to the city's southernmost suburbs. American contractors were in charge of the north.

The job was easy—boring even—as their primary duty was to observe. In fact, the most action they had seen in all their time on the contract was the smuggling of a group of Romanian Gypsy girls to Thailand by way of Italy at the hands of one of the world's most notorious drug and human traffickers, Arthit Domaphong. Julian's team was prepared to take down Domaphong before he crossed the French border, but at the last minute, they were instructed to pull back. The entire scene was incredibly frustrating and his boss was a demanding asshole. His next job as security detail for a warlord outside of Bukavu in eastern Congo was sure to be much more exciting with better perks. Still, he decided that his paycheck meant more to him than trying to make sense of the situation and instead thought it best to bite his tongue and bide his time.

"I asked you a question, Julian," the voice interrupted.

"Sorry, sir, poor cell reception. Yes, I heard you and yes, I understand."

"Good, and don't forget that I'm the one who pays you. President Hartenau-Hesse needs to know what's happening on the ground in order to bolster his legislation. I, on the other hand, require something quite specific, but equally important to the safety and security of our nation. Just be certain that you give me exactly what I want when I ask for it."

"Yeah, I've got it."

"Don't bother me until it's finished. I have other pressing matters."

With that, the line went dead. Julian rolled his eyes and sauntered downstairs to prepare for what was sure to be just another routine trip to the South Commune.

Chapter Sixteen

Though the weather was quite cold, Sofi decided to wait outside for her mother's return home from her first day of work. She thought the fresh air might do her some good since she spent nearly every minute of the last three days indoors. She also desperately needed to clear her mind.

Ever since Lulu told her about her mother's alleged banishment, her thoughts had been preoccupied with trying to determine the veracity of Lulu's story. She also grappled with the guilt she felt for keeping it from her mother.

She sat on the step and pulled her necklace out from beneath her layers of clothes. She turned it towards the sky and watched the shallow rays of the winter sun dance off the locket's impossibly blue sapphires. She marveled at its size and wondered if there was more to this very interesting, and increasingly enigmatic, piece of jewelry.

This necklace seems too big to be just a pendant.

She continued to study the locket, turning it back and forth in the palm of her long, thin hand, but was soon startled by the crackle of gravel.

Surprised and excited that her mother was back a bit early, Sofi let the locket fall to her chest. But it was not her mother. The imposing figures of four large men seemed to be coming straight for her. She froze.

Oh no…these must be the men that Lulu told me about!

Unprepared and scared, she stood motionless for a few moments longer, strangely fascinated by the ominous vibe the men exuded as they strode down the path. Though Marko told her not to fear the suited gadjé, every instinct in her told her to run. Remembering Lulu's warning, Sofi pulled her eyes away from the quickly approaching men and walked into the trailer as nonchalantly as she could, locking the door behind her.

I wonder what they want?

Instead of staying in the small living room where she could run the risk of being seen, Sofi hid in her sleeping area and pulled the curtain closed. She slowly peeked out the small window above her cot and noticed that three of the men had already surrounded the trailer, nosing around and obviously looking for something. The fourth, clearly the leader of the group, casually approached the front door.

Though she could see him knock, the sound made her jump. Her heart pumped with fright. She had absolutely no intention of opening the door, let alone talking with that man, especially with her mother gone.

"Hello, there!" The gadjo at the front door sounded friendly enough as he called out in Romani. "Don't be scared, we just want to talk with you. Is your mother home?"

Sofi was alarmed to hear the man speak Romani.

They know I'm in here!

Not sure how best to proceed, she slowly inched her way past the galley kitchen and into the living room. She took a deep breath and reached for the front door, but stopped short when she heard her mother's smooth, deep voice on the other side of the door.

"Good afternoon, gentlemen. Can I help you?"

"Yes, and good afternoon to you, too. My name is Julian. These are my colleagues. We represent a local charity organization."

"You don't look like you work for charity." Nadja said without so much as a smile.

"Is that so?" Julian snickered, amused by the small, sassy woman. "Well, in our line of work, we visit neighborhoods like the South Commune to offer our services. We heard from Marko that you recently arrived here from Bulgaria."

"Yeah, that's right."

"Please know that should you need anything, anything at all, just ask. You'll see us around here pretty often."

"We have everything we need, thank you," she replied curtly.

"If you wouldn't mind, miss, could you please tell me your name and a little bit about yourself? Where do you come from and how many are in your family? You see, we like to know how many people are in each zone we visit for logistics purposes. You know, for things like how many clothing and food donations we need to solicit each month so we can better assist you."

"Well, as I told you, we are in no need of additional clothing or food, but thanks for your offer. Should we need something in the future, I'll contact you. Now, you if you'll excuse me. It's getting cold out here. Goodbye."

Nadja turned her back on the man and walked towards the front door. Sofi, anticipating her, opened the door as soon as she reached it.

"Do not show yourself, Sofi," Nadja instructed in a forceful whisper. "Shut the door and lock it behind you."

Before Sofi closed the door, she stole a peek at the suited men who began to walk in the direction of Marko's trailer.

"Where'd the other one go?"

"Sofi, I told you to close that door!"

"But Mama, there were four men earlier, but only three are walking back now. I don't see the fourth."

Nadja looked angry and worried. She blew past Sofi and slammed the thin, metal door shut.

"Draw all the curtains, Sofi, and put that damn necklace of yours inside your clothes!"

After the door was locked and the shades were drawn, Nadja sat down with Sofi, who was a bit shaken.

"I'm sorry to have upset you, honey, but there's something not right with those men. They remind me of someone from long ago."

"I know, Mama. They're creepy!"

"Marko thinks they're friendly, but I don't trust them. If you see them again, I want you to go inside. Do not open the door or speak to them or tell them who you are. Do you understand?"

Sofi silently nodded her head.

"And I definitely want you to keep your necklace hidden, as I told you before. I cannot stress enough how important that is. Okay?"

"Yes, Mama, okay. I'm sorry! I was just admiring it while I was waiting for you to get back, but then I saw those men. They were so scary! I got startled and forgot to put it back in my shirt. It won't happen again."

"Alright," Nadja replied with a sigh of relief.

She pulled off her coat and smoothed down the strands of black hair that stuck to her face during the walk home. She went over to the basin to wash her hands and returned to find Sofi standing next to the window, nervously peeking through a small corner of the drawn curtain. She felt sorry for frightening her, but she could not risk anyone hurting her only child. She also hoped that the episode with the gadjé would not ruin the plans they had for their mother-daughter afternoon.

"Why don't we have a little snack? That will give me a chance to warm up a bit before we walk to the shopping area. You still feel like exploring, don't you?"

"Sounds great, Mama. I'd like to get outta here."

While Sofi had not spent the day alone, she looked forward to checking out Paris' southern suburbs, as well as spending some quality time with her mother.

"But, wait. Is it safe for us to leave? What if those men are still out there?"

"Good point, honey. Let's leave in an hour. They should be long gone by then. And if, for some reason, we happen to run into them again, we'll just ignore them and walk away. We can't let them spoil our day. After we explore the area, we can come back here and get ready for dinner. Don't forget that we've been invited to eat with Marko and Anka."

"I like them, Mama. I hope they'll be our friends."

"Me too. But just remember that even though they seem to be very kind people, it's always best to take time in getting to know someone before allowing them to get too close. It's almost impossible to know the true intentions of others, especially those who are new to our lives. Keep that in mind as you get to know them, and when you go to school."

Sofi thought about her deep and revealing conversations with Lulu, a weird lady she barely knew. Her mother was usually spot on when it came to assessing the character of others. She began to worry that maybe she shared too much with her new neighbor.

Could Lulu have been lying to me? Maybe I shouldn't have spent so much time with her?

Sofi bit her bottom lip and looked down, concerned that she may have made a mistake that could not be undone.

"Everything alright, Sofi?"

"Oh! Yes....yes, Mama. Everything's fine."

While Nadja and Sofi prepared for their outing, the four gadjé convened in front of Marko and Anka's large trailer unit.

"Julian, did you see anything?"

"Not really. They drew the curtains before I could get a good look inside. But I saw something around the girl's neck. It looked like an expensive piece of jewelry."

"Maybe she stole it?"

"Probably. I just happened to see it because it was so friggin' big. But a lot of Gypsies wear jewelry. I don't think it's of much importance."

"Well, you'd still better mention it to the boss."

"You're right. That asshole wants to know every stupid detail."

"So we've got a description of the mother. Wow, she looks like a kid herself, doesn't she? Hard to believe that she's got a teenage daughter. Then again, these people tend to start early."

Julian shrugged his shoulders. "Yeah, I don't get them, but they seem harmless enough. Not our problem, though."

"That's for sure."

"Marko will supplement the information we're lacking—I'm sure of it. Doesn't take much to persuade him."

"Yeah, let's hope he's here."

Julian banged on the fiberglass door of the Lubvic's trailer home. Anka opened the door with a big smile, expecting to see someone other than the same intimidating man who treated her husband so roughly one week ago.

"Hello, Julian….and gentlemen."

Their hardened faces made her wince. She remembered the conversation she partially overheard between Julian and Marko last week. It ended very unpleasantly, which made her uneasy—scared even. Though she was not privy to her husband's dealings with the suited men, she knew that they had some sort of control over him. She definitely not want them in her home, especially while she was alone.

"Is your husband home?" Julian's question was more like a demand.

"He's not here at the moment, but he should be finished with his shift in about an hour and a half. Come back then."

"That's fine, Mrs. Lubvic. And don't worry. We won't stay. Just be sure to tell Marko that we need to speak to him about your new neighbors—tonight."

"Which new neighbors?"

"The only new neighbors you've got. Those two women, the mother and daughter from Bulgaria."

"I see. Well, coming back tonight isn't a good idea."

"Is that right?"

"Yeah. They're joining us for dinner. If you come back, it will be very…well, it'll be awkward. No offense, of course."

"Ah, I see." Julian remarked, looking satisfied. "I suppose it would be untoward to interview your husband about your guests while they're present. So never mind then. Enjoy your evening. And see you soon," he said with a wink.

"Goodbye, Julian." Anka started to close the door, but Julian blocked it with his hand.

"One more thing."

"Yes?"

"Forget we came by."

"What do you mean?"

"Oh, you know what I mean," he said smugly.

"Fine. I won't tell anyone you were here."

Anka watched the men step off the porch and march down the path. She wished she never had to see them ever again. While she was somewhat curious to know why they were always so eager to talk to her husband, her fear of the truth kept her from pursuing the matter. She tried to talk herself into believing that whatever dealings Marko had going on with the gadjé in the black suits was nothing to worry about.

"I can't live that way, and I won't," she said as they walked out of sight. "We're going to have a lovely evening with our new friends without any interruptions. Everything will be fine."

Chapter Seventeen

"So tell me, Julian. What did you learn about those Roma women in the South Commune?"

"We had some trouble communicating with them. Both were suspicious of us. The mother pretty much slammed the door in my face. I don't understand why. Marko was supposed to tell them to trust us."

"Forget about that idiot. These women are likely wary of all non-Roma. Typical Gypsy behavior. Remember, they live on the fringe of society. Many never mix with the outside world. That's probably the case with these two. But if that's all you've got, I will be very disappointed, Julian. I hope you haven't called to waste my time."

The austere voice was impatient, which would have caused Julian to worry if not for the fact that he had quite a bit of information to share.

"Of course not, sir. We obtained the intel you desired. It was all too simple in the end. A sketch of the mother should already be on your fax. Do you see it?"

"Not yet, but go on."

"We also paid a visit to Marko at the train station. You know he's very protective about his job and would do anything to keep his position."

"Ah, yes. That's the way you keep that fool in line. Keep reminding him that the fate of his job is in your hands, and he'll provide you with whatever information we need. So what did he say?"

"He told us that they came from the same Bulgarian province he's from—Dobrich. They lived in a village about an hour and a half outside Varna. The mother is very small. In fact, she looks like a kid. She has long, black hair and usual Gypsy coloring. She and her daughter came to France so the daughter could attend public school after her Gypsy school in Bulgaria closed. The mother's name is Nadja and her daughter, who's probably around sixteen or seventeen, is called Sofi. She appeared to be tall and quite unlike her mother. I couldn't get a good look at her, but she's very light-skinned. Doesn't look like most of the other Gypsies."

The voice on the other end of the phone began to hack and sputter. Julian listened in disgust to what sounded like spitting, then slurping.

"Say that again."

"Again, sir?"

"Yes!"

Julian reiterated the information and waited. The voice on the other end was silent for some time.

"I'm looking at the fax now," he finally said. "Yes... yes. This is why I pay you the big money. You and your team have done well. You can expect a bonus for the information you've provided today."

"Thank you, sir."

"I have one more question for you. Did you obtain their last names?"

Julian thought back to his conversation with Marko.

"Yes. I believe Marko said the family name is Vadoma."

"Vadoma!" The sinister voice repeated it back slowly. "Ah, yes. You have done very good work, indeed. Come to my office tomorrow morning. You'll be paid in full, plus the additional wages I promised to you and your team upon successful completion of this assignment. You'll receive instructions tomorrow for ensuring absolute confidentiality should anyone ever question you about this matter. After that, I never want to see you or hear from you again.

"Yes, sir, but I don't understand. The contract doesn't expire until next month."

"Never mind that—unless you feel like sticking around. As I said before, you and your team will be compensated for the full duration of the contract plus the reward. I can guarantee that you won't be disappointed tomorrow so long as you continue to follow my instructions."

"Yes, sir."

"Be at my office at ten sharp. Bonsoir."

With that, the line went dead and Julian was left holding the phone to his ear, completely dumbfounded. He had no idea how two insignificant Gypsy women from a remote Bulgarian village could possibly be of such intense interest to one of the most powerful politicians in Europe.

Chapter Eighteen

"Thank you both for a wonderful evening," Nadja said warmly. "Dinner was delicious."

"Sofi, don't forget those French phrases I taught you tonight. You can use them at school on Monday." Marko grinned, remembering Sofi's distinctive Eastern European pronunciation of some of the more difficult French phrases. It was very cute.

In the year and a half that he and Anka had been in France, Marko acquired limited working proficiency of the language. He was happy to share his skills with two willing pupils, especially since his wife showed little interest. He was sure that Sofi, with her sharp memory and want of learning, would speak fluently in no time.

"I'm going to write everything down as soon as we get home so I can keep practicing," Sofi promised. She mouthed some new phrases to herself, swung her cape around her shoulders, and pulled on her fuzzy cap.

"Adieu! See you tomorrow."

The night wind was a jolt to Nadja and Sofi, who were still adjusting to France's cold climate. The two linked arms and hurried down the path, but Nadja stopped abruptly just before they reached the halfway point between their trailer and the Lubvic's.

"Sofi, honey, we forgot the French dictionary."

"Can't we get it tomorrow?" Sofi shivered. She wanted to get back inside and stay put for the rest of the evening.

"I know it's cold, but you said you wanted to practice in the morning. Why put off till tomorrow what can be done today?"

"But Mama…"

"Marko and Anka will both be at work tomorrow. Run now and go back for it. I'll walk ahead and put on some tea. It'll be ready by the time you get back."

They shared a smile and Sofi sprinted back to the Lubvic's trailer. Nadja could not help but laugh a little as she watched her daughter's quick stride. Her long legs seemed to fly in every direction. With the next burst of cold wind, she pulled her coat close and ran the rest of the way home.

She was pleased to find that the trailer was nice and toasty. She felt thankful to have a warm place to stay, despite its small size and dingy appearance. She pulled off her mittens and laid her coat on the stool next to the doorway, rubbing her tiny hands together.

After taking not two steps inside, she stopped cold. Three gruesome men, completely bald and heavily tattooed, emerged from the bedroom.

"Good evening, Nadja," one of the men purred in Bulgarian. "We've been waiting for you."

"Who are you and what do you want?" Nadja demanded, trying to mask her fear. She stood motionless, but her eyes darted around the room looking for a heavy object—anything that she could use as a weapon.

"Didn't anyone ever tell you not to come to France little girl?" another mocked. He kicked a chair across the living room and laughed. "Tonight marks the end of the road for you."

"What are you talking about? Leave me alone and get out of my house!" Nadja cried as they circled her.

"Where's that daughter of yours? I hear she's all grown up."

"Yeah, I'm looking forward to testing her out. We're gonna take her for the ride of her life!"

"No! You must have the wrong person. I don't have a daughter. It's just me who lives here!" Nadja shouted. "Now I told you, get the hell out!"

Nadja's pronouncement did not make a difference to the men. They violently ransacked the trailer. Then, one of them went back into the bedroom and returned with two large, red cans. He drenched the carpet, furniture—everything in sight he soaked with gasoline.

"Where is she!?" they demanded furiously, losing their patience as they continued to prowl around the trailer like a trio of dobermans.

"I don't know what you're talking about!" Nadja screamed back in desperation. "Who are you?"

Frustrated, the largest of the three lunged at Nadja.

She was horrified at the sight of him and nearly vomited from fright. His eyes were two different colors; one brown, one gray—almost colorless—as if it had been damaged. A deep, uneven scar ran across his face and his skin was heavily pockmarked. With his tattooed hand, he grabbed her by the back of the neck and forced her face to meet his. With his other hand, he pulled hard on her long braid until her chin was raised to the ceiling. Nadja's eyes fixed on a heavy black swastika on the side of his thick neck. The blood flowing through his carotid artery made it pulsate.

He lifted her off the floor by her jaw and smiled sadistically. Nadja thought she heard a cracking sound in her ears. She tried to kick but her tiny feet just dangled in the air.

"Where in the hell is that daughter of yours?" he hissed into her ear.

"I—I told you. I don't have a daughter," she barely choked out.

"You're lying!"

The man threw Nadja hard against the wall, then slammed her head off a wooden end table. She gasped for breath and tried to get up, but she was paralyzed. Her only thought was protecting her daughter. She prayed with all her might that Sofi would be held up at the Lubvic's.

She tried again to stand, but the room swirled and slowly faded to black.

Sofi banged on the Lubvic's door. "Come on, Marko, it's freezing out here!"

"Did you forget something?" Marko laughed at the sight of Sofi, who danced around the landing like a puppet, shivering visibly and teeth chattering.

"Yes, I fff—forgot the ddd—dictionary. Sss—sorry."

"Come in! You must be frozen. You could have just picked it up tomorrow, you know."

Sofi practically jumped inside. To her delight, she was greeted with a gust of warm air.

"It's so cold in France, Marko! How do you stand it?"

"Oh, the body grows accustomed to it. You'll see. By this time next year, you won't feel it as you do now."

"Ah, Sofi, you've come back!" Marko turned and smiled at his wife as she entered the living room. "You forgot the dictionary…but I guess that's why you're here."

"Yes, indeed."

"Well, take your coat off and have some hot chocolate before you head back. I know it's not a long a walk, but it's so cold out there tonight."

"Thank you very much, but Mama is back at the house. She's making some tea as we speak."

"Okay then, no problem. But hang on for just a few minutes. I forgot to give something to your mother earlier. I'd planned to bring it over tomorrow with the dictionary. But now that you're here, you might as well bring it back with you."

"Sure."

"Wait here. I'll be right back."

Sofi chatted away with Marko as Anka disappeared into the kitchen. She must have forgotten where she had placed it because Sofi could hear a bit of commotion. She looked over at Marko, who was grinning broadly, accustomed to his wife's habit of misplacing things at the most inopportune times.

After a few minutes, Anka emerged, flustered.

"Are those gloves?"

"Yes! I found them at a little stand at the square. They're rubber cleaning gloves, but they're so pretty, don't you think? And look, these rubber flower thingies on the palms are for scrubbing. They're so cute. I couldn't resist. Your mom can use them at work. I don't know, maybe she'll think they're silly...but they'll protect her little hands, at least." Anka chuckled and slapped Sofi playfully with one of the gloves.

"I think they're fun. Mama will love them!"

Sofi picked up the gloves and the dictionary and made her way to the door. "Thanks again for the dinner, and for my Mom's present."

"It's our pleasure! You and your mom are always welcome here."

Bracing herself for the next burst of cold, Sofi walked outside, hands full. The wind had picked up, so she walked at a slow pace, battling each blustery blast. Though she tried to be careful, she managed to drop the dictionary twice.

"The tea is probably cold by now," she muttered.

As she continued on her way, she could not help but think how different their lives had become in such a short time. True, they lived in a small, shabby shack instead of their quaint and cozy brick home in Bulgaria, but here they had friends and opportunity, two things they never had before. Her mother had a job. And, her first day of school was tomorrow.

When she reached the last stretch of her walk, she sighed in anticipation of her first sip of hot tea, but as she reached the top of the knoll, her heart sank. Huge, dark clouds rose from the top of their trailer.

"Oh no! Mama!"

She dropped the dictionary and gloves and ran as fast as she could. When she got close, she saw Lulu outside screaming for help. The young Popazov couple was also outside. They wanted to do something, but were powerless against the blaze. All three stood helpless, watching the flames grow more and more forceful with each gust of wind.

"Thank God you're okay!" Lulu cried when she saw Sofi. "Is your mother inside?"

"Yes, she must be! We've gotta get her out!"

"No, you can't go in there! The flames are too strong. I think the place is going to collapse!"

"How did this happen?"

"I don't know! The fire must have spread so quickly because of this wind. I don't know what to do. None of us have phones! We can't call the fire department."

"I'll run up to Marko's," Mr. Popazov yelled. "I know he has a cell phone."

Sofi and Lulu watched Mr. Popazov hurry away to find help. The neighborhood was eerily quiet save for the crackling of the burning trailer and the cries of the Popazov's baby in the distance. The screaming infant was soon overpowered by a loud shatter. The front window had blown out. A plastic tarp covering the roof was melting. Bright orange flames leapt across the structure, engulfing it.

"Lulu, I can't just stand here and let my mother die! I need to help her! She's probably suffocating....or burning alive!"

"No, Sofi, you mustn't go in there! You might not come out! Besides, I don't understand why your mother wasn't able to get out. Was she asleep?"

"No." Sofi brushed off Lulu's question, which seemed pointless. "I don't care! I'm going in."

"Sofi, no!"

Before Lulu could hold her back, Sofi raced to the front of the trailer. Without hesitation, she hurled her body through the front door. She was met by a dense wall of black smoke. It encompassed her, filling her nostrils, throat, and chest. She covered her mouth and nose with her cape to shield herself, but it did not help. The smoke strangled her.

Unable to see and barely able to breathe, Sofi instinctually dropped to the floor and felt around for her mother, slowly crawling past the opening of the tiny galley kitchen and into the living room. She tried to call out, but she swallowed more smoke as soon as she opened her mouth.

On her way to the bedroom, a large piece of the ceiling crackled loudly and crashed to the floor. She covered her head with her hands just in time to save her eyes from the fiery hot ash. Sizzling embers burned holes into her gloves. She felt like she had been stung by a swarm of bees.

"Mama! Where are you?" she finally managed to yell.

After maneuvering around a burning chair, Sofi made her way into the bedroom. There, she found Nadja motionless on the floor. A large contusion distorted the right side of her face. Her right eye was completely swollen shut, and she bled from the mouth as if she had been punched or kicked. Her skirt and blouse were torn and Sofi thought she saw blood on her legs.

"Oh, my God! No....no!"

Not knowing what to do, Sofi tried to lift Nadja's head, but stopped when the sensation of warm liquid touched her skin. She looked down in horror. Her gloves were saturated with her mother's blood. Her hands began to shake uncontrollably. Screaming, she tore off the gloves and hurled them across the room.

"What happened to you, Mama?" she cried passionately. "Mama, wake up. Please!"

Sofi shook her mother urgently, but Nadja did not respond. Crying, she bent low, placing her face next to her mother's, and gently kissed her cheek.

"Mama? Can't you hear me? Oh, dear God—help us!"

The flames had yet to reach the bedroom, but they were quickly closing in. She knew that if she could not wake her mother, they would both be trapped. Sofi shook Nadja again. This time, she opened her left eye.

"Mama, you're alive!"

"Sofi, get out of here now," she commanded in a whisper.

"No! I'm taking you with me. Come on, get up!"

"You're in grave danger. You need to leave. Go out the back window now. They're watching."

"Who's watching? Who did this to you?"

Nadja tried to answer but she did not have the strength. She closed her eyes as if she would go back to sleep.

"Mama, no! Wake up," Sofi demanded. "Wake up!"

Nadja forced herself to turn away from the beautiful light that seemed to beckon her home. She could not leave her daughter just yet. She lifted her eyelid and, despite her injuries, managed to give her daughter a very serious look.

"Listen carefully, Sofi. Leave. Show yourself to no one."

"Why, Mama? Let me help you. We can leave together!"

By now the flames fully engulfed the trailer and Sofi could hear part of the roof collapse.

"My dear girl...I'm dying. You must leave me here. Trust no one. Tell no one you've escaped."

"Where do I go, Mama? What will I do?"

"Your necklace is a locket. Open it. Use the orb the dragon holds. You'll know what to do...." Nadja's voice trailed off. Her eye rolled behind her head.

"What does that mean? Mama, please!"

Sofi tried to lift her mother, but Nadja was dead weight. All she could see were flames. The entire trailer was ablaze and completely swallowed by thick, black smoke. The air had become even thicker than before, and Sofi could feel the lack of oxygen in her lungs. Her chest was burning and tight, and her mind was foggy. She hurried to the back window and kicked it out. Remembering her mother's orders, she pulled her slim frame through the small window's opening and landed in a heap on the ground behind the trailer. Though her sight was blurry, she managed to run away from the camp. She crawled up the hill behind the trailers towards an area of dense, evergreen thicket, not far from the train tracks.

She pressed her stomach to the ground to conceal herself in the dark shadows of the brush. From here, she saw the South Commune from a completely new vantage point.

When her vision cleared, she caught a final glimpse of the trailer she called home for less than a week. It was consumed by the fire. After a minute, it exploded, along with Sofi's heart. She wailed in agony knowing that her mother, the only person who ever loved her in her entire life, had perished.

Lying hidden amongst the evergreen branches, Sofi put her head in her arms and wept. She felt as though her heart had been torn from her chest. She angrily pummeled the earth beneath her, refusing to believe what had happened.

The echoing cries from the South Commune's inhabitants were soon drowned out by the distant screams of a fire truck's sirens that grew louder by the second. They were too late to save her beloved mother, her best friend in the world, her everything.

Sofi stayed hidden, sobbing facedown in the frozen dirt for what felt like hours. As what remained of the trailer, and her mother, continued to burn, she never raised her head; that is, not until she heard an unexpected sound. Someone was laughing nearby. She lifted her head, but otherwise stayed completely still. Her mother's final warning was branded in her mind.

Three enormous men with shaved heads stood less than ten yards away. They were covered in tattoos and wore leather jackets and heavy boots. Their presence was terrifying. One brandished a bowie knife and danced around, laughing like a madman. Another took long drags from two cigarettes he smoked simultaneously. The biggest man had a grisly scar that ran the entire length of his face. He lifted his massive head to the sky and smelled the air like a wolf.

Sofi forced herself to control her sobs. Once she quieted down, she realized that she could understand every word of their conversation. They were Bulgarian.

"I think it's safe to say that tonight was a success."

"How'd you like the sound my fist made when I beat the shit out of that Gypsy whore?"

The men laughed hysterically.

"Did you see the look on her face when I grabbed her by the neck?"

"She weighed, like, nothing! I tossed her into the bedroom like she was a doll. Bitch barely made a thud."

Sofi threw up in her mouth. Hearing them ruthlessly brag about the way they punished her innocent mother was too much for her to take.

"I thought for sure that daughter of hers wasn't gonna show. But then she did—just like you said and right on time."

"Yeah, she was so brave, the way she ran in to save her poor, little mommy," the largest man said mockingly. "Pretty stupid, too, because she never came out. And there's no sign of her out here."

"So we're good to go, then."

"We'll know for sure tomorrow. But we all saw her run in. There's no way she survived that explosion."

"Won't the fire department do a forensic report or something?"

"Maybe, probably not. These people are the scum of the earth. They won't waste their time investigating this. At least they don't bother with cases like this back home. If the French do, I'll be shocked."

"Yeah, we got nothing to worry about. That Gypsy bitch burned alive, just like her whore mother. Wish we had a chance to have some fun with her first!"

The crazy one with the knife laughed like a devil.

"Alright, let's head back. We can report to the boss that it's done. Then it's payday. Cha-ching!"

All the while Sofi listened, her emotions whirled— grief, anger, frustration, and sadness, but above all, pain. Her head swam with images and sounds she wished she had never seen nor heard. Her mother was beaten by a gang of thugs, left for dead, and burned alive. She was left completely alone and could trust no one. Someone out there wanted her dead. According to the conversation she just heard, they thought that she already was.

What am I going to do?

Sofi sobbed into the singed remains of the cape her mother crocheted for her just before their trip. The tears came uncontrollably and they stung her face, which had been scraped by the piece of burning ceiling that nearly crushed her. Her chest was heavy and sore from inhaling so much smoke. She struggled to breathe the icy air that whipped through her torn clothing. She was determined to stay there all night and die of hypothermia, but her survival instincts kicked in when her physical pain grew to match her emotional pain.

The evergreens provided a light shield from the powerful winter wind that barreled through the air like a locomotive. She pulled herself into a seated position and wiped the icy tears from her swollen eyes. What used to be her home was now nothing more than a heap of charred rubble. Realizing that her mother's remains were among the wreckage, Sofi started to cry again, this time with loud, powerful sobs. After a few minutes, she pushed back the tears from the raw skin of her crestfallen face and forced herself to calm down.

The firemen stayed on the scene for some time, attempting to control the blaze, but they ultimately gave up. The night's forceful winds made the fire dance across the rooftops of the nearby trailers, placing the neighbors at risk, so they turned their attention to making sure that the fire did not spread.

Squinting to make out those in the disbanding crowd, Sofi was able to pick out the Lubvic's. Anka was obviously distraught, huddled in a little ball on the side of the lane with her head in her hands. Marko, strangely, was not at her side. Instead, he paced back and forth a good distance away from the crowd, talking animatedly on his cell phone. Sofi also noticed the Popazov family and a few other neighbors that looked familiar. They were grouped together, clearly shocked by all that transpired. She watched the fire crew secure the area, hang caution tape, and after a few hours, leave. The group of frightened spectators dispersed soon thereafter. The night became still, calm even, as if nothing had happened. It was surreal.

Sofi knew she had to do more than just sit in the bushes all night and freeze, although the thought crossed her mind several times. Though she wished with all her might that she, too, had died, she was clearly alive, and relatively well considering all that had occurred. That being the case, she cleared her mind as best she could to formulate a plan. She wondered if she should seek out Marko, but something told her not to bring him into this. She remembered her mother's warning about trusting new people and Lulu's heads-up about Marko's mouth. And, despite her grief, she decided to listen to the pit in her stomach that sunk deeper and deeper each time she watched Marko vigorously pace the length of the crime scene while on his phone. His reaction seemed detached, cold even, especially for someone who witnessed such gruesome tragedy befall his friends.

She mentally combed through the faces of each person who had gathered around the crime scene and realized that one person was conspicuously missing.

Where was Lulu?

Sofi thought about the conversation she had with her mother earlier that day about being cautious around strangers and trusting new people.

No way. Sofi was adamant. *Besides, Lulu tried to stop me from going inside. There's no way she wanted this to happen. Those men wanted both of us dead, not just Mama. They said it themselves. Lulu tried to keep me safe.*

As soon as Sofi recalled the events of earlier, the realization of her mother's murder hit her hard and square in the face like a pair of brass knuckles. She winced from the blow. She tried to prevent the flood from coming again, but there was nothing she could do to stop the hot tears from filling her sore eyes. They boiled over like lava and streamed down her ice-cold cheeks.

"She's dead! Mama is dead!"

For the third time that evening, Sofi wished that she could have joined her mother in death instead of being left alive—cold, hurt, frightened, and completely alone—in a world that despised her.

"Most Holy Lady, please help me!" she cried whole-heartedly from her soul, looking towards the stars.

The moon was high and bright in the sky. It cast a cool, faint light on the earth. The scary, bald men were long gone, so Sofi felt safe enough to sneak out from beneath the evergreen thicket and carefully make her way back down to what was left of the trailer. Taking lengthy strides, she came upon the heap of ash and rubble in no time.

This was, perhaps, the worst moment of her entire life. She could not bear the sight of the remains, let alone the smell. Vivid pictures of her cherished mother, lying beaten and surrounded by flames, flashed through her mind like scenes from a horror movie.

She made herself turn her attention to next door, which was uncharacteristically dark and quiet for this time of night. She snuck around back to see if she could awaken Lulu. She realized that although she was likely in grave danger, there was no way she would be able to make it on her own without some sort of miracle. Her clothes were burnt and torn, her face was sore and scraped, and she had no money, no connections, and a limited grasp of the French language.

Surely Lulu will help me.

Sofi was willing to risk the dubious possibility that Lulu had ulterior motives. Even if Lulu did, she reasoned that she would rather deal with it, if and when the time came, instead of facing the freezing night completely alone.

"Lulu!" she hissed. "Wake up!"

Sofi tapped lightly on Lulu's bedroom window. "Lulu! It's me, Sofi."

Oddly, there was no response. She peered into the window, but Lulu was not in her bed. She went back to the rear door and knocked, but there was no answer.

Convinced that Lulu was her only hope, Sofi banged desperately at the back door, which caused it to creak open. She warily stepped inside and realized that Lulu was not there.

By now, she was in survival mode. She hurried to the living room where she ditched her singed cape and swapped it for one of Lulu's warm sheepskins sweaters and a wool pashmina. She then went to the washroom to examine her face in the small mirror that hung over the sink. The sets of abrasions on her cheek and neck were, thankfully, not serious, but they stung. She washed her face and hands, attempting to wipe away evidence that she had been caught in a fire. After all that happened tonight, she did not know who else might recognize her in this city, or who else might want her dead. She quickly scanned the trailer to see if there was something—anything she could take with her that could be helpful—but stopped short.

Here I am, a Gypsy thief.

She took a breath and grabbed ten euros and whatever bits of change sat on top of the counter.

"I'm truly sorry, Lulu."

Figuring she had already spent too much time lingering in Lulu's trailer, Sofi prepared her escape from the South Commune. As she turned to leave, she recollected one more, and very important, thing.

Earlier that day, Lulu showed her a map of Paris. She had pointed out the location of some of the city's major sites, such as the Eiffel Tower and the Arc de Triomphe. She remembered that Lulu placed the map, along with a pocket French dictionary, in a drawer to the right of the stove. She forced the sticky drawer open with a knife, grabbed the map and dictionary, and stuffed them into one of the sweater's pockets. Mimicking a group of Muslim women she saw during the train ride to Paris last week, she wrapped the wool pashmina over her head and across her mouth to hide her face. She ran out as quickly and quietly as she had come; back up the little hill, through the evergreen thicket, and onto the train tracks, which she planned to follow north until she reached the nearest train station.

Chapter Nineteen

Sofi stared at the large clock that hung above the timetable of RER trains. From her travels on the rails less than a week before, she remembered that these trains ran into the heart of Paris, and this particular station stayed open all night. She knew she needed to get far away from the South Commune. She also needed protection from the below freezing windchill. Still, she was clueless as to where she would go.

By now it was nearly one-thirty in the morning and Sofi was completely spent—mentally, physically, and most of all, emotionally. As she sat quietly, unable to think, the tears started to come again. She angrily brushed them away and forced herself to concentrate on devising a plan.

This was no time for her to fall apart. There were people who wanted her dead, and she had no one but herself to rely on. She knew that her mother would want her to fight and never give up, just as Nadja had done so many years ago when she was apparently banished from everyone she knew and loved.

That's why Mama was so strong. She had to be. For me. I can do this for her...

With renewed strength, Sofi went over the events of the past few days; her visits with Lulu, her times with Marko and Anka, and the last wonderful afternoon she ever spent with her Mama. She thought about all the people they met and all the things they did since arriving in France. Her thoughts hovered over the strange, intimidating men in suits she encountered earlier that day, and the disgusting animals she overheard that night. Both frightened her and gave her a creepy feeling inside.

The men I saw tonight weren't the same men I saw earlier. Are they somehow linked? Maybe it's just coincidence...maybe I should just go back to the South Commune?

"I can't go back," she declared, determined.

With her mother's final warning ringing in her ears, Sofi fought through her weariness and tried to remember her mother's words verbatim. She knew her Mama would never leave her without helping her as best she could. Excruciating as it was to imagine herself back in the fire, she knew she needed to remember every word her mother said to her before she died.

As she drifted deeper into thought, Sofi reached down out of habit and pulled her locket from beneath Lulu's sweater. She mindlessly twirled the locket's chain in her fingers for a while, then held the piece firmly in her hand. As the memories of her mother's death became more vivid and painful, the tighter she squeezed, inadvertently pressing the large sapphires into her hand so deeply that her palm began to throb.

It took her a few moments to separate the physical sensation from her emotional torment. She looked down and saw that the locket's strange coat of arms created an impression in her hand. She traced the outline of the coat of arms with her index finger and considered the significance, if any, of the pendant. It was then she remembered. Her mother told her that the necklace was actually a secret locket and she wanted Sofi to open it.

Sofi began to study the locket very carefully. She admired it countless times since her mother gave it to her and always had a feeling that there was more to it than its obvious uniqueness and exquisite beauty. Her mother's words now made perfect sense. She searched for a clasp that would unlatch the locket.

I should have known this wouldn't be easy.

In fact, no matter how closely she looked or how many different ways she turned the piece of jewelry, she could not seem to figure out where or how the locket was supposed to open. There was no evidence of a line around its perimeter that would indicate a break in the solid gold; no sign of a soldered hinge, nothing at all that hinted at how to open the mysterious cerulean locket.

What else did she say? Sofi struggled to remember. *Oh yes! Mama said to use the orb and that I'll know what to do.*

In the dim light of the Villeneuve-Prairie train station, she was relieved to finally see that the sapphire orb in the center was actually a handle that opened the locket.

"It's so obvious now!" she exclaimed, surprised that she never seen it before, but impressed by the locket's clever design. Never in a million years would she have noticed it without her mother's help.

Before she could open it, she heard footsteps and quickly stuffed the locket back into her sweater. She wrapped the pashmina over her head like a hijab and draped it over the front of her face to hide from the approaching figure. Hanging her head low, she pretended to nap, but snuck a peek from the corner of her eye at the person who made his way towards her. Her heart raced.

Oh please, please, leave me alone! she prayed, terrified that one of the bald, tattooed men had come to finish her off.

She considered running, but thought better of it. No sense drawing any unnecessary attention to herself. Instead, she sat still and tried to control her panicked thoughts.

As the figure drew closer, she could see that he was no threat. He was young, blond, and tan like a surfer. He wore a puffy coat and a huge backpack. He mumbled something to himself in what sounded like English while looking impossibly perplexed. In one hand, he held a Métro map; in the other, a French to English dictionary. He scratched his head, trying to make out the timetable of trains that was posted on the wall. They did not match the map he was using. Clearly, he had yet to realize that this was the RER train and not the Métro. He peeked over at Sofi for a second with a pleading look, as if he would ask her for help, but she kept her head down.

Satisfied that he was not out to kill her, Sofi looked from side to side and reached back into her sweater. She pulled the locket's sapphire orb, which opened a little door in the front. Hoping for a miracle, she reached inside and found a tiny, rolled piece of parchment paper tied neatly with a pretty blue ribbon. Before opening it, she took another sweep of the station. The young backpacker was still the only other person around. She carefully untied the ribbon and unraveled the scroll.

Written precisely in elegant calligraphy was a name and address of a person she had never heard of before. She began to worry, searching her memories to determine if the name sounded even vaguely familiar. She came up empty. Perplexed, she read the address again.

16 Rue des Rosiers, No. 3, 75004, Paris, France…that can't be too far away. Mama must have wanted me to find this person. Maybe this is the reason why she gave me this locket in the first place. Did she know we were in danger?

Sofi committed the name and address to memory before returning it to its place inside her locket. She looked at the timetable and saw that the last train of the evening would soon depart, so if she wanted to reach her intended destination tonight, she would need to move fast.

She brushed herself off and hurried over to the ticket window. The attendant slumped behind the desk, nodding in and out of sleep. She reached into the pocket of Lulu's sweater, pulled out the dictionary, and made her best attempt at conversational French.

"Pardonnez moi, si vous plait?" she said timidly. It was strange to hear herself recite a completely foreign language. Though the words she used were correct, her quiet tone was not loud enough to awaken the sleepy Frenchman.

"Monsieur? Si vous plait? Her voice was stronger this time, as she grew more desperate with each word she uttered. "I need your help!"

"Oui! I'm awake!" the man nervously squeaked, leaping out of his chair and losing his hat in the process. He looked around anxiously, like a little squirrel that had misplaced his acorns, and began to fidget with the papers in front of him. All the while he did not seem to notice Sofi, though she stood directly in front of him.

"Monsieur! Hello?"

At the sight of Sofi he gasped, then awkwardly disappeared beneath the counter. A moment later, he popped back up wearing his hat. This time, he was perfectly composed.

"Bonsoir, mademoiselle," he purred, raising an eyebrow and giving Sofi a silly grin. "May I help you?"

"Oui, monsieur. I would like to take the train to Rue des Rosiers."

"Rue des Rosiers…in the fourth arrondissement?"

"Je suis désolé, monsieur. Je ne sais pas!"

The man looked Sofi up and down. Though lovely, she appeared to him to be a very sad sort of person. She was dressed like an Eastern European with a distinctive accent, but her features looked entirely French.

"Where exactly are you going? What's the address?"

Sofi recited it perfectly from her very sharp memory.

"Ah, oui! Absolument!" The man was pleased that he could help. "You're going to a very historic neighborhood. Le Marais, home of the Pletzl."

Sofi looked at him blankly.

"The Pletzl! It's the Jewish quarter. You should not look so unhappy, young lady. It's a lovely place."

Realizing that she probably did not understand him, he slowed down and spoke very loudly. "Listen carefully," he all but yelled, "you are going to Le Marias, understand? It is in the fourth arrondissement. If you get lost, just ask for the Pletzl. Say, the Pletzel," he instructed.

"The Pletz—"

"Right!" he interrupted. "Now, you'll need this." He handed her a map showing the two transit systems she would utilize on her journey. "Here," he pointed, "this is the RER train. And this is where you are right now—Villenueve-Prairie, see? He circled the starting point. "This is the D line, which is green, understand?"

Sofi nodded affirmatively.

"Now, you want to take this all the way to here." He took his pen and drew a square around another stop, Gare de Lyon. "There, you get off the train and look for signs that look like this." He showed Sofi a picture of a sign, which read Métro.

"See, like this. Do you understand?"

Sofi asked him to go over it one more time so she could memorize the directions, then she repeated back everything he had explained.

"Excellent, mademoiselle! Okay, at Gare de Lyon take Métro One, which is yellow, to Saint-Paul." He drew a large box around Saint-Paul so Sofi would not forget. "Now listen, this is important. When you get on the yellow line, make sure you go in the direction of La Defense. See what I mean?" He showed Sofi on her map and she nodded. "Rue des Rosiers is very close to Saint-Paul. You should have no trouble then. Are you sure you understand?"

"Yes, I understand." Sofi pulled out the ten euros and showed the attendant. "Do I have enough money for a ticket?"

"Of course! You have just enough money to make it to Le Marais." He took the ten euros and gave her a ticket and change.

"Now, when you get to Gare de Lyon, you need to buy a new ticket for the Métro—line one, yellow. Okay? Buy a new Métro ticket at Gare de Lyon," he shouted, hoping she understood. "Your trip should take thirty minutes. But make sure you catch this next train since it's the last one from this station. It's coming now. Hurry!"

The man shook his arm at Sofi, encouraging her to run to meet the train that had just pulled up.

"Merci beaucoup, monsieur!" Sofi yelled back and waved as she ran to the train. She managed to board just before the doors closed.

Though she was unbelievably drained, she felt more alert on the train from Villenueve-Prairie to Gare de Lyon than she had ever been. She watched intently as the bright fluorescent lights inside the car cast an unattractive hue on the faces of the few other passengers who slumped in their seats.

Never before had she lived in a city of any size. Apart from the first and only trip she took with her mother to Paris, she had never traveled by train, or by car, for that matter. In Bulgaria, she walked everywhere. Though she loathed the lengthy train ride from Bulgaria to France, she now felt fortunate that she at least had some travel experience under her belt. Without it, she would have been completely at a loss.

At the next stop, a group of twenty-somethings barreled into the car. Still afraid to draw attention to herself, she turned around very slowly and inconspicuously studied them. They were musicians. They carried various instruments and were dressed in flamboyant costumes, maybe on their way back from a gig. Sofi marveled at the purple pleather miniskirt and pink tights that one of the girls wore and stole a long look at the lime green sneakers and mohawk of another. Watching them put her at ease a little, and she allowed herself to relax into her seat, pulling Lulu's sweater tightly around her. She wondered what her mother might have worn when she was part of the taraf so long ago.

Once she began to think of her mother, it was not long until her thoughts went back to all that had transpired earlier that evening. Struggling to maintain her composure which was by now extremely fragile, she could not keep a large, single tear from falling from her eye. The tear was then followed by another, and then, another. Feeling herself falling apart, she pushed back her tears, sat straight up in her seat, and battled her thoughts. She forced herself to focus on the present, which helped to push the images of her mother's bloodied body out of her mind.

What am I going to say when I get there? Will this person even know who I am? Will he even be there?

She practiced a little dialogue in her head, using her French dictionary to learn some new words that might be useful to her later.

When the train reached Gare de Lyon about twenty-five minutes later, Sofi was the first to hop off. A few other passengers followed, but to her relief, they went about their business without paying her any mind.

After the train pulled away, Sofi looked around Gare de Lyon in amazement. The station was expansive and striking with multiple levels, colorful billboards, and the largest timetable she had ever seen. Though it was well after two in the morning, the place was far from empty. A constant stream of travelers walked by Sofi with their luggage in tow.

Remembering the attendant's instructions, she followed the Métro signs down several flights of stairs and through a long tunnel, which opened to a brightly lit platform with thick, metal columns painted a garish yellow. She looked around, unsure if she was in the right place, but soon noticed a large sign, which read, *Paris Métro Line One*. She hurried over to the ticket window and spotted a single employee who was getting ready to close up shop. She tapped nervously on the glass.

"Si vous plait, monseiur. I need a ticket."

This man was not as friendly or helpful as the attendant at Villeneuve-Prairie. Seeing a young, miserable, and poorly dressed girl before him, the man grunted dismissively. He put out his hand and tapped his foot impatiently. Sofi quickly reached into her pocket and pulled out five euros.

"One ticket to Saint-Paul, please."

"Make sure you get on the next train. It's the last one of the night. If you miss it, you'll have to come back in the morning." The grumpy man dumped the ticket and change on the counter and quickly shut the blinds.

Taking a seat on a nearby bench, Sofi waited for the train to arrive. To keep the almost constant flow of tears from reaching past her throat, she buried her head in her Métro map and looked for her destination, which she was relieved to see was very close.

Several minutes passed before the final train of the evening came to a screeching halt on the tracks. As she boarded the car, Sofi looked back to a clock that hung in the middle of the platform's main wall.

No wonder I'm so tired. It's nearly three in the morning!

Sofi yawned loudly but decided not to sit down. Since the train ride would be short, she did not want to risk falling asleep. The last thing she needed was to miss her stop.

The train arrived at Saint-Paul minutes later, though it could not have been soon enough for Sofi. Exiting the train carefully as not to make a wrong turn, she followed a person who looked as though he knew where he was going. After climbing a flight of stairs, she could tell she was approaching ground level. She looked past the final flight of stairs and saw a sliver of the cold, dark sky.

A loud metallic sound clashed behind her. She jumped, nearly stumbling on the steps, but was relieved to see that it was just a Métro worker locking a large metal gate.

"No more trains this evening, mademoiselle," he called. "The Métro is closed until daybreak."

"Monsieur, si vous plait! Which way to Rue des Rosiers?" she asked breathlessly through her tears, which had inexplicably started to fall again.

Without looking up, he pointed in the direction of a one-way street. "Straight down Rue Malher and take a left."

Caught up in an intense wave of momentary exhaustion, Sofi could not move. The man looked up at her, intending to shoo her away, but was surprised when his eyes met a pitiably desperate-looking young person. He wondered what on earth had happened to her that night. Feeling compassion for Sofi, who appeared to be the same age as his own daughter, the Métro worker softened his tone and stopped fiddling with the sticky lock.

"Listen, chéri, this is a safe part of town," he said. "You will be fine. Go up the steps then turn to the left. You will see Rue Malher. It's very close. Walk down Rue Malher and take another left on Rue des Roisers. What number on Rue des Roisers?"

"Sixteen, sir."

"You'll be there in minutes, you'll see. And try not to worry, dear. I'm sure everything will be okay."

Chapter Twenty

Sofi thanked the man as best she could and hurried up the stairs. When she reached the top, she was relieved to see that the Métro worker's assessment of the neighborhood was spot on. This area seemed quite safe and comfortably awake at three in the morning, though not bustling. Several of the area's quaint restaurants and bars were just closing their doors. Though heavy metal gates hung over each of the many shops that lined the main thoroughfare of Rue de Rivoli, Sofi could see that they were pretty and well-kept. She turned left onto Rue Malher, just as the Métro worker had instructed, and found that the one-way street was quiet save for the distant bark of a noisy Pomeranian. After only two minutes of walking, she turned east onto Rue des Rois-es, the street of the rosebushes. Walking briskly across the cobblestones, she glanced around at the little Jewish shops and colorful restaurants sandwiched between high-end clothing boutiques.

Taking in the stillness of the scene before her, she slowed her pace and eventually stopped in the middle of the street. The hot tears on her ice-cold cheeks stung unbearably, adding insult to her injurious night. The smell of smut on her clothes was overwhelming. She looked up at the stars and inhaled deeply, letting the night air fill her chest. The fresh sensation against her smoke-stained lungs made her cough. Raising her chin to the navy blue sky, she groaned.

"Mama, if you can hear me, please help me."

Sofi's legs carried her to the intersection of Rue des Roises and Rue Ferdinand Duval. The white light of a black wrought iron lamppost illuminated a large wooden doorway, which was situated between a bakery and an accessories shop. The pleasant picture in front of her was so opposite from the dingy trailers of the South Commune. It was hard to believe that these two worlds were separated by just thirty kilometers.

She reached building sixteen in moments.

Now what?

This was, indeed, her intended destination. She worried that the person she would meet inside would turn her away—or worse.

How will I ever explain why I'm here in the middle of the night?

She looked down at the cement stoop outside the front door and considered camping out there until sunrise, but then thought better of it. Those men might still be after her.

Biting her lip and holding her locket tight, Sofi pushed open the heavy iron door and stepped inside. She figured that apartment number three must be on the third level, so she tentatively made her way up the detailed staircase and walked over to the only door on the floor. Mustering all her courage, she gave three hard knocks.

No answer.

With the knot in her stomach growing larger and tighter by the minute, she felt as though she might vomit right there on the doorstep. After several moments of silence, she decided to give it another try. She told herself that if no one answered this time, she would wait in the stairwell until morning. She banged again, harder this time, and paused.

Still no answer.

By now she was totally dejected, miserably depressed, and terribly fatigued. Her legs gave out beneath her and tried to grasp the banister, but it was too late. She collapsed. She tried her best to stand, but didn't have the strength. She felt like giving up. Her eyes brimmed with tears and she crumbled to the floor, defeated. Her chest heaved and her frame trembled uncontrollably.

This is the end for me.

Through her convulsive sobs, she thought she heard a creaking sound. She lifted her head to find that the door of apartment three was open, revealing a fiercely attractive young man. Sofi was stunned.

The man looked back and forth several times, obviously confused, and scratched the top of his head. At first he did not realize that Sofi was even there. When he finally looked down, he caught sight of her, piled in a soot-stained heap at his doorstep.

From the look on his face, he clearly did not know how to react to the unexpected sight of this lovely, yet thoroughly depressed and horrendously dirty, young woman. She was obviously in some sort of distress. She looked French, but her odd, mismatched attire appeared to be that of a Gypsy.

"Was that you banging on my door?" he demanded.

"Je suis désolé, monsieur. Please don't turn me away." Sofi tried to put on a brave face and brushed away her tears. "I'm looking for Isaiah Becerra."

"Who wants to know?"

He spoke so quickly that Sofi could not understand him, but she nonetheless launched into the story she had practiced in French on the train.

"My name is Sofi. A bad thing, a very bad thing. Fire. Please help." She tried to speak as best she could, but her nerves caused her to forget the words.

The young man looked at her quizzically. She was so forlorn, so sad. And he could not understand a word she was saying.

"Please, sir. Help me."

"Listen, I don't know who you are or what you want but it's late. Go home to your parents. Go on, now. Go home."

"Please!" she cried out in utter desperation. "Help me!"

Frustrated that she could not communicate her situation more fully, her tears flowed furiously.

"Please, Isaiah Becerra. You are supposed to help me…" she hoarsely choked out, this time in Bulgarian. She looked up at Isaiah one last time, eyes full of sorrow, cheeks wet from crying.

Isaiah rubbed the sleep from his eyes and ran a hand through his thick, black hair. Though he truly felt sorry for the girl, he had no time to trifle with Gypsy theatrics. He had a very busy morning ahead of him. In just a few hours, his least favorite person in the entire world, Philippe Roubert, would lead an emergency meeting in the President's office. Still, something about the girl pulled at his heart strings.

"Look," he said more gently, "if you need some money, I think I have some spare change lying around."

Devastated and completely devoid of hope, Sofi threw her hands over her face. Her shoulders slumped miserably. The locket, which she had been grasping so tightly, fell back to its place at her heart. As it dangled at her neck, the sapphire orb caught the rays of the hallway's dim overhead light, and it sparkled directly into Isaiah's eyes. He squinted, then caught sight of the prominent gold and sapphire piece.

"Let me see that," he quickly commanded as he reached for the locket.

Frightened by the man's unexpected touch, Sofi cowered.

"Where'd you get this?" he ordered in Bulgarian.

Sofi's mouth gaped. She was shocked that this Spanish-looking man who lived in a Jewish neighborhood of Paris spoke perfect Bulgarian.

"This?" Sofi grabbed her locket protectively and recoiled again. "This is mine. My mother gave it to me."

"Did you steal it?"

"No! I'm no thief. As I told you, it's mine. It's a family heirloom. It's all I have left."

Since his tone was getting him nowhere, Isaiah tried a different approach.

"What did you say your name was, if you please?"

"My name is Sofi," she answered back. "My mother is…" Her voice broke momentarily before starting again. "My mother *was* Nadja Vadoma. She gave me this locket for my birthday and told me it was a family heirloom. She was killed tonight by a group of men who burned down our home." The tears came back in full force now, and her chest heaved and shook as she struggled to speak. "Before she died, she warned me that I was in danger. She said to open the locket. I found your name and address inside. I have nowhere else to go."

Isaiah's eyes widened. He put his hand to his forehead, clearly flabbergasted.

"Could it be?" he asked himself aloud in French.

"What did you say?"

"Excuse me," he answered, quickly switching back to Bulgarian. "What did you say your mother's name was?"

"Nadja Vadoma."

"Sofi," he said very kindly, "would you please come inside so we can talk privately? I can see you've been through a lot tonight. I promise you'll be safe here, and I won't do anything to hurt you. Do you understand?"

Sofi could not speak. She managed only to shake her head. Isaiah reached down to help her to her feet, but she was very unsteady.

"You're not well. Let me help you," he offered.

"No, no. Thank you, but I can manage…"

She attempted to take a step forward but instead teetered back. Her head was swimming and she could not see clearly through her tear-stained eyes.

Isaiah, on the other hand, could no longer hide his pity for the doleful young woman. Her physical exhaustion and mental anguish were painfully obvious. Though she was covered in ash, her undeniable beauty showed through. In an impulsive move, he reached around her slender body and effortlessly hoisted her into his arms. With ease, he carried her across the threshold and into his large and richly furnished apartment. He looked at her curiously while holding her close, attempting to connect with her onyx eyes.

"How old are you, Sofi?"

"Sixteen," she said, turning her face to avoid his stare. She had never been so close to a man before, let alone a handsome one. He smelled musky and she liked it, which made her quite uncomfortable.

"Is that so?" He shook his head in disbelief. "Sixteen. Well, it would be right."

"What would be right?"

Isaiah did not reply. With the utmost care, he placed Sofi down on a very comfortable, and obviously expensive leather armchair. Though it appeared that she could crumble from fatigue at any moment, he was surprised to see that she forced herself to sit perfectly upright, either too terrified or too suspicious of him to move. Her dark eyes darted wildly around the room as if she was planning an emergency escape route.

"Sofi," he said softly, "I promised you before that I wouldn't do anything to hurt you. I believe I may be a close friend of your family."

"You knew my mother?" Sofi's expression instantly flashed bright with hope.

"No. I'm sorry to say that I've never met your mother."

"Oh."

"Do you know who your father is?"

"No, I never knew my father. My mother never told me anything about him. Not even his name," she said, continuing to avoid his gaze.

"I see. Well, your mother somehow knew to send you to the right place. By the looks of you, I assume you now know that there are people who want you dead. In truth, I had no idea you existed until you showed up here. But things are starting to make sense to me now. But please, be still and try to relax. You must be totally exhausted."

She was. Most of Isaiah's words just swirled in her head, making little sense. The lacerations on her face burned while the rest of her body was freezing. She had not noticed before, but her teeth were chattering, and by the look on Isaiah's face, she figured she must look quite wretched.

"Please excuse my appearance," she said, finally making eye contact. "I was trapped in a fire that killed my mother." With her last sentence, the tears came again. "I didn't know what else to do!" she blurted out through her sobs. "My mother told me to open my locket, and that's how I found you."

Something about the stillness of the room, the softness of the chair, and the warmth of Isaiah's scent caused Sofi's head to swim.

"They wanted both of us dead," she mumbled. "I'm next. They want to kill me...to kill me..."

Sofi's voice drifted off as her eyes began to close. The more she fought sleep, the heavier her lids became.

"It's okay, Sofi. Rest now."

Isaiah watched Sofi sleep for some time, wondering what on earth had happened to her. Her smooth and lovely face was marked with a cluster of abrasions on one side and her eyes were red and visibly swollen from what appeared to be hours of crying. Curled in the fetal position, she hugged one long, thin arm around herself. With her free hand, she clutched the locket tightly. In her sleep, she muttered something incomprehensible.

Isaiah moved closer to Sofi and covered her with a blanket, then stretched her long legs onto the nearby leather ottoman. He considered putting her in bed, but did not want to risk waking or frightening her. Instead, he reached for his cell phone and called Amié at the Palace. He would have to miss Roubert's all-important Saturday meeting.

"The world doesn't revolve around you, Roubert," he said after hanging up the phone.

With that, he latched the dead bolt of his front door with extra emphasis and returned to Sofi. It was not long before he, too, was lulled to sleep by the sound of her soft, steady breaths.

Chapter Twenty-One

As daybreak turned to morning, the winter sun's rays gradually filtered through the floor to ceiling windows of Isaiah Becerra's comfortable flat, filling the living room with warmth. His first waking thought was the poor, young girl who sought refuge on his doorstep in the early morning hours.

In the light of day, and with a few additional hours of rest, Isaiah considered the potential scenarios surrounding his mysterious guest. He studied Sofi's physical characteristics—her straight nose, full mouth, creamy rose complexion, and distinctive height. He also calculated her age against the limited information he had about René's past life. Though he tried hard to fight against the clues right in front of his face, he was eventually forced to concede that Hartenau-Hesse blood possibly flowed through her veins.

If her familiar features did not provide adequate support for her lineage, the unmistakable sapphire studded locket bearing the royal Hartenau-Hesse coat of arms was a dead giveaway. In fact, the crest at the top of the coat of arms was identical to the one that was etched into the President's gold and cerulean sapphire signet ring, which he wore

every day since Isaiah first met him over a decade ago. O
course, the best and most accurate way to determine th
veracity of his supposition was to administer a DNA test, bu
that would certainly not be possible at present.

Isaiah wondered how René could turn his back o
his daughter, but concluded it was out of the question. Cer
tainly, if René knew he had a child, he would have taker
care of her without hesitation. There was no question o
René's profound sense of duty.

He knew he needed to talk to René as soon as possi
ble, but he was not looking forward to it. While the two
could discuss any topic, no matter how personal, the mer
thought of their impending conversation gave him heart
burn.

What if I am completely wrong about all this?

As Isaiah continued to gaze at Sofi while wrestling
with ideas about what to do, she started to stir. Still in th
comfort of sleep, she smiled serenely and stretched, flutter
ing her eyelashes before resting back into the armchair. Afte
settling back into her position, she popped up quite quick
ly—eyes wide and scared. She searched the room helplessly
as though she were lost in a fog.

"Sofi, it's okay. You're safe. It's me, Isaiah. Remem
ber? You came here last night."

She looked into Isaiah's eyes, which were an capti
vating shade of greenish hazel in the morning light, and
breathed a sigh of relief.

"I'm sorry, Isaiah. I think I forgot where I was. Las
night was such a nightmare. I thought I'd dreamt it. I can'
believe it's real!"

No sooner did she utter the words did a flood of painful images rush to the front of her mind. She broke down, remembering the beaten and bloodied face of her dear mother, nearly dead on the floor of their burning trailer.

"Listen, Sofi," Isaiah said, "you've got to be hungry and thirsty, plus you seem to have a few cuts on your face and hands that must sting. Why don't you take a warm shower while I will run next door to grab some breakfast. You don't have to be afraid. I won't hurt you."

Sofi thanked Isaiah quietly, feeling unsure as to how she was supposed to act. She was unaccustomed to being alone with a man. Admittedly, she never had extensive contact with anyone outside of her small community back home, with the exception of the few short-lived friendships she made in the South Commune. In fact, she had never even been inside of a gadjé home, other than during her time spent with the Laporte's when she was a young child.

"Thank you, Isaiah. I'm so sorry to have brought you such trouble," she blurted out apologetically through her tears. "I cannot tell you enough how grateful I am for everything you've done."

"I've done nothing yet, believe me."

Isaiah disappeared into his bedroom to rummage through his drawers and pulled out a pair of A.P.C. jeans, a Lacoste tee shirt, and a Marc Jacobs hoodie.

"Obviously I don't have any women's clothing here, but you can wear some of my things," he called out. "You're tall, so you won't look absolutely ridiculous."

He looked back at her and laughed nervously, trying not to admire her soft face and dark, glossy tresses.

"Um, there's fresh towels in the bathroom. You won't be disturbed." Isaiah's speech was a bit muffled as he threw on some clothes, brushed his teeth, and came back into the living room. "I'll be back in twenty minutes with something to eat. There's juice in the fridge. Make yourself...comfortable."

He stole a glance back at Sofi one last time before he left.

She certainly is a beautiful girl, and young. God, I hope the neighbors don't catch sight of her.

He fretted momentarily, but his concern passed. He felt such pity for her. He, too, knew the pain of losing a parent to tragedy.

Back in the apartment, Sofi struggled to pull herself together. After a few minutes of staring into space, curiosity got the best of her and she began to look around. A fireplace with a magnificent mantle was flanked by ornate built-ins filled with books in French, Italian, Spanish, Hebrew and Greek. French doors led to a balcony overlooking the Pletzl. Each piece of carefully selected furniture was covered in soft, chocolate leather. A Persian rug covered the reclaimed wooden floors. Sofi turned her back to the windows and noticed a contemporary open-concept kitchen complete with all the bells and whistles, though it appeared to have never been used.

As she robotically surveyed the design of the space, she mindlessly touched her cheek, but drew her hand back. The sting of her abrasions burned hot under her skin.

Figuring that a shower was probably a good idea, she made her way to the bedroom. She saw where Isaiah neatly placed some clothing for her on his enormous canopy bed. To the right of the bed was a pocket door leading to the master bathroom, which was beautifully tiled in a surprisingly modern design for such an obviously old building. Closing the bathroom door, she realized there was no need for her to turn on a light. Sunlight streamed through a large skylight above.

This man must be rich, she thought as she undressed and stepped into the large and very complex shower.

She looked for a faucet, but there was not one to be found. After what felt like hours of anxious confusion, she finally noticed a contraption that appeared to be a touch-screen computer with a myriad of options.

Sofi never used a computer before. Undeterred, she took a breath and set her sights on the screen, which gave options for water, steam, and other French words she did not recognize. After a few missed tries, she found her way to the right button. Perfectly warm water sprayed from the walls of the shower in every direction. Awestruck, she all but jumped into the stall, letting the shooting jets massage her sore and banged up body. The soothing water also helped to clear her mind.

Not long after she finished showering, Isaiah returned with a bag of groceries and the morning paper.

"Hi," he said awkwardly.

Clean and dressed in slim cut designer clothes, Sofi looked a lot less like a vagabond and much more like a runway model.

"Hello, Isaiah."

"Um...how are you feeling?"

"Better," she answered truthfully, combing her fingers through her damp hair.

"After I left, I remembered that I hadn't shown you how to turn the shower on. I hope you didn't have any trouble."

"No trouble at all." She bit her lip as she lied.

"I thought maybe you'd like to try some Jewish brunch foods. Croissants, salmon pancakes, and matzah brei."

Sofi's eyes lit up with Isaiah's mention of food. Though she was still shell-shocked by all that had happened in the last twelve hours, she could not deny her natural teenage need for sustenance. Leaving her trepidation behind, she literally followed her nose to the completely foreign, yet enticing, spread.

"I'm starving," she confessed as she sniffed the salmon pancakes with interest. "Thank you."

"It's no trouble." Isaiah looked sheepishly at Sofi, embarrassed by his own prejudice. He found himself increasingly surprised by, and attracted to, Sofi's gentle voice and articulate manner. "Bon appetit."

"Aren't you going to have some, Isaiah? You must be hungry."

"No, no. I don't eat breakfast…only coffee." Isaiah smiled into his travel mug and breathed the aroma. "Actually, Sofi, I want to show you something." He pointed to the morning newspaper. "The fire you escaped made the front page."

Sofi looked at him with dread.

"Never mind. We'll talk about it after you eat. Just try to relax for now. I'm not going into the office until later, so we'll have time to talk."

Chapter Twenty-Two

"So, Mr. President, I see your young aide decided not to grace us with his presence this morning," Philippe Roubert hacked out sarcastically. "Is it too early for the man or does he refuse to work on his Sabbath?"

"Neither," René responded flatly, annoyed by Roubert's narrow remarks. "He has a pressing family matter that requires his immediate attention. He'll join me later today."

"A family matter? Ha! Wonder what that boy is up to," Roubert smirked. "Well, at least we won't be bothered by his constant interruptions."

Roubert sank into the silk cushions of the Louis XVI armchair and reached into the breast pocket of his pin-striped sport jacket.

"Really, Roubert, it's six-thirty in the morning! Don't you ever take a break from those things?"

In all the years René's knew him, the thing that tried his patience the most was Roubert's seemingly constant attachment to his cigars.

"This is my breakfast," he replied nonchalantly from the side of his mouth while toasting the cigar's foot. He blew pungent black smoke in René direction and laughed heartily.

"Come on, man. Good God!"

"Well, well, René! You are quite the agitated one this morning." Roubert was amused by the President's irritated tone, which was quite the opposite of his typically collected self. "What's happened?"

"You really want to know? *This* happened." René threw the morning paper on the glass coffee table. "Take a look at the headline.

Roubert squinted hard to make out the print on the front page.

"René, you know I can't read this! It's too small." Frustrated, he flung it back down. "Read it to me."

"Fine. The headline reads, *Neo-Nazis prime suspects in Roma murder by fire.* Shall I continue?"

"Go on."

Last night, two Roma burned to death in their trailer home, located in Choisy-le-Roi's growing Gypsy camp, the South Commune Firemen found the remains of two women, one of whom sustained serious injuries including a broken jaw and multiple fractures to the face. Witnesses identified the victims as a mother and daughter who recently came to France from Eastern Europe. Witnesses also say they saw three suspicious men, described as skinheads, loitering around the camp that night.

These deaths come on the heels of President Hartenau-Hesse's recently introduced Roma Expulsion legislation that remains hotly contested by Socialist leaders in the National Assembly. Despite widespread protests by international human rights organizations, and mounting violence against Roma in Western Europe, the MFF continues to adamantly endorse the legislation. Opponents of the measure believe that

Hartenau-Hesse's decision to back such a controversial bill may hurt his chances for reelection.

Incensed, René crushed the paper between his massive hands and let it fall to the floor. Roubert, on the other hand, sat very calmly, much to René's annoyance.

"So what do you want me to do about it, René?"

"What's wrong with you, Roubert? Have you nothing else to say? You're the one who called this meeting."

"I don't know what you want from me. So some Gypsies died in a fire. So what? What does that have to do with anything we're working on?"

"It has everything to do with this legislation, that's what! This article, and many others like it, implies that the legislation and the sentiments around it are responsible for the death of these women and others. Our strongest selling point is that we have the public's support. But their backing is beginning to wane as more tragedies like this come to light."

He turned his back to Roubert and paced the length of the north wall of the Golden Room.

"You came to me in early fall with disturbing reports about the living conditions of the Roma, and the activities that were taking place in their illegal camps. Then, you provided my team with a shocking and detailed follow up—reports of prostitution, human trafficking, rampant disease, terrorist infiltrations, and God only knows what else. But, all this while, we've seen little actual, targeted violence against the Roma. No uprisings and generally fewer problems than those that our neighbors to the East have been dealing with all these years."

Roubert responded by rolling his eyes, which irritat
ed René even more.

"Until the legislation was introduced, France had
zero reported incidents of violence against the Roma by our
citizenry. And, there's been very little known neo-Nazi activ
ity here in recent years. In fact, the last report of a hate
crime committed by skinheads was five years ago in that case
with the West African tradesman. Then, one week after we
introduced the legislation, we receive a report about a group
of men that beat a Roma man to death in Grenoble. Re
member that?"

"That was an isolated incident."

"No, it wasn't. The following week, three Roma
teens outside Lyon were arrested and beaten by the police
One of them died!" René's voice began to swell with anger
and frustration. "Now, we've got to deal with this situation
that's right under our noses. Two defenseless women—one a
minor—burned alive!" René kicked the crumpled paper and
sent it flying across the marble floor. "This isn't what I want
ed, Roubert. This expulsion policy is causing too much tur
moil. It's divisive. We've got to go about this another way
Clearly, some of our citizens think they have the right to take
the law into their own hands and we, the government, are
not providing a good example for them. We're showing them
that lives of Roma are of lesser value, not to mention the
fact that I'm getting trashed in the media because of it. I
don't want my name or my administration associated with
this any longer. I'm pulling it out of the Assembly."

As René stomped around the Golden Room, continuing to rant about the fire, he failed to notice Roubert's

color turn from beet red to stark white. When he finally turned around, Roubert was sweating profusely.

"Roubert! Are you alright?"

"Yes, dammit!" Roubert waved his hand dismissively at René and wiped his head with his handkerchief. "I'm fine. I just need some water. Maybe you were right about the damn cigar." He tossed the stub in the general direction of the ashtray.

René poured Roubert a glass of water, then called for Amié to bring them breakfast. When he returned to Roubert's side, he cooled his tone significantly, concerned that his forcefulness may have been the cause of Roubert's episode. He quietly watched the old man, who guzzled the water.

"Hang in there, old friend. Would you like me to call the doctor?"

"I said I'm fine, René," Roubert snapped. "I think I just need something to eat. The water definitely helped."

He straightened his posture, then wiped some small puddles of water that gathered on his shirt and tie.

"I don't know, Roubert. Maybe I should call the doctor."

"You will do no such thing!" he replied, sharply. "Look, I'm feeling better already. I'm ready to continue whenever you are."

"Are you quite sure?"

"Yes, of course I am. I don't want to be here all goddamn day! Believe me, I'm not going to die from hunger. Let's get on with it."

"Very well, then." René marveled at the old man's stubbornness, unsure how long Roubert could continue to keep up with his lifestyle. "As I was saying," he continued but this time more sedately, "we've recently seen a spike in the number of hate crimes against the Roma. There were only a few instances worth mentioning before the expulsion policy was introduced, but we've since had three gruesome cases in one month and the international media outlets are all over them."

"Well, you've hit the nail on the head there, René. It's the damn media, not the policy! They're skewing public perception with their liberalistic views, as always. Here's what you do," he pointed hard at René's chest. "Put a bug in the ear of the press secretary. Hold a press conference so the media can get their facts straight. Hammer them with the reasoning behind the expulsion policy. You know, the human trafficking and prostitution in particular. You'll win them over, I'm sure of it, and you'll continue to have the public's backing. But this talk about pulling our legislation is absolutely ludicrous! Now is the time for you to show strength."

"My mind is already made up. I'm just letting you know as a courtesy, Roubert. I told you, I'm going to go about his another way."

"I can't accept that. Listen—these setbacks have less to do with the expulsion policy and more to do with people who are fed up with paying higher taxes to support a group of people who are not French, who don't want to be French and who do nothing but drain our resources. Thieves and liars they are! These Gypsies provide no value, no services, nothing whatsoever in return for their ever-growing presence here."

René looked away and vehemently shook his head.

"Look, I know you feel somehow responsible for what happened to those two women last night," Roubert pressed on, "but I'll let you in on something..." he inched his way so close that René could feel the old man's cigar breath seep into his skin. "I know everything there is to know about those two Gypsies because I've had my people watching the South Commune camp for months. Nothing good comes from that place, I can assure you. Yes, the women were a mother and a daughter, that part is true. And, it's sad what happened to them. Very sad. But, the article neglected to include some very important facts."

"What do you mean?"

"Those women who died came to France very recently from Bulgaria. Like typical Gypsies, the mother had no job in Bulgaria. She came here without a valid work permit. They moved into a broken-down trailer that was stolen from the nearby garbage dump. As soon as they got here, the mother was hired by the Sherpus Hotel. They are notorious for employing Romanians, Bulgarians, and Gypsies. They brought her on as a maid—off the books, of course, so she wouldn't pay taxes out of her wages. She also planned to enroll her daughter in Choisy-le-Roi's public high school, paid for by whom? The taxpayers, of course! They were breaking our laws, René, and taking advantage of our good people. We've seen what these people have done to our neighbors. When the UK, Sweden, and Ireland lifted their restrictions a few years ago, they were absolutely flooded. The UK expected that 15,000 would come per year. Actual numbers are closer to a million in just a few years. We cannot have the same for France. You've got to understand that. Our citizens do! These women should be used an example of why we still need the restrictions and why passage of the expulsion policy is vital."

René listened quietly to Roubert's assessment and nodded.

"I feel badly about what happened to them, I really do," Roubert continued smoothly. "But think about it. They are a microcosm of what's going on here in France and throughout Western Europe. These Gypsies sneak into our nations illegally in droves! For each one who comes here and stays, they bring ten more along with them. These two women who died decided to come only after someone from their village back in Bulgaria suggested it. And they, in turn would have encouraged others to do the same. That Gypsy camp in Choisy-le-Roi is comprised almost entirely of nomads from Bulgaria and Romania and their numbers are growing exponentially. They live in extremely poor, dangerous conditions, yet they want to stay! It's their nature to live in squalor. Can't you see that? They come to take advantage of our social programs, and that hurts our citizens. In my estimation, and in light of this tragedy, the expulsion policy is needed now more than ever!"

René reclined in his chair and thought about it for some time before responding.

"You know, Roubert, you make an interesting argument, but you seem to completely disregard the human aspect in all this." He paused, considering his next words carefully. "These Gypsies—or Roma, I should say. They are people like you and me. We can't just ship them away like cattle."

"Like you and me? Oh no. You may equate yourself to them, but keep me the hell out of it!"

"Come, Roubert. We both know that many of them are not what they seem. I know you won't want me to say it, but I keep going back to the days before I was President. To a time before I even entered politics. Ever since I saw the headlines this morning, I've been thinking about my own experiences, my...my personal encounters with the Roma people many years ago. People like Nadja and her family. I know you couldn't have forgotten her. Surely, they were not like the people of the South Commune. Despite everything that happened, no one could deny her intelligence, her talent, and most of all, her humaneness. I sometimes wonder what her life is like today. She and her family would be so hurt if they knew about the Roma expulsion policy."

"Don't you dare start with that sentimental nonsense! I don't want to hear a word of it! There's absolutely no need to bring her up. No connection whatsoever. She's irrelevant!" Roubert angrily responded.

"Is she? That woman who died in the fire could have been someone just like her."

"We're talking about important national security matters here. Not your old feelings for some cheap carny act!"

"Cheap carny act! What the hell is wrong with you, Roubert?"

"Nothing is wrong with me. It's *you* who needs to get your head on straight. I don't want to hear any more!"

"My God, just listen for one moment. Hear me out!"

"René," Roubert said harshly, spitting with each word, "you sound like a lovesick nincompoop! I don't want to hear it! I mean it. That woman is long gone by now. Your mother would be very displeased to hear that you've been taking a trip down memory lane. And I'm sure Viviane wouldn't appreciate your meandering thoughts!"

"Meandering thoughts!?" René's voice boomed. "What the hell is that supposed to mean?"

"You know exactly what I mean! How would your wife feel if she found out you used to screw some Gypsy scum?"

"Roubert! You are out of line!"

"Am I? You're the one who brought her up. Wake the hell up, man! I'm concerned about the security of our nation and the best interests of our citizens. You're over there reminiscing about an old girlfriend!"

"You have absolutely no right to mention my wife, disrespect Nadja, or question my loyalty to France," René shouted back. "I thought that after all these years, we'd be able to talk about the past with civility. I see now that I was wrong. I should never have mentioned it. It's none of your business anyway."

"Of course you were wrong. You are most of the time," Roubert responded vindictively. "It's a good thing you've still got me to guide you. And, for the record, it is my business! It was back then as it is today. But I'm through talking about that woman. I never want to hear her name mentioned again."

Thoroughly aggravated, Roubert reached for his cane. "You'd better think about what I said before you make some half-baked decision based off old feelings that were nothing more than the desires of an oversexed playboy. You may be the President now, but just remember that I saved you from the biggest mistake of your life. Never forget it. I did that for you!"

"And don't you forget to whom you are speaking. Despite anything that happened in the past, I am your President and you will address me respectfully, Roubert." René's eyes flashed as he spoke.

"If what happened ever got out, you would have been sitting behind a desk at some law firm, and all your political aspirations would have been destroyed. I don't want to hear another word about it. If you want to reminisce about that Gypsy tramp, talk to that yes-man of yours. Not me. I have other things on my agenda today. I'm done here."

Roubert turned to leave and the room fell silent except for the echo of his rosewood cane against the marble floor. René, too infuriated to speak, stood motionless. He listened to the old man shuffle across the sprawling office towards the heavy double doors. He made no effort to help as Roubert struggled to open them, and did not flinch when the doors slammed shut.

Bigoted son of a bitch! No use trying to change his mind. Words wasted on ignorant ears. That old bastard always has to have the last word!

René pressed his fingers to his temples, frustrated by Roubert's perniciousness as well as his own weakness in dealing with him.

Why do I let him get to me like this after all this time?

He bolted from his seat and, with leaping strides, found his way to his favorite thinking spot in front of the north windows. He stared out into the winter gardens wearing a bittersweet expression. He pictured the first time he saw Nadja at his family's estate in Varna. Her lithe young body swayed alluringly to the strange music. Her smooth face was bright like a star. It glowed under the light of the silvery summer moon. Her impossibly dark eyes, nearly enveloped by a set of thick, black lashes, pierced him. Her enchanting voice was deep and strong, soaring through the night air and across the Black Sea.

It wasn't meant to be…

If not for their forced separation, he might never have reunited with his childhood sweetheart, who ultimately became his wife, his best friend, and the love of his life.

I hope you are living a happy life, Nadja, with healthy children and a husband who loves you. You deserve nothing less from this world.

Chapter Twenty-Three

Sofi listened intently to Isaiah as he translated the cover story of Le Parisien. Each word he read, she relived. She thought that some rest and a fresh perspective of the tragedy might shed some light on what she experienced the night before, but by the time Isaiah finished the article she felt only more confused, angry, and miserable.

"So you're telling me that two people died in the fire?" she asked in disbelief. "No, there's no way! The reporter has gotta be wrong. I swear to you, it was only Mama and me in there and clearly, I escaped."

"Are you sure you didn't see anyone else? Could someone have followed you inside?"

"I didn't see anyone else, but I guess I can't be sure. With all the flames, I could barely make out a thing. When I finally got out of there, the smoke was so thick and black. It was nearly impenetrable."

"Impenetrable? Really?" Isaiah hid a smirk. Despite the awful circumstances, he was increasingly enjoying the company of the surprisingly expressive teenager, but he quickly turned his thoughts aside. This was no time for him to find amusement in the linguistic idiosyncrasies of his young guest.

"After I ran in, I couldn't find my mother. When I saw her lying there, there wasn't anything I could do for her. I just let her die! It's all my fault!"

"But Sofi, the article says that the firemen found the remains of two women. Someone else must have gone inside the trailer after you," he prodded as gently as he could. "Can you think of who that may have been? Who else was there when the fire started?"

"I don't know!"

"Sofi, I know you want to push last night out of your mind, but this is very important. Try to concentrate. Try for me."

Sofi looked tentatively at Isaiah. His hazel eyes were full of compassion. Knowing that his intentions were true and realizing the significance of remembering every detail, she took a deep breath and cleared the confusing jumble of horrific images from her mind. She tried to focus her energy on remembering exactly what transpired less than twelve hours ago.

After a few moments of silence, her eyes opened wide, as if she had a painful epiphany. It finally dawned on her why her neighbor was nowhere to be found when she went to her trailer for help after the fire.

"Dear God, it was Lulu!" she cried.

"Who is Lulu?"

"Luluja Hlutev. Our neighbor. I was just beginning to get to know her. She was very kind to me right from the start. It was very strange, though…"

"What was?"

"Well, she told me that she recognized my mother from the times she spent in Bulgaria as a girl. Apparently, her uncle and my grandfather were close friends. They came from the same town in the Ukraine."

"You're right, that's strange. Did your mother ever talk to this woman?"

"No. Mama got a job at a hotel right away, so while she was at work, I spent time with Lulu. Actually, Lulu told me what she knew about my mother's past, but I decided not to tell Mama. I knew it would upset her."

"Why is that?"

"Well," she hesitated. "My mother never talked about the past or our family. It's always been just the two of us and she wanted to keep it that way. Back home, we were sort of...isolated, I guess you could say." Sofi started to stare off, but caught herself just in time before slipping back into despair. "Lulu said that my mother was banished from her village a long time ago. Based on other things she said, I figured that the reason might have been because my mother was pregnant with me. Lulu never said that, but it was implied."

"So other than what Lulu said, you know nothing about your family or your father?"

"Nothing at all. Mama didn't allow me to ask questions. Over time, I became...disinterested, I guess. Until I met Lulu, that is." Sofi's voice shattered. She put her face in her hands and cried, "I can't believe she's dead, too! And it's all my fault. This is all too much to take!"

Isaiah reached out to Sofi and put his arms around her. She found comfort in his touch.

"I know this is hard, but just try to focus for a mo
ment longer. Did anything else happen that night to mak
you think that it was Lulu who went in after you?"

"She was the only other person with me after ou
neighbor ran to Marko's for help. Now that I think about i
when I snuck over to Lulu's trailer after the fire, she wasn'
there. It was really weird. It was as if she'd disappeared. He
place was unlocked. It seemed like she'd been home earlie
The neighbors always said that she kept to herself, and sh
rarely left her place. I couldn't imagine where she coul
have gone."

Sofi took a long pause. After a few minutes, she sa
up and looked straight at Isaiah.

"I'm positive that it was Lulu who died with m
mother. It's the only logical explanation. She told me not t
go inside, but I ignored her. In fact, I pushed right past her
Our trailer was completely in flames, but I just ran in with
out thinking. I remember that Lulu reached for me. Sh
tried to stop me from running into the trailer, but I ra
straight towards the door," her voice now trembled. "I want
ed to save my mother, but I failed—and I killed Lulu in th
process!"

Convinced that Lulu was dead as well, Sofi could n
longer stop the tears from coming. She found that once sh
began, it was nearly impossible to stop. She knew that befor
long, she would slip back into the same, despondent stat
1she feared had become her permanent companion.

"Look at me," Isaiah said fervently, taking her slender hands in his as if he could read her thoughts. "None of
this is your fault. You've got to realize that! Lulu did you a

great service, whether she knew it or not, because whoever wanted you dead probably thinks that you are."

"You mean because the firemen found the remains of two women instead of one?"

"Precisely," he responded. "Think about it. Unless the perpetrators saw Lulu go into the trailer after you, the person behind all this thinks that you died in the fire along with your mother." Isaiah's words caused Sofi to wince. "Sorry."

"It's not your fault, Isaiah. This pain just won't go away. I don't think it ever will." She looked down, dejected, and sat quietly for some time.

Uncomfortable with Sofi's miserable silence, Isaiah began to think aloud.

"This article quoted some of the witnesses. None saw Lulu go inside. They all say that it was you, or someone matching your description. See, here it says:

The two were a mother and daughter who recently moved to the South Commune from Bulgaria. Several witnesses said they saw the daughter run into the burning trailer shortly before it collapsed.

Lulu must have gone in to try to pull you out before the trailer collapsed," he surmised. "Yes, if what you say is right, the perpetrator probably thinks that you're dead. I'd actually be willing to bet on that."

Sofi could not say a word. Instead looked into Isaiah's eyes with a pleading look.

"Look at it this way," he said gently, "whoever wanted you dead likely believes that he's already accomplished his goal. Still, it's imperative that we find out who is behind this and fast. If you are who I think you are, I'd wager that the person responsible for your mother's death knows your true identity and wants to keep it a secret."

"True identity? Why would that matter? I'm nobody."

"Sofi, you could never be a nobody." Isaiah smiled at her, then paused, searching in vain for the right words. "Sofi, the man who may be your father is a prominent person here in France."

"Oh."

Sofi did not know what else to say. She stirred in her seat and wondered what Isaiah could mean. The very mention of her having a father was surreal. He was a person she had only dreamed about, more like a figment of her imagination than a real, live person. She never realized that he actually existed.

"You said you know my father, or at least the man you believe may be my father. Does he know about me?" Sofi asked.

"I can guarantee that the man who I believe may be your father does *not* know about you. He's a good and honorable man. If he knew he had a child, he would have taken care of you right from the start. I promise you that."

Isaiah's response satisfied her for the present.

"So what should we do now?"

"You are going to sit tight and wait for me. I'm sorry, I have to leave you alone again for a little while. But I need you to stay here, out of sight. We can't risk anyone seeing you, do you understand?"

"Yes, of course." Sofi shuddered at the reminder that she still could be in very grave danger.

"Remember, we don't yet know who's behind all this, so I think it would be wise not to take any chances. Please make yourself at home while I'm gone. Watch television, do whatever you'd like...though by the looks of you, you're probably ready for a nap," Isaiah added, seeing Sofi yawn. "I'll be back soon."

Isaiah strode into the Élysée Palace at a quarter past eleven, well after the six-thirty Saturday morning meeting with the insufferable Philippe Roubert. He was anxious to see his friend, the President of France. He stopped short of entering the Golden Room when his eyes met Viviane Hartenau-Hesse, the First Lady of France. She stood protectively behind her husband, who stared intently at the Palace's gardens. He looked rather upset.

"Excuse me," Isaiah began apologetically, "I hope I'm not interrupting. I can come back later, of course."

"Ah, Isaiah, you're here. Thank God." René was obviously pleased to see him. "When you called earlier, you said there was something urgent we needed to discuss," René continued. "What's going on?"

"Yes, Mr. President, it's extremely important, but—" he stopped short and looked at Viviane nervously. "On second thought, this can wait. You appear to be otherwise occupied and I'm sincere when I say that I don't wish to bother you and the First Lady."

"It's alright, Isaiah. I was just getting ready to leave, so if you have some business matters to discuss with my husband, please stay." Viviane gave Isaiah a warm smile. He was always a favorite of hers, though they butted heads from time to time.

"Thank you, Mrs. Hartenau-Hesse, but this is no business matter."

"I see. No matter. I'll leave the two of you to talk in private."

She glided out of the room and was gone in an instant, leaving René and Isaiah alone. Just as his wife could sense Isaiah's anxiety, René could feel it, too.

"Isaiah, what's happened? Amié said you had an emergency last night."

"I did, René, though I'm fine and my family is fine. It has little to do with me, actually."

"Then who is this about?"

Isaiah scanned the room with his hazel eyes like a skittish rabbit. "Are you sure we're completely alone here?"

"Yes, of course! Isaiah, you're acting so weird. What the devil is going on?"

"René, I have something to tell you, and I don't quite know how to say it."

"You can tell me. Just spit it out."

"No, no," Isaiah reconsidered. "Perhaps this should wait for another time." He worried that he should have done more reconnaissance before bringing this matter to the President's attention.

"Isaiah, you've really built up the suspense. There's no turning back now. Did you come here to tell me you're resigning?"

"Resigning!" Isaiah laughed nervously. "No—it's nothing like that..." His voice trailed off, trying to figure out the best way to dive in.

"Get to it! What's this all about?" René demanded.

"Well," he stammered, "late last night, or rather, very early this morning, an unexpected visitor came knocking on my door. I think—that is, I suspect she may belong to you."

"What on earth is that supposed to mean?" René was growing impatient.

Isaiah looked down and wrung his hands. He noticed the crumpled front page of Le Parisien that René chucked a few hours earlier.

"So, you've read today's paper?" Isaiah asked.

"Yes, of course."

"Did you see the front page article about the two Roma women who were burned to death in a fire?"

"Yes, indeed. Very sad. Tragic."

"Well, there's more to that story. I know who died in the blaze."

"Really?"

"Yes. I'm—I'm sorry to tell you this, sir. I have good reason to believe that one of the women who died in the fire was—well, it was Nadja Vadoma."

René stared at Isaiah incredulously. Since his argument with Roubert, he had been thinking about Nadja all morning. In fact, Viviane rushed to be with him after he called to tell her about the reason for their fight. Viviane knew that his past with Nadja really affected him. In fact, it was something they had to work through together early on in their romantic relationship.

"Isaiah, how can that be? And how could you possibly know that?"

"Remember how I told you a visitor came to m
door last night? Well, she's a teenager. Her name is Sol
Vadoma. She claims to be Nadja's daughter."

René sat straight up in his chair and looked at Isaial
with an expression that was half shock, half hope.

"Nadja has a daughter? How did she find you? Wa
she injured in the fire? What's her name again?" he aske
rapidly.

"René, please just listen. The girl, Sofi, knocked a
my door in the middle of the night. She was very distraught
Totally dejected, actually. Her clothing was burned and cov
ered in ash and dirt. She had cuts on her face and hands. A
first, I thought she was a Gypsy beggar, so I turned her away
but then I saw a huge gold and sapphire pendant around he
neck, which made me do a double-take. When I inspected it
I immediately recognized it as the Hartenau-Hesse coat o
arms. In fact, it looks like a companion piece to your ring
Those cerulean sapphires are so distinctive."

René's eyes followed Isaiah's to the gold and sap
phire ring that René always wore.

"Sofi explained that it was actually a secret locket—
a gift from her mother for her sixteenth birthday," Isaial
continued. "She also said that my name and address were
hidden inside. She showed me a tiny scroll. My name wa:
written perfectly in beautiful calligraphy. She also told m
that she tried to rescue her mother from the fire, but tha
Nadja had been badly beaten. Just before she died, Nadj
told Sofi that she was in great danger."

"Oh, dear Lord!" René lamented. "Well, where i
her father? Is he still in Bulgaria? We must help her to re
unite with him."

"Um…that's the thing, René. She doesn't know her father."

René was dumbfounded. He pictured Nadja being beaten by a gang of skinheads and left to burn alive in a Gypsy trailer camp—her daughter left behind, frightened and all alone.

"How could this be?" he asked.

"I don't know. But René, the girl says she's *sixteen*. And she has that locket," Isaiah reiterated.

René did not respond.

"René," he continued, "in all these years, have you heard anything from your mother concerning Nadja or her family?"

"No, not once. After Roubert and my mother discovered our relationship, they forced our separation. I believe they hid it from everyone, including my father. Of course, over time I understood why they did it, and I was beholden to them. But back then, I was still very immature and selfish. My mother made me see that it was the best thing for Nadja, and for me. If her parents found out about us, she would have been ostracized by her community. With me gone, she could go on to live a happy life with her people without the shame of anyone knowing that she had been with a man outside of marriage, let alone a non-Roma."

"She must have been very young at the time."

"Yes, she was only seventeen, though I didn't know that until Roubert found us out. I was much older than Nadja. It was so wrong of me to pursue her. And I could have found myself in a heap of trouble. I've never forgiven myself."

"So you don't know what became of Nadja, then?"

"I just assumed she went on with her life. After our separation, I asked about her constantly. But, after coming up empty for over a year, I decided to leave it alone. It was better for the both of us that way. I always imagined her happy and settled, singing in the taraf and surrounded by her family. How did she ever end up here in France? In a Gypsy camp no less? And alone with a daughter?"

"I don't know the specifics, René."

"You said that Nadja's daughter is sixteen?"

"Yes."

"You think I'm her father."

"Yes, I do."

"Well…it would make sense, wouldn't it."

"It is, at the very least, possible."

There was nothing else for René to say. He walked across the room and plopped onto one of the sofas.

"So now what?"

"There's a relatively easy way to find out if she's yours. We can do a paternity test. I'll tell you, though, she looks a lot like you."

"Really?" René chuckled softly to himself. He tried to suppress the glimmer of hope that was growing in his heart.

"We need to call Viviane right away. I want you to tell her everything you told me. Then I want to see the girl."

"With all due respect, you're not worried about how Viviane will react?"

"Of course. But Viviane is my best friend. Always has been. Very early on in our relationship, I confided in her the heartbreak I felt after being forced to leave Nadja behind in Bulgaria. I felt like she was ripped away from me by my mother and Roubert. I also felt incredible guilt. I questioned my character, my integrity—hell, even my sanity. It took me a long time to get over what happened. Viviane and I have been friends since before I could walk, Isaiah. It was she who helped me make sense of it all. We have no secrets between us. So, now that I know, she needs to know."

"I'll have Amié send for her, then. Before I do, René, I should stress that we need to handle this very delicately. Obviously we need to be mindful that this doesn't get leaked to the press. Beyond that, Sofi and I have reason to believe that this was no random act of violence. There's someone out there who wanted both Nadja and Sofi dead. Before she died, Nadja warned the girl that she was in great danger—that she had to stay hidden. There's got to be more to the story."

"You believe this has something to do with me?"

"Absolutely. There are too many coincidences. Nadja and Sofi arrived in Paris only a few days ago. No other Gypsies at the South Commune were harmed that night except for them. And, Sofi told me that after she escaped the fire, she hid in some bushes near the train tracks and overheard three men talking about how they beat her mother. Poor thing is really damaged by what she witnessed. At first, I was concerned that perhaps you were in danger as well. Now, I suspect that whoever is behind this wanted to keep Nadja and Sofi away from you. Maybe someone was watching and tracking their every move?"

René flinched. "What did you just say?"

"I said that someone must have been watching them."

René thought back to his conversation with Rouben earlier that morning, including the additional details he had about the women who died in the fire, the fact that he had his people watching the camp for months, and the way he turned ill at the mention of Nadja.

"Isaiah, is the girl safe?"

"Yes. She's at my flat and I'm confident that no one knows she's there. She's probably asleep by now considering the night she had."

"That's fine. Isaiah, after we talk with Viviane, I want to see the girl as soon as possible. Can you arrange for us to meet at a secure location?"

"Of course."

"This must be discreet. I have an idea as to who may be behind all this, but I need to be sure before I start throwing around accusations. Without proof, this could really blow up in my face. But above all else, your primary objective is to keep Sofi safe. Promise me that."

"Absolument, Mr. President. I promise."

Chapter Twenty-Four

"Are you quite sure she's yours?" Viviane rose from her chair and took a turn around her East Wing office. She was surprised, though not shocked, by the news. "This isn't the first time someone has claimed to be your offspring."

"We won't know until a paternity test is administered, though the girl's story certainly makes sense," René responded. "But she has made no claims. Neither did her mother."

"The girl has no apparent reason to lie, at least from what I've been able to ascertain," Isaiah added. "She doesn't know her father's identity. She said that her mother kept it a secret from her. I believe that the girl knows very little about her family."

"Of course, she must still traumatized by what happened. It will be difficult to piece together a clear picture of her situation," Viviane remarked.

"Maybe Nadja was trying to protect Sofi by keeping her hidden all these years?" Isaiah wondered aloud.

"Perhaps," René replied. "Although, I have a sneaking suspicion that Nadja was forced into silence. After we were separated, I received no substantive answers from my

mother or Roubert about Nadja's well-being, despite m
questions. Do you think one of them may have known tha
Nadja was pregnant?"

"René, come on. You don't seriously believe tha
your own mother would keep something like that from you?'
Viviane could not fathom that sweet Amalie could be capa
ble of such deceit. "I'm more suspicious of Roubert. I knov
that you try to see the best in him, and he has, admittedly
done a lot for you over the years. But we all know his ten
dencies. He detests the Roma people. And he's always beer
obsessed with your career."

"I share similar thoughts about that, but we need tc
talk to Sofi first. We can't throw around accusations that wc
can't substantiate. We must tread lightly—gather as mucl
information as we can," Isaiah reminded.

The conversation stopped when Isaiah's cell phonc
rang.

"My apologies, I need to take this. I'll be back."

As soon as Isaiah left the office, René hurried over tc
Viviane. He took hold of her by her shoulders and tried tc
make eye contact. Obviously, she was upset, but he had expected her to be angrier. He searched her face for answer:
but came up blank. Her expression was indeterminable. He
wanted to say something comforting, but could not find the
right words.

Viviane stared back at him coolly, anticipating wha
he was trying to do.

"René, you don't have to say anything. I'm fine. And
although I'm surprised by this—this *revelation*, I am by nc
means astounded."

"Honestly, Viviane, I thought you would have react-
ed differently. How could you not be shocked?"

"We didn't start our romantic relationship until we
were thirty years old. I was well aware of your past relationships and your propensities with women. Don't forget, I've
known you all your life, and I've always accepted all of you
—the good and the bad. None of the things you did in the
past ever made me stop loving you. I may feel disappointment as a result of your past indiscretions, but what's done is
done. I just have to make sense of this on my own and continue to move forward. You're going to have to do the
same."

A lump formed in René's throat. He had a wild
youth, to say the very least, and Viviane was the one person
in his life who never judged him for it.

"When we grew older, I knew I could trust you because you were always open and honest with me," Viviane
continued. "The fact that you told me about Nadja—her
background, her age, and her position in life, was a testa-
ment to your trustworthy character. You never had to tell me
any of that. But you did. And I knew it wasn't easy for you."

René hung his head, overcome with emotion and
furious with himself for causing his wife to be caught in the
middle of such confusing and distressing circumstances yet
again. Sensing his struggle, Viviane wanted to reach out to
her husband to comfort him, but stopped short. His actions
and his actions alone put them in situations like this.

"It's less about what you've done in the past and
more about how you proceed from now on that really matters. That said, I believe that you were born to be a father. I
knew it the moment Rosamonde was born. I miss her so

251

much, and my heart still aches for her. I long for her to be with us. I wish it was me who had died instead of her. In a sense, I did die. But now, you have second chance. Even if this girl is not your daughter, we can't simply turn our backs on her. She is motherless and completely alone. We must help her if we can. And, if it turns out that she's yours, I believe I can accept her as our daughter in time."

René looked down at Viviane and held her hands to his chest. "Are you sure?" he asked passionately

"Yes, I'm sure," she replied, but not with the same fervor.

"I never meant to hurt you. I want you to know that. I *need* you to know that. If I'd known about the girl's existence, I would've told you. I would've taken care of her, for God's sake!"

"I know, René. You don't have to try to convince me about that. After all these years, I know you well enough to be sure that you would never turn your back on your family." She reached up to pat René's cheek with her hand. "And I'm fine. I'm actually better than fine because we might have a daughter." Viviane tried to smile.

After a few moments of silence, Isaiah returned, announcing his arrival by noisily fidgeting with some papers.

"Are we ready?" Viviane turned her back to René and called from across the room.

"Yes, it's time."

"Meet me in the Presidential Suite of the Four Seasons in one hour," René instructed. "I'll be waiting."

"And, Isaiah, I shall accompany you," Viviane said smoothly.

"I don't think that's a good—"

"Come, Isaiah!" she quickly interrupted. "Marcel will drive."

Isaiah watched in amazement as the First Lady of France darted into 16 Rue des Roises without being noticed.

To avoid unwanted attention, Viviane insisted they take a Renault Clio instead of her usual ride, a black Citroën C6. Isaiah unenthusiastically went along with her idea, thinking that the people of France could not be so easily fooled. Apparently, he was wrong.

"Marcel, pull the car around the corner and wait for us in the alley," Isaiah said.

Though Viviane's face was concealed by an Hermès headscarf and oversized Chanel sunglasses, her frame and style were extremely recognizable. Isaiah did not want to take any chances.

He rushed into the building and hurried up the steps, but Viviane easily beat him to the third floor.

"Is this it?" she asked casually.

"Yes, number three," he wheezed, trying to catch his breath. "Wow, you got up here fast!"

"I'm in better shape than my husband," she said with a wink. "It seems so quiet in there. Are you sure she's still here?"

"She's probably asleep. Remember, she was up most of the night and almost died in that fire. She's very fragile."

Isaiah turned the key and the two entered his apartment, which was bright and warm. Though they moved slowly, they still managed to frightened Sofi. She jumped from the couch and darted behind it like a startled rabbit.

"Hey, hey! It's okay. It's me, Isaiah," he said in Bulgarian. "You're safe."

"Yes, of course," Sofi replied, embarrassed. "I must have fallen asleep."

She tried to pat down her impossibly long hair which seemed to be everywhere. All the while she did not notice Viviane; that is, until she spoke.

"You look just like him," Viviane declared, though she intended to say it to herself.

Surprised, Sofi stood up and straightened her shirt, unsure of what to say to the glamorous woman who seemed to be inspecting her.

"Oh! Um…hello. Please excuse me—"

"It's alright," Isaiah gently interrupted. "This is Mrs. Hartenau-Hesse. There's no need to worry. She's a friend."

He walked over to Sofi and motioned to her to sit down next to him. Viviane settled into a nearby armchair.

"I hope you don't mind, but I told Mrs. Hartenau-Hesse much about what we discussed this morning. I believe she will be able to help you."

"Sofi, darling…" Viviane began carefully, but stopped short. The sight of this girl, who so much resembled her own Rosamonde, was nothing short of shocking. She could not help but to gape at her striking chestnut hair, the exact shade as Rosamonde's, which cast a golden halo around her head in the afternoon sun. Her perfect cream and roses complexion and long, straight nose were typical of the Hartenau-Hesse family. She thought about how much Sofi looked like René when he was a teenager—long and slim, yet graceful, like a thoroughbred—exactly the way she pictured Rosamonde would have looked had she grown up.

"Bonjour Madame Hartenau-Hesse," Sofi said tentatively in French.

Viviane cleared her throat and tried again.

"Sofi, it is a pleasure to meet you. I am here because..." she struggled for an easy explanation, but decided to just come out with it. "I am here because my husband, René, may be your father."

Sofi concentrated on Viviane's words very carefully, but was not sure if she fully understood. She noted that the woman's name and face seemed familiar. Before she could piece together a response in French, Isaiah jumped in.

"Viviane, Sofi has only been in Paris for a few days. I've noticed that she seems to understand if I speak slowly, but she still has some difficulty formulating cohesive sentences."

"Sofi, why don't you speak in Bulgarian," he then turned to Viviane, "and Mrs. Hartenau-Hesse, you can speak in French. I will translate. That way, you can converse more meaningfully."

"Bonne ideé," Viviane responded. "Sofi, if you please. What did you wish to say just a moment ago?"

"It's a pleasure to make your acquaintance and thank you so much for offering to help me. Please forgive me if I speak out of turn, but you seem familiar to me. We've never met before, but I feel as though I've seen you somewhere. What did you say your last name is?"

Viviane smiled after Isaiah's translation. She was pleasantly surprised to hear that Sofi was so articulate, and apparently intelligent as well, though she assumed that Isaiah must have taken liberties in his translation.

"My last name is Hartenau-Hesse. You've probably seen my picture."

With her gloved hand, Viviane pointed to a photo accompanying an article in the style section of Le Parisien. Sofi smiled broadly.

"Of course, you're the First Lady of France!" she exclaimed. "Just the other day, I read that you and the President recently returned from a trip from America. I saw a photo of the two of you getting off the plane. But wait..." she trailed off, looking at Isaiah for an explanation.

"Mrs. Hartenau-Hesse is married to the President of France," he responded.

Sofi paused for a moment. She could not help but smile with surprised delight, then immediately felt shy. Her cheeks colored and she looked down, resting her chin on her hand.

How similar she is to my husband! Viviane marveled. Sofi's pensive expression was exactly the same as René's when he concentrated on a serious matter.

"Mrs. Hartenau-Hesse, you said that you believe that your husband may be my father. Are you telling me that my father is the President of France?" She was incredulous, not believing her own words.

"Yes, Sofi, it's entirely possible. My husband is René Hartenau-Hesse. We believe that you may be his daughter."

Astonished, Sofi looked away. She did not know how to process the information.

"How could this be?"

"Many years ago, before I married René and before he entered politics, he had a relationship with a Roma girl named Nadja Vadoma. They met by chance at a summer gala hosted by his parents at their family estate in Varna. Nadja was one of the musicians. In fact, she was the lead singer. Her taraf was extremely popular and toured much of Europe."

"Why does his family have an estate in Varna?"

"René is of mixed nationality. His late father was Bulgarian. His father was a Bulgarian prince."

"So the story Lulu told me was true?" Sofi whispered as she touched her cheek with her hand.

"Who's Lulu, dear?"

"She's a woman Sofi met at the Gypsy camp in Choisey-le-Roi," Isaiah interjected.

"You mean to tell me that she randomly met someone here in France who knew about her mother's relationship with René?"

"Sort of. Sofi, please explain to Mrs. Hartenau-Hesse how you met this woman, Lulu."

"Well, Lulu lived in the trailer next door to where my mother and I were staying. She said she recognized my mother, and that she knew her when they were young. Just as you said, Lulu explained that my grandfather was part of a taraf in Varna and my mother was a singer. She said that her uncle and my grandfather were founding members of the band. Of course, I wasn't sure if I believed her because my mother never told me anything about her past or our family."

"Where's this woman now?"

"I don't know. Isaiah and I think she may be the other person who died in the fire with my mother."

"I see."

Isaiah provided further details about Lulu's situation to Viviane quickly in French.

"I'm so sorry about your mother, and your friend. Please believe me, I wish I could do something to take away your pain. I, too, know what it is like to tragically lose someone you dearly love."

"Thank you." Sofi tried to contain the overflow of tears that poured from her eyes. "Do you know anything else about how my mother came to know your husband? You said she met him at his parents' estate a long time ago."

"Yes. After he and your mother met, they started a secret love affair—secret because it was forbidden on both sides. Your mother was very young, just about the same age as you are now. It wasn't long, though, until a friend of René's family discovered them. To protect his future political career, and to shield your mother from the punishment she would receive from her people for having a relationship, a—a *sexual* relationship, as an unmarried girl, the friend told René's mother. Together, they decided to separate them. In the end, René went back to Paris, continued his studies, and entered politics. He was told that your mother went back to her everyday life with her own family, and that she would be free to marry one day and live happily without anyone ever knowing about their indiscretion.

"Oh." Sofi took a long pause to let Viviane's explanation sink in. "I learned recently from Lulu that my mother was brought before the Roma court and later banished from her village. Lulu implied that it was because of some scandal. Maybe my grandparents found out about their relationship? Or maybe my mother told someone else who betrayed her?"

"That's quite possible, Sofi. Based on everything we've been able to piece together, I think it's likely that your mother became pregnant as a result of her relationship with René, but didn't realize it until months after their forced separation. It's hard to hide a pregnancy, as you might imagine. With your mother being so young at the time and unmarried, it could be that she was banished because of it. Since René is an outsider, it probably made her pregnancy unforgivable. Or, maybe she refused to tell her family who the father was? That could be why my husband had no idea that you ever existed."

"That would explain a lot," Sofi conceded.

"But, before we sort all of that out, we still need to deal with the person or persons who pose a threat to you. Isaiah and I think that someone out there knows about you and wants you kept away from René. This attack happened only days after you moved to Paris. And, while I know it appears random, the coincidences are just too striking—at least for me."

"I agree, Sofi," Isaiah added. "I also think somebody knew that you might run into trouble here. Maybe your mother, maybe someone else? Considering what you found in that locket, and the fact that your mother warned you about being in danger, it could be that you both were targeted."

Sofi shook her head and looked away. She knew they were right, but she did not want to believe it.

"When you lived in Bulgaria, did you ever have any problems? That is to say, did you ever feel as though you were in harm's way?"

Sofi knew what Isaiah meant. Of course, they faced all sorts of problems in Bulgaria like a segregated school system, no jobs, and harsh treatment from both the gadjé as well as most of their Roma neighbors. Still, she never felt unsafe as she did in Paris.

"No, Isaiah. We never had that kind of trouble before moving here."

"Alright. Well, let's assume that all of our suppositions are true. What if the person who wanted to hurt you and your mother is linked to those who hid your existence from René all those years ago?"

Viviane did not like where this conversation was heading, but before she could refute Isaiah's budding theory, her attention quickly turned Sofi, who was shaking.

Sofi had tried her best to be brave, but it was no use. Earlier that week, she moved clear across Europe, leaving the only home she had ever known. Secrets about her family history and her mother's past were unexpectedly revealed to her by an unlikely source. Someone out there had nearly succeeded in killing her. The only person she loved in the whole world, her mother, died less than twenty-four hours ago—murdered at the hands of neo-Nazis. On top of all that, it was entirely possible that she could be the secret, illegitimate daughter of the President of France.

"This is too much to handle," Sofi cried, trembling. "I think I'm still in shock about everything that's happened."

"Oh, you poor girl!"

Viviane was at Sofi's side in an instant, cradling her as she sobbed into her jacket.

"I'm sorry…"

"Don't say another word. This is *not* your fault. Just know that you are safe here with us," Viviane whispered to Sofi in French. She held her close and stroked her chestnut waves, just as Nadja would have done. "We won't speak about this until it's absolutely necessary. And not another word from you, Isaiah," she warned.

Isaiah nodded miserably and bolted out of his seat. He paced around the room, angry that there was not more he could do. Though he knew this girl for less than a day, it tore him apart to see her grappling with so much pain.

"We're going to find out who did this to you, Sofi. I promise you that. I won't rest until we get to the bottom of this!"

Viviane looked over at the visibly agitated Isaiah, who by now was stomping across the hardwood floors. She had never seen him like this before—so emotional and fervent.

What is it about these Vadoma women that captivates men so much? she wondered. *Isaiah had better get a handle on his emotions sooner than later. We certainly don't want a repeat of last generation's tragedy.*

After a little while, Sofi's sobs quieted. She felt ashamed for displaying her emotions so vehemently to two people she barely knew. Hurriedly, she wiped the tears from her swollen eyes.

"Sorry for my outburst. I'm alright now, and I'm ready to do whatever needs to be done to apprehend my mother's killers."

"If it's alright with you, we would first like to take you to see my husband," Viviane gently offered. "He's anxious to meet you. We would also like to determine if you are indeed, his daughter."

"How do we do that?"

"If you're willing, we will take you to our physician who will administer a paternity test. It's painless and quite easy from what I understand."

"Of course. I want to know."

"Very good. Now, since that's settled, I need you to know something." Viviane looked at Sofi very seriously. "Regardless of the results, I promise that we will help you. We will do everything in our power to help you find out what happened to your mother and bring the perpetrators to justice. We will not leave you by yourself. Understand?"

"Yes, I understand."

"Now, gather whatever things you need quickly. We will leave through the back entrance. With luck, no one will see us."

Sofi stood up and looked at Isaiah. He was staring through the windows, his forehead pressed against one of the panes. He watched the bustling Pletzl below, brooding.

"Isaiah," Sofi softly interrupted his ruminating. "Mrs. Hartenau-Hesse is ready for us to go now. Thank you so much for lending me your clothes."

"Keep them. They're clean and warm." He looked her up and down and smiled. "Besides, they look good on you."

"Isaiah!" Viviane interjected loudly. "It's time to go. Now."

Chapter Twenty-Five

Sofi turned her long neck around as far as she could, trying to absorb as much of the beauty and splendor of the Four Season's Grand Lobby that her eyes could process. Ornate dentil moldings framed the perimeter of the room. Four Calacatta marble statues, each one representing a season of the year, shone brilliantly under the sparkling light of an enormous Swarovski crystal chandelier in the style of Louis VX. Several beveled mirrors framed in gold were placed strategically around the room to reflect the chandelier's glow.

Viviane and Marcel paid little attention as they led the way to the corridor of elevators. Sofi lagged behind, so Isaiah guided her along by the elbow. Before being whisked into the private elevator, she strained to take one last glance at the colorful, oversized flower arrangements that flanked either side of the main entrance, and the bold tapestry of Botticelli's Venus de Milo that hung behind the Belgian black marble concierge desk.

Following her first-ever elevator ride, she was ushered through a pair of exquisitely crafted double doors that opened to the penthouse suite.

"Oh my," she whispered as she was steered through an oval-shaped foyer to an elegant sitting area. It was absolutely the largest, most lavish, and sophisticated room she had ever seen in her entire life.

At first, Sofi was so distracted by her surroundings that she did not notice the very tall and striking man in the next room. When she did, she was immediately taken aback. He looked like he stepped out of the pages of a fashion magazine. He appeared to be somewhere around the same age as Viviane, perhaps in his mid-forties, though she could not be sure. His thick chestnut hair, the exact same shade as Sofi's, had a noticeable wave to it. He was graying slightly at his temples, which enhanced his extremely attractive and charismatic look. He wore an exquisite navy blue suit, perfectly tailored to his strapping frame.

"Voilà, mon chère. Regarde!"

Viviane gently nudged Sofi ahead, bringing her face to face with the handsome stranger who gazed at her in amazement.

"Sofi," he began warmly, "thank you for coming. I am René Hartenau-Hesse."

He took a long pause. Staring intently into Sofi's black eyes, he could feel tears welling in his own.

"You have your mother's eyes."

Upon further inspection of his could-be daughter, René observed her undeniable resemblance to him, as well as to little Rosamonde. Carefully taking one of her long, slender hands into both of his own, he began to speak again, this time in perfect Bulgarian.

"I wish I could adequately convey the depths of my gratitude to the Lord God for bringing us together today. I am beyond distressed to hear about the death of your dear mother. She was a wonderful person—strong, brave, and full of life. Long ago, I loved her very much. She will be dearly missed."

Sofi could feel warmth and emotion radiating out of René's hands as he held hers. Tentatively, she tilted her chin upwards to meet his gaze and looked into his eyes, searching for answers. She could easily see herself in the face of the man before her; his long, straight nose, full lips, and slightly heart-shaped face. His complexion was identical to hers. They even shared the same, constant rosy glow in their cheeks as if they had just come in from the cold.

Sofi stood like a statue, wishing she could express what she was feeling inside. Looking at this man brought her much-needed comfort, but it was followed by a surge of intense guilt for allowing herself even a moment's respite from her constant grief. Her feelings were so fragile, so delicate, that she could snap at any second. Her mother was dead, beaten to a pulp and burned to ashes, yet here she was in a beautiful Parisian hotel suite. As she grappled with her fear, sorrow, confusion, and doubt, she thought she heard her mother's voice, clear and strong, in her ears.

Let go of your fear. They will take care of you.

She looked up, forgetting everyone else in the room. She wondered if her mother could possibly be near, but she saw nothing. She looked around the room and blinked her eyes, but still, no sign of her mother.

Am I going crazy? she agonized.

"Sofi, you're safe," Viviane said, misinterpreting her panicked expression. "We won't let anything happen to you."

Sofi jumped at the sound of Viviane's voice, which was so close, and looked at her blankly.

"Did you hear me, Sofi? We will take care of you." Viviane looked at her with alarm, then at her husband, no knowing what to do.

"Sofi, are you okay?" René said, lightly shaking her.

"I'm fine," she replied faintly, as if she had just awoken from a dream. "I'm—I'm fine, just…confused. This is all so unreal." She put her fingers to her temple and let her head fall lightly on her hand. "I don't know what to feel. It's like I feel nothing and everything at the same time!"

"Sofi, I can't imagine what this must be like for you. You've been dealt an unimaginable blow. It'll take time for you to heal. But we're here to help you."

Sofi felt tears brimming in her eyes, but this time they were welcome. They did not burn her throat and eyes or cause her to sink into an even deeper state of despair. Instead of trepidation, a sense of relief washed over her. For the first time since the fire, she truly believed that everything might be okay.

Trembling under the weight of her emotions and the stress of the entire situation, Sofi instinctually buried her head in René's chest. He wrapped his arms around her tightly, wishing to never let go. As he rested his chin on top of her chestnut mane, he locked gaze with his wife, whose eyes were wet with tears. She nodded to her husband, encouraging him to comfort the girl who was so clearly in need of love.

Unbridled joy washed over René. He knew he should push it away until he knew for sure, but the feeling was so strong, so sure, that he was willing to take the risk.

Shaking away a single tear, René cleared his throat and bent down ever so slightly to look his daughter in the eye.

"You are my daughter. I'm sure of it. And I am so happy to have found you."

Sofi allowed René and Viviane to soothe her as she wept. In some sense, it seemed natural and right to be with these people, even though they were little more than strangers.

After awhile, the trio was interrupted when Isaiah entered the room.

"Excuse me, Mr. President," Isaiah said apologetically. "I'm sorry to disturb you, but Dr. Krauss is here to administer the paternity test." He looked over at Sofi's tearstained face and grimaced. It pained him to see her in such distress.

"Alright, Isaiah, send him in." René looked back at Sofi and Viviane. "I didn't realize Dr. Krauss would be here so soon."

"Are you nervous, Sofi?" Viviane asked.

"A little. Is this going to hurt?"

"No, not at all. Dr. Krauss will swab our mouths and then he will test the samples. From my understanding, it usually takes a few days for the results to come back. But, he assured me that we would know by the end of the day," René promised.

"So we'll know for sure very soon, then?" Sofi looked hopeful.

"Yes, we will, but I want you to understand something. I don't need the paternity test to tell me that you are my daughter. I can feel it." René spoke ardently and put his hands on Sofi's shoulders. "We are only doing this as a for-

mality. I can't pretend that I am not the President of France
But I want you to know that if I had it my way, we wouldn'
need this test. I'm confident that you are my daughter."

"I can't help but feel the same way," she confessed
"But I think it's a good thing that Dr. Krauss is here. You're
right. As the President of this country, you must be protect
ed."

René stared at Sofi incredulously, shocked by her
keen perception, despite her sheltered life in Bulgaria.

"Excuse me," Isaiah interrupted. "Sofi, this is Dr
Krauss."

"Hello, Dr. Krauss. Pleased to meet you." Sofi said
politely in French.

"The pleasure is all mine, Sofi." Dr. Krauss smiled
widely at the lovely girl before him. "She looks like you, Mr
President."

"Incredible, isn't it?"

"Indeed. Well, mademoiselle," he said, turning back
to Sofi, "what I need from you and the President should only
take a moment. First, I'm going to take this swab and extract
samples from the inside of both of your mouths. I'll then
run the samples through a series of DNA genetic tests. Now,
these tests usually take at least twenty-four hours to process,
but being that this is a special case," he winked kindly at
Sofi, "I have a team of scientists on standby ready to get to
work. So, with your permission, Mr. President, we will call
you with the results in a few hours. Of course, if you are
dissatisfied with the news, you can be retested, but I would
like to point out that DNA genetic testing is the best and
most accurate way to determine parentage. Do either of you
have questions before we begin?"

"I'm ready whenever you are, Sofi."
"I'm ready, too. Let's do this."

Chapter Twenty-Six

Sofi slumped in the oversized sofa across from he could-be father, struggling to focus. After again recounting all the events that occurred over the past several months, she felt absolutely drained, as if an evil scientist sucked all thought and reason out of her mind. Still, she realized that even the smallest detail could be vital in apprehending the people who murdered her mother, so she tried with all her might to tell René and Isaiah the most accurate story possible. However, after nearly two hours of constant talking, explaining, and thinking, she had to stop and take a break.

"So that's what happened leading up to us moving to France."

She sighed loudly and sunk deeper into the couch, touching her brow weakly with the back of her hand. Viviane noted her weariness over thirty minutes ago. She entered the room with a tray of tea, sandwiches, and savories.

"I think now is a good time for us to take a pause gentlemen. Sofi, dear, would you like some tea?"

"Oh, yes! Thank you, Mrs. Hartenau-Hesse."

"Please, call me Viviane."

"But....I couldn't."

"I insist. It's my particular wish."

"Sofi," Isaiah interjected. "I have to ask. Didn't it seem like a rather sudden scheme on the part of your mother to pick up everything and leave Dobrai?"

"Isaiah, I said it's time for a break," Viviane reminded him, this time not as gently.

"With all due respect, Mrs. Hartenau-Hesse, it's very important that we learn as much as we can as quickly as we can. There's someone out there that poses a great threat to Sofi!"

"Be that as it may, I must insist that she be allowed to rest! The girl is exhausted, can't you see that?"

Viviane and Isaiah continued to argue in French. Sofi could not understand a word they were saying. She was too tired to concentrate. Their speech came quickly and without pause. Now, alone with her thoughts and fighting despair, she wrapped her arms around herself and closed her eyes tightly, hoping it was all a dream. But when she opened her eyes, nothing had changed. Isaiah was still there, hovering, while Viviane and René conversed quietly in the next room.

"Ah, you're awake," said Isaiah. "Are you up to answering just a few more questions, or would you like to stop for today?"

"I'm pretty tired," Sofi confessed, covering a yawn. "I want to help as much as I can, though. I just don't know if I'm thinking clearly." The combination of worry and fatigue caused the tears to come again, but she fought them.

"In that case, we'll go on for only a few more minutes, then you can rest, alright?"

"Yes, that sounds alright."

"Very good."

Isaiah called for René and Viviane, then got up to pour a cup of tea for Sofi.

"Sure you're up for this?" René asked protectively.

"Yes. I'm feeling better now," Sofi said between sips.

"She's certainly resilient, is she not?" remarked Viviane to René in French.

"Indeed," René replied while smiling warmly at Sofi. "That's a brave girl. We have just a few more questions."

Sofi nodded. "Okay."

"You told us just a little while ago that your mother's plan to come to France seemed sudden. Based on what I knew of Nadja, I find it hard to believe that she would relocate you clear across the Continent on a whim. There must have been a good reason."

"It was sudden," Sofi conceded. "I was against the move at first, but Mama insisted that we would have a better life in France. She said I'd be able to go to school, maybe even study at a university someday. Ultimately, that's what convinced me. That's always been my dream—to go to university. But you're right in your assessment of her. Mama always thought things through. Even before she spoke, Mama would carefully consider what she wanted to say before she said it."

Talking about her mother in the past tense caused Sofi's voice to buckle, but she pressed on.

"In the weeks leading up to our move, she seemed trapped. Like she wanted to escape. There was urgency and stress in her voice. Her behavior was sometimes erratic. I never saw her like that before. It was like was willing to take risks in order to leave."

"Did you have a difficult life in Bulgaria?" René asked awkwardly. "That is to say, were you...were you very poor?"

"Life was life. We didn't have much interaction with our neighbors. They didn't seem to like us very much. I only had one friend in school. Everyone thought I was pretty weird."

Sofi looked down, slightly embarrassed to admit in front of Isaiah that she was so unpopular among her peers.

"We were excluded by almost everyone. We were very...*different* from everyone we met, whether they were Roma or gadjé. Few people from our village ever spoke to us, so we felt isolated. Even though she never complained, I think Mama felt it more than me."

Her voice was now raw with emotion as she remembered her mother's loneliness. She struggled to hold back tears.

"Mama was very solitary. As I got older, I realized that everything that my mother did was for me," she looked away and took a brief pause, but composed herself quickly and started again. "My Mama loved to be in church. She also loved to garden. But when we were not together, Mama was by herself, always. We had a warm house and plenty of food, which is much more than our neighbors had. I suppose that was strange, since Mama hadn't worked in years. Mama told me that she saved a lot of money, though. We always had everything we needed, plus books. I always had a present at Christmastime and for my birthday. I wasn't aware that we struggled. For me, the worst part of life was school. Our instructors were....well, let's just say that the could be very cruel."

"Do you know how or where your mother got the money to pay for your house, your food?"

"I'm not sure. I asked once, a long time ago, but got into trouble for it. We always seemed to have enough money, unlike our neighbors. She just said she was good a saving money."

"Sofi, was there anything leading up to your move that you either saw or heard that seemed strange or out of the ordinary?" Isaiah asked, trying to understand what prompted Nadja, an apparently careful, intelligent, and de liberate woman, to hurriedly leave the only country she had even known.

Sofi sat quietly for a moment. She thought back to the weeks leading up to their departure and her brief encounter with the curious stranger.

"Actually, now that you mention it—on the day my school closed, I came home and found Mama talking to a rich-looking gadjo. He didn't come in the house. They were standing in the yard, hiding behind the trees."

"René, what is this word, gadjo, that she continues to use?" Isaiah asked, confused.

"Sofi, you're referring to a non-Roma, correct?" René wanted to be sure.

"Yes, of course."

Isaiah's curiosity was piqued. He could think of only one thing that a wealthy man would want with a poor Gypsy woman.

"So what did your mother and this gadjo talk about?"

"I have no idea," Sofi continued innocently. "Mama was upset, but she wouldn't tell me what was wrong. As soon as the gadjo saw me walking up the lane, he got in his car and left. But he didn't seem surprised to see me."

"What kind of car did he drive?"

"His car was gorgeous. It was one of those big, fancy ones. All black. A Mercedes, I think. It had a fancy, round symbol sticking straight up on the hood."

"How did he interact with your mother?" René asked. "Did he seem threatening?"

"No! Not at all. The man was very nice to her, or at least it looked that way. He seemed to be kind...gentle even. You know," Sofi looked away as she thought about that day, "the man was familiar to me. I'd seen him before on a few occasions, but several years ago. The last time I saw him besides that day was when I was still in junior high."

"Think back to when you saw him in the past," Isaiah gently prodded.

Sofi closed her eyes and searched her memories.

"I remember...he came to our house before, but just like this past time, he didn't come inside. He just stood on the landing at our front door and talked with Mama. I saw him give her a package and an envelope full of money. When they saw me, he left."

"He gave your mother money? Are you sure?"

Sofi noticed René and Isaiah share a concerned glance, so she took it upon herself to provide the backstory.

"Yes, he gave her money, but it's not what you think. Later, I asked Mama why he had given her money. She said that the man stopped by our house at the request of Mr. and Mrs. Laporte. You see, when I was small, my mother worked

for the Laporte's. They were a nice Canadian family. Mr
Laporte was a hunter, so he had a house in Bulgaria not far
from our village. Mama told me that the man stopped by to
give her money for work she did for the Laporte's a few
years back."

"What about this Mr. Laporte? How well did you
know him?"

"I remember him very well, but I was little when my
mother worked there. He and his wife were always so kind to
us."

"Where are they now?"

"I don't know. Back in Canada, I guess."

"Something about this story doesn't add up. It just
doesn't sound right," René remarked. "Sofi, what did the
man with the Mercedes look like, this gadjo."

Sofi sighed deeply, wishing their questions would
end.

"Well, like I said, he drove that very fancy car. I never
got close to him, but he always wore the same thing—a
black wool suit, a black overcoat that reached his knees, and
a hat. Sort of like what a limo driver would wear in a
movie."

"Sofi, did the man have a driver or did he drive the
car himself?"

"He drove."

"He's a chauffeur," René deduced. "How strange!"

"I guess," Sofi said. "Funny thing," she continued,
grinning, "he bowed super low—it was kinda dramatic—
and he tipped his hat to Mama like she was royalty or something."

Sofi's description of the man and the words she used sparked something in René.

"No!" he declared adamantly. He bolted out of his seat and marched across the room, then turned and looked at Sofi intently. "Do you remember anything else about him? Really think now! Height, weight, features..."

Sofi's cheeks flushed. She felt pressured to give the right response.

"Um, he was taller than my mother, obviously, but not taller than me. He was maybe like this." Sofi stood up to illustrate the man's size in comparison to her, which put his height just above her shoulder. "When I saw him the first time, he had dark brown hair but the last time I saw him, it was gray. I could tell when he lifted his cap. He had a slim, almost neat build, and he moved very smoothly, gracefully even. He wore a pin on his lapel, I think. Actually, the colors of his pin were gold and blue— kind of like my locket, but I can't be sure. He also had very shiny shoes. Oh, and a kind face. He seemed really nice."

As Sofi spoke, René began to stomp around the room, his arms crossed and forearms flexed.

"René, what is it my dear?" Viviane knew that familiar look. "What are you thinking?"

"Isaiah, translate Sofi's description of the man to Viviane, then ask her who it sounds like," René barked.

As Isaiah repeated Sofi's words, Viviane began to chuckle. She immediately pictured a familiar friend who looked and acted very similarly to the man she described, and whose very proper and old-fashioned manners struck her as comical at times. However, looking at her husband's

agitated expression, she realized what this meant and imme
diately changed her tone.

"There's no way. Absolon would never have hid
something so important from you, René. Besides, it's entirely
too coincidental."

"Exactly. It's way too coincidental, therefore not a
coincidence at all. Sofi's description reeks of Absolon. That's
him to a tee. I've got to get him on the phone."

"René, no, not yet. We don't know if we can trust
him with this information," said Viviane. "I'm sorry, René
but if he hid Sofi from you all this time, maybe we can't trust
him at all?" Viviane worried.

"Excuse me, please, but are you referring to your
mother's driver, Absolon?" Isaiah interrupted, needing clari-
fication.

"Yes, of course."

"Well, I'm with Viviane on this. I think this is entirely too premature. He's not the only chauffeur in Bulgaria
The man Sofi described could have been anyone. Besides,
René, you and Absolon are very close. Do you really think
he would hide your own child from you?"

"Excuse me, what are you saying?" Sofi piped in.

She could only make out bits of the conversation,
but she could tell it was important. Though her comprehension of the French language was improving exponentially,
she simply could not keep up with their quick speech.

"Sofi, everything's fine." Isaiah rose from his seat
and walked around the coffee table to sit closer to her
"We're trying to determine who this mystery man could be.
We have an idea based off your description, but we can't be
sure just yet."

"I see."

Sofi looked down, disappointed. She wished she could remember more to help them figure out what could have brought her mother to France. She mindlessly reached for her precious locket and began to twist its chain around her fingers, then held it tightly to her chest. René could not help but watch how Sofi's long, delicate fingers deftly slid across the chain, and the way the locket's cerulean sapphires sparkled in the afternoon sun.

"I have the companion piece to that locket, Sofi," René said quietly as he showed her his ring. "These pieces were my grandfather's, Stefan Alexander Hesse by Rhine, Prince of Bulgaria. You can see the Hesse crest here on my ring, and the full coat of arms on your locket.

Sofi's eyes widened with interest. It was the first time her thoughts did not flash with images of her mother's beaten body or charred remains.

"Didn't you tell Isaiah that your mother gave this locket to you for your sixteenth birthday?"

"Yes."

"Have you any idea where she got it? Was it something that she saved for you, or did someone give it to her?"

"Well, she told me that she was saving it for my sixteenth birthday, but I had never seen it before then. She said it was a family heirloom. When I figured out how to open it and found Isaiah's name and address inside, I figured he was a family member or friend of my mother's."

"When exactly did she give you the locket?"

"A few days before we left for France."

"May I?"

279

Sofi reached around, pulled the chain over her head and carefully laid it in René's hands. He turned it back and forth, staring at it in amazement.

"I have not seen this piece for some time. I thought it was lost."

"Does it have a story behind it?"

"Oh yes!" René looked at Sofi and was pleased to see that her curiosity was genuine. "Our family coat of arms dates back to the darker days of Bulgaria's history, when the Ottoman Empire ruled."

"Really?" Sofi sat up, hoping that more of the story was to come.

"You want to know more?"

"Yes, please."

"Very well then," he said smiling. "During the later part of the fourteenth century, the Ottoman Empire invaded the Balkans. When the Bulgarian Empire was conquered in 1396, the Bulgarian dynasty was disbanded and the people were enslaved. Around that time, one of our ancestors, the beautiful Princess Alexia S'miranda, had the unfortunate happenstance to catch the eye of the Sultan, Mehmed II. At first, Mehmed wished to take her as one of his many wives. However, one of his sons, Zilmar, notorious for his excessive brutality and depravity, petitioned that she become his first wife instead. Mehmed happily granted his son's wish. Of course, Princess Alexia had no say in the matter. She knew she had to marry Zilmar. If she refused, her entire family would be slain."

"Oh, how terrible!"

"Yes, but there's more. What was especially heart-breaking was that the news came just one week before she was to marry her true love, Alexandru II, the Prince of Moldavia, who was voivode of a moderate-sized militia. To save him from certain death, Princess Alexia told Prince Alexandru that she changed her mind about wedding because she had fallen in love with the Sultan's son. The Princess bravely journeyed to Turkey with the Sultan's caravan. She was then locked away in a turret of one of the Sultan's many palaces while preparations for the wedding commenced.

Back in Bulgaria, Prince Alexandru was beside himself with despair. His thoughts bordered on madness. He decided to follow Princess Alexia to Turkey, traveling all the way alone on horseback.

On the day of the wedding, he disguised himself like a Turk and snuck into the Palace with the rest of the wedding guests. When he caught sight of the exquisite Princess, her beauty took his breath away. She was like a sparkling gem, draped in a rich, cerulean fabric. Her face was covered with an indigo silk shield so that only her eyes were visible. Though she looked calm to the hundreds of strangers who gathered to witness the wedding, Prince Alexandru knew better. He could sense she was terrified. When the marriage ceremony ended, he saw a single tear fall from her eye just before Zilmar grabbed her and carried her away.

Seeing his love in the arms of the Turk, Prince Alexandru's grief turned to anger, prompting him to action. He assembled as many dissidents, rogues, and warriors as he could. His plan was to lay siege to the palace, kill the Sultan's son, and save Princess Alexia. Of course, it was an ill-fated scheme, as his mishmash of an army was no match for the powerful Turkish forces that awaited him at the palace. Though he fought valiantly, his army was overcome and he was soon captured.

Face to face with the merciless Zilmar, Prince Alexandru knew that death awaited him, but he was still without fear. The Sultan's son enjoyed torturing the innocent. He picked up a dagger, taking it upon himself to slowly kill Prince Alexandru. To further his sadistic delights, he forced Princess Alexia to watch her lover's death from the balcony of her turret.

The sight was unbearable to witness. Princess Alexia wished she could do something to save her love and put an end to her husband's reign of terror. As the Sultan's son approached Prince Alexandru, Princess Alexia saw her chance. She hurled herself from the balcony, landing on Zilmar and knocking him to the ground. His temple caught the corner of a sharp rock and he was killed instantly. Prince Alexandru ran to meet the Princess, who had risked her life to save his, but he realized it was too late. The dagger that the Sultan's son intended to use on him pierced Princess Alexia in the heart. She took her last breath while looking into the eyes of her true love.

Our family coat of arms pays homage to the courage of Princess Alexia and Prince Alexandru. The golden dragon you see here depicts the Sultan's son, and the bright cerulean sapphire he holds represents Princess Alexia. Here, of course, is Prince Alexandru. He is the lion, wearing a sapphire crown. Finally, the cross in the center signifies their martyr-like triumph over the Turks as well as the two pillars of the House of Hartenau-Hesse— fearlessness and self-sacrifice."

"That's an amazing story. Did it really happen?"

"Well, it's the family legend. The tale has been passed down from generation to generation. It's meant to instill in us certain qualities that are essential in a leader. We must be brave and strong, but also generous and altruistic. As a child, I loved the story of Prince Alexandru and the Princess Alexia. I used to envision myself as the Prince, fighting bravely against the evil Zilmar. Years ago, before my father passed away, he promised me that my firstborn child would wear this locket. He knew it meant a lot to me."

No sooner did René speak the words did he stop and sit straight up, as if he had been poked with a cattle prod. He looked at Viviane, eyes wide and full of hurt.

"It was my mother! She knew all along."

"What? Wait, what are you saying, René?"

"She gave this piece to Nadja to give to Sofi, I'm sure of it." He got up and stormed around the room. "My father promised this locket to my firstborn child. Mother was there when he said it. He felt so strongly about passing on this piece to his grandchild that he even put it in his will. It's so obvious now. I should have realized it sooner!"

"Oh, René," Viviane went to her husband and held his hand, trying to soften the sharp sting of his mother's alleged betrayal.

"She must have known that Nadja was pregnant, but she kept it from me and forced Absolon to help her. He would never have hidden anything like this from me unless he was coerced into it. Look at the writing on this slip of parchment. It's in Absolon's hand! He probably hid it in the locket when he gave it to Nadja hoping that Sofi would one day find it. I am almost sure of it! Absolon often expressed his admiration for Isaiah. He told me on several occasion that Isaiah was someone I could always trust."

René looked over at Isaiah as he continued to speak "It makes sense that he would include *your* name and addres inside this locket. And thankfully, you did exactly what Ab solon anticipated you would do—bring my daughter to me."

René took a deep breath. He had managed to keep his temper in check for many years, but this level of treach ery, apparently at the hand of his own mother, pushed him to the edge.

"All this time, she has been lying to me—keeping my child from me! Unbelievable! And even after we lost Rosa monde, she never told us the truth. How could she?"

While Viviane attempted to comfort her visibly livid husband, Isaiah moved closer to Sofi to translate what had been said. She felt the energy in the room shift. Isaiah could see Sofi's distress. He could hardly bear it.

"Isaiah, are you saying that his own mother kept me a secret?"

"Yes, I think that's what they believe. And I'll tel you something, it makes a lot of sense. Right before Christ mas, René's mother, Amalie, didn't want to join the family in Versailles for the holiday, as they do each year. It was only after much persuasion that she decided to come. Oddly though, she wanted to leave Absolon in Bulgaria all alone, which was quite unexpected since he usually travels every where with her—especially now that she's older. At first, Amalie was unyielding and said there was something at home that needed to be monitored closely, or something to that effect. In any case, René didn't believe her excuse, par ticularly since he and Absolon are so close. You see, Absolon is like a second father to him, especially since René's father pushed him so hard when he was young."

"René didn't have a good relationship with his father?"

"Not so much. Let's just say it was complicated. Anyway, in the end, Viviane and René persuaded Amalie to come to Versailles *with* Absolon. But it took a lot of convincing."

"So you think that Amalie didn't want to come to Versailles for Christmas because she needed to make sure that someone was monitoring Mama and me in Bulgaria?"

"It certainly could be a possibility. It appears as though Absolon went to see your mother before Christmas. My guess is that he reported back to Amalie that Nadja was leaving Bulgaria. Amalie likely didn't want to leave Varna without being positive that someone would be there to watch over the two of you to make sure you didn't leave without her knowledge."

"Isaiah...you don't think that Amalie had anything to do with the fire, do you?"

Isaiah touched Sofi lightly on the arm and smiled. "I sincerely doubt she was involved with any of that. Amalie is a good woman. She's actually quite likable, though somewhat dramatic, and even more so in her old age," he said with a wink. "My guess is that Amalie may have been protecting the two of you in her own way."

Isaiah stopped and looked into the next room. René was bent over a large desk, phone in hand, while Viviane stood by his side rubbing his back.

"He looks really mad," said Sofi quietly.

"Oh yes, he's furious. By the looks of things, I bet we'll have some answers sooner than later."

"Why, who's he calling?" Sofi asked.

"Probably his mother. This could get ugly."

Chapter Twenty-Seven

"How could you do this to me?" René screamed through the phone. "I am your son, your only child!"

"René, dear, I—" Amalie's aging voice crumbled under the weight of her son's booming shouts.

"You knew this whole time but you never said a word. Even after we lost Rosamonde. You watched us grieve, you saw our pain, and you never once decided that it might have been a good time to tell us that I had another child!" René's voice turned scary as he snarled into the telephone.

"Darling, let me come to you. I'm still here in France. Absolon can get me to Paris in no time."

"Don't even talk to me about Absolon! Apparently, the two of you were in cahoots."

"Oh René, please. I know this is a serious matter, but enough of the theatrics! First off, Absolon and I were never in 'cahoots,' as you say. I forced him into this scheme. He was opposed to keeping this secret from the very start. Also, I can assure you that we looked after Nadja and Sofi diligently. They always had a warm home, plenty of food, and above all *safety*. For years, I prayed that they would always remain under my protection. I shuddered to think what could have happened to them if they ever left us. But then they did leave, despite Absolon's warnings. Now look what has happened!"

"It took a tragedy for me to find out that I have a daughter. You could have just told me, Mother. I would have handled it. But instead, you meddled in my life, treated me like a child. How dare you!"

"René, you are my son. I will always put your needs ahead of my own."

"Yeah, right."

"Sixteen years ago, you were not equipped to handle the situation. Think about where you were in your life. Consider how your future would have changed. I would have gladly welcomed little Sofi into our family if circumstances were…different."

"What circumstances? You mean because Nadja was a Gypsy?"

"Oh, René, it's complicated. Surely, you know that Sofi is not the first illegitimate child the Hesse clan has ever produced. You know that it didn't matter to me who Nadja was or where she came from, though it certainly would have made a difference to your father. But there's more at work here, René, and I assure you that I had good reason for keeping Sofi from you. It was for her own safety!"

"Is this your way of trying to tell me that Sofi is still in danger?" René asked bluntly.

"With you watching over her, no. But René, you cannot be so trusting. I know I'm probably the last person you want to see right now, but I must come to the Palace with Absolon this very minute. We will tell you everything."

"We're not at the Palace." René's voice was cold and distant.

"Where should I meet you then?"

"Meet me? Are you delusional? What makes you think I'd wish to see you now—or ever? I can't trust you. I'll never trust you again!"

"Oh, René…"

"You betrayed me, Mother, and kept me from my own flesh and blood! Because of your lies, my daughter's life is at risk. I will not lose her. I will not lose another child!"

"I swear to you that I had your best interests at heart. For sixteen years, I made it my mission to keep Sofi and Nadja safe. You can fault me for everything else, but I am not the one who wanted to hurt them. I tried to shield the girl, for God's sake!" Amalie cried, voice trembling.

"Shield her from what?"

"I know that nothing I can possibly say or do can make this right. But please…please, there's so much more to tell. I must see you."

René said nothing.

"Son, are you still on the line?"

"Very well," he replied flatly. "Instruct Absolon to bring you to the Four Seasons. You know the drill."

"I'll be there shortly, René. But remember what I said. Do not speak of this to anyone else until we've had the chance to talk."

"Oh please, Mother. I would never do anything to harm my child."

With that, René hung up, and after a moment, hurled the phone against the wall. He whirled around and slammed the door with so much force that the entire room shook.

Isaiah and Sofi heard his fit from across the suite. Sofi, not knowing what to do, got up and inched her way towards the door.

"Isaiah?" she said nervously.

"Try not to worry. René isn't upset with you. Everything's going to be fine. Believe me, he'll take care of it."

Isaiah could see that Sofi was not convinced.

"Hey, let's dig into these sandwiches and play cards," he offered. "Ever hear of Pinochle?

Viviane looked squarely at her husband, who was tearing up the room like a coked up rock star.

"What in the hell is the matter with you?" she yelled as René kicked a chair. "I said, that's enough!" She threw a magazine at René's head, narrowly missing him.

"Hey!"

"Knock it off! You're behaving like an idiot!"

Though Viviane was cognizant of her husband's pain, she had put up with enough of his antics. Now was the time for rational thinking and strategic action on his part, not blind emotion and fits of rage. Besides, it was his year of womanizing that created this state of affairs. No one else was to blame.

René rubbed the side of his head and turned around slowly to face his beautiful wife, who looked like a tigress. After a decade of marriage and a lifetime of friendship, he could count on one hand the number of times she raised her voice to him.

"Pull yourself together," she growled. "Yes, your mother was beyond wrong to hide Sofi from you, but let's be real. Do you actually expect me to feel totally sympathetic to *you*?"

René started to protest, but he knew she was right. He could have prevented all of this.

"My concern lies with Sofi," Viviane continued. "She is completely innocent in all of this. She's done nothing wrong, but look at the horrors she's faced. But you..." she snarled, pointing a finger at René's chest, "this is *your* fault."

"My fault?" he responded petulantly.

"René, I shouldn't have to tell you that you could have done more. You should have acted like a man and not a hormone-crazed teenager when Nadja needed you all those years ago. Be honest with yourself and with me. How hard was it for Roubert to convince you to leave her after he explained all the trouble that your affair would have undoubtedly caused you? Was it really that difficult of a choice?"

René could not respond. Instead, he looked at his wife blankly and set his jaw, preparing himself for more.

"You left that young girl completely alone—and pregnant, no less! Now of course, I know you well, René. Surely, you could not have known that she was pregnant. If you did, I'm convinced you would have taken care of your child. But, you knew that Nadja would be heartbroken without you, and that she would be exiled from her community if her family ever found out about your affair. You did nothing to ensure Nadja's safety or well-being after you left her. If you think you did, you're deluding yourself."

"Well, what was I supposed to do back then?"

"Take accountability for your actions, that's what You thought that everyone else around you would take care of your messes, as they always did. Well, look what has happened as a result! In the next room likely sits your daughter a guileless girl, who is just one year younger than Nadja was when you seduced her. She was the very same as Sofi, no doubt—naïve to the outside world and sheltered from the desires of men like you. Yes you. A lawyer. A budding politician. A rich aristocrat. A man of the world! And, on top of it, you were nearly thirty years old!"

"But you forgave me for all of that years ago, my darling!" René pleaded. "I told you about my past, my... *predilections*. And you accepted me."

"Yes, you were honest with me about Nadja and about all your other women when we started our relationship. And, it's true, I accepted you despite all of it. But I won't accept a man who makes excuses for his own bad behavior and blames other people for his own mistakes."

"Sofi is not a mistake, Viviane."

"Don't twist my words, René! You know I didn't mean that and I certainly didn't say it. Sofi could never be a mistake. It is *you* who made the grave error of bedding an impressionable teenager. A child! Then you abandoned her in her greatest time of need. Your actions weren't just cruel René, they were criminal. Can't you see why your mother did what she did? She was protecting you."

René turned from his wife and her cutting words. He could not raise his eyes to meet hers. The sharp truths she spoke tore at a wound he had hidden away in his heart many years ago. She was entirely right. His fiendish treatment of women in his youth was the catalyst of this situation. He paced around the room, nervously wringing his hands.

Viviane stood apart. She knew that the kind and respectable man she married was so opposite from the immature, callous playboy she dated years ago, the one whose poor choices were now wreaking havoc on their lives. Biting her tongue and holding her pride, she fought to keep a level head, if not for her husband's sake than for Sofi's.

"So what did your mother say on the phone, René? Did she have an explanation?" Viviane asked.

"Well....yes, she did," he said while avoiding his wife's penetrating gaze. "As you guessed, Mother says she had good reasons for hiding Sofi, mostly to protect me but also something about how she and Absolon were shielding Sofi from danger. Mother wants to come here to tell me the details in person. She believes we can't trust our friends. I'm sure it's just a lame excuse for her to see me, but—" he stopped to look at his wife, "I believe I already know who else might be involved. I just need her to substantiate it."

"You didn't mention anything about that earlier."

René said nothing.

"Aren't you going to tell me who it is?"

René eyed his wife cautiously, rethinking his mother's words.

"Are you kidding me, René?" Viviane's green eyes flashed irately as she read her husband's thoughts. "You don't trust me? I am your wife!"

"Darling, please, let's just wait until we hear what Mother has to say," René begged.

"You son of a bitch! I'm the only one who has stood by your side through *everything*. How dare you question my loyalty to you? I've done nothing but love you all my life….and look where it has gotten me! After all the women, all the unwavering support I gave you year after year as you chased your political dreams. I am rewarded with a dead child and your illegitimate teenage daughter at my doorstep. Thanks, René," she said icily.

"Dammit, Viviane, I'm *sorry*!" René tried to take hold of her thin frame, but she pushed him away.

"Don't touch me!"

"What can I do?"

"Nothing."

"Bloody hell!"

"Just get out of here, René. I need some time to myself."

"No! Viviane, I know I've done nothing but wrong. But I need you now more than ever. I can't do this alone!"

"You are so selfish! Get away from me."

"For the love of God, I said I'm sorry and I mean it!"

René attempted to embrace her again. This time Viviane did not pull away from his familiar touch.

"How could you do this to me, René? All I've ever done is love you…"

"Forgive me, darling," he whispered. "This all happened years ago. Please, forgive me."

Though revelations concerning René's past indiscretions injured her deeply over the years, Viviane knew that his actions were not aimed at hurting her. His connection with Nadja, and the life he led before their marriage, took place before she came into the picture—romantically, at least.

"René, this cannot be about us right now. As much as I want to get up and run out of this hotel suite, I know that we must focus on the situation before us instead of dwelling on the past. There's plenty of time for that later."

René winced. "Viviane…"

"Sofi is going through the cruelest pain right now—the loss of her mother, the only constant in her life. It's also pretty clear that she feels responsible for the death of the woman who tried to save her."

"You're right. Of course."

"We must be a united front. That said, I want you tell me who you think is behind all of this."

"Well," René sighed, "I've got a sinking feeling that Philippe Roubert may be responsible."

"Roubert!?"

"Yes, I—"

"Mr. President, I'm sorry to disturb you," Isaiah called from behind the door, "we've received a call from Dr. Krauss. He said he couldn't get through on the landline."

René and Viviane looked across the room to the phone, which was lying on the carpet in several pieces.

"Let's continue this later," he whispered to his wife, who responded with a nod. "Come in, Isaiah," he called.

"I'm sorry."

"It's fine, Isaiah," René said calmly. "Do you know the results?"

"Yes."

"Well?"

"Sofi is, indeed, your daughter. A courier is bringing us the results as we speak."

René slapped his thigh and pumped his fist.

"Aha! I knew it! This is great, just fantastic, I—"

He stopped short, remembering his wife.

"Are you alright with the news?"

"I'm fine."

"Um…I'll leave you now, Mr. President," Isaiah said sheepishly while closing the door.

"I knew she was your daughter from the minute I laid eyes on her."

"Did you?"

"Of course. She looks just like you….and Rosamonde."

"Darling, I —"

Viviane brushed past René and left the room, pausing in front of Isaiah.

"Thank you for everything you've done to unite my husband with his daughter. I'll never forget it for as long as I live."

Isaiah nodded.

"And now, my dear," Viviane continued warmly making her way toward Sofi, "I assume Isaiah told you the news."

"Yes."

"This will be the start of a new life for you. Anything you can imagine is possible now. And you can be sure that your father and I will always be here to take care of you. You will never be alone from now on."

"Oh, um, thank you so much, Mrs.—I mean, Viviane. I'm sorry, I don't know what to say…" Sofi's cheeks colored as she tried to formulate some sort of coherent response in French.

"It's alright, Sofi," René's deep voice gently interrupted. He tenderly took her hand into his. "I know this must be incredibly shocking for you."

"It is."

Sofi was distracted by the comforting sensation her father's hand created in the palm of her hand, which moved quickly to her heart.

"I want you to know what joy it brings me to know you are my daughter. I also want you to know that your mother was —" he stopped, not knowing how to continue, then began again. "Your mother was very special to me. She was... she was like an angel. Innocent, pure, incredibly kind. Completely the opposite of *me*."

"Why are you telling me this?"

"I need for you to understand that I never intended to hurt your mother, or you. Had I known you existed, I would have been there for you. You see, from the time I was a young man, I struggled deeply with many...*passions*. I had a lot of demons and I dealt with many women. You could say that I was a womanizer. When I met your mother, who was all sweetness and goodness, I wanted to be like her, to get as close as I could to her. I'd been going down a dark path for a long time, so I thought that she would save me from who I'd become."

He looked away and cleared his throat. This was too difficult for him to do alone. He glanced towards the spot where Viviane had been standing, hoping she could help him explain to Sofi, but she was gone. René sighed.

"Sofi, I don't know what to say to make you understand how important you are to me, except by sharing with you how much your mother meant to me. Though our time together was brief, she opened my heart by showing me the importance of love and respect. You may not believe me, but I did respect her. You were conceived out of love."

Sofi did not know what to say. She had never heard anyone talk about love or relationships openly before. It was awkward.

"With your permission," he continued, "I would like to hold a memorial service for your mother, as well as for your friend who saved you. Then we can bring your mother's remains to my family's church back home in Bulgaria, Saint Paraskeva Petka in Varna."

"Yes," Sofi choked out. She hadn't realized until now that she was crying again. "I'd like that very much."

René could not bear to see Sofi in such anguish. Each one of her sobs was like a punch to the gut. Desperate to lessen the sting of her wounds, he quickly switched the subject.

"Speaking of Varna," he said, trying to be cheerful. "Viviane and I are scheduled to visit next month, and I hope you will want to join us. I can't wait to show you the Hartenau-Hesse estate, Aytos Manor, as well as our lands and the church our ancestors built."

He looked at Sofi, whose tears had yet to stop. She was listening, though barely. Rene tried again, but this time he took both her hands in his and bent down, as if she were a little child, to meet her tear-stained face.

"When we go to Sveta Petka, you may be surprised to see that there is a familiar lion depicted on the iconostas of the church, bowing his head before the Cross and offering an orb-shaped gift. You see, the same lion is here on your locket, part of the Hesse Royal Coat of Arms. It depicts Prince Alexandru. Remember?"

Recollecting their family's tale, Sofi's mouth relaxed into a tiny smile. She met her father's gaze and clasped her locket.

"You are part of a powerful and respected family, Sofi. You should be very proud. I'm so looking forward to making up for lost time with you. I want to know everything about you and your life in Bulgaria. And, I hope you will want to learn more about our family history, your ancestors. I feel as though God gave Viviane and me a second chance to be parents. I promise you that we will not squander it."

"What do you mean, second chance?"

"Viviane and I had a daughter together, Sofi. Your sister. Her name was Rosamonde. After trying for many years, we didn't think we'd be able to have a child. So, we gave up hope. But then, when we least expected it, Viviane became pregnant with Rosamonde. She was the sweetest, cutest little thing we'd ever seen. But she passed away a few years ago."

"She died?" Sofi whispered. "Oh, I'm so sorry." She turned to look at Isaiah. "That's what Viviane meant before, back at your flat, when she said she knew what it was like to lose someone she loved?"

"Yes."

"Rosamonde was the miniature version of you, was she not Isaiah?"

Isaiah nodded his head, still amazed by the surreal resemblance.

In that instant, Sofi understood completely. She knew this moment was as bittersweet for them as it was for her. They all shared traumatic loss that would stay with them forever. For each of them, the person they cherished most in the entire world was taken away.

It was not long before Viviane returned, followed by an incredibly regal-looking old woman and man of middle age wearing a black wool suit and cap. Sofi immediately recognized him. He was the man in the Mercedes who visited her mother only weeks before they left Bulgaria.

"My dear, darling boy!" the woman cried melodramatically, arms outstretched towards René. "Come to me, my son!"

"Hello, Mother."

René's response was mechanical and monotone. He made little attempt at civility. He likewise made no effort to accept the embrace she offered and instead eyed the woman warily as if she were a vagabond.

"Allow me to present my daughter," he said. "Sofi, meet your grandmother."

Chapter Twenty-Eight

Septuagenarian Amalie Hartenau-Hesse stood majestically in her mink coat, matching hat, and canary diamond chandelier earrings. With her discerning blue eyes, she looked her only grandchild up and down with an indeterminable expression.

"I am your Grand-mère Amalie."

"Pleased to meet you, Grand-mère," Sofi replied gently in French, unsure how she should act.

"Well, she knows French! And how prettily she speaks! That's very good, very good, indeed," she said, nodding her head approvingly. "René, darling," she called, "you must get this girl some proper clothing. She's dressed like a boy!"

"Mother, please. Are you seriously going to talk about her attire right now?" René was not to be trifled with this evening, or sidetracked by his mother's attempts to diffuse the situation. "Just give me your coat and sit down," he commanded exasperatedly. "Absolon, please sit here, across from Mother. I know you also had a hand in keeping Sofi a secret from me, so I'll need answers from you, as well."

"Yes, sir."

"Isaiah can you take Sofi into the next room fo
some tea and sandwiches?"

"Don't you think I'll be able to handle what she'
going to say?" Sofi interjected.

"I just don't want you to be upset more than you
already are."

"I'm okay, promise. I just want to know what hap
pened—what she's been hiding from us all these years.
think I deserve to know the truth. And I want to hear it from
her."

"Of course, Sofi, you're right. You need to know
what happened, perhaps more than any of us," René con
ceded. "Isaiah, please translate for Sofi."

René took a seat directly across from Amalie, who
tried to hide her uneasiness by avoiding eye contact. She
looked around the room aloofly, then began to fidget with
her necklace. Undeterred, René began coolly and formally.

"I find it unnecessary and redundant to reiterate the
sentiments I previously made known to you by phone. As I
am sure you are aware, they have not changed."

"I know, I know," Amalie said, waving her hand
dismissively as if she were swatting a fly. Her tone irritated
René even more.

"As you both know, someone is responsible for the
death of Sofi's mother, and that same person likely wanted
Sofi dead as well. If you have information that can help us
identify the perpetrator or people involved, I need to know
now. Otherwise, we have nothing further to say to each oth
er."

"René, I'm sorry for the pain we put you through,
truly I am —"

"Mother, I told you, I don't want to hear it!" René interrupted. "And, incidentally, I believe you misspoke. You should have said, 'the pain *I* put you through.' Not 'we.' Absolon had no choice but to keep this secret from me."

"Be that as it may, René, I did *not* speak incorrectly. I meant 'we.' You are wrong to assume that I was referring to Absolon as well as myself. I was actually speaking about that mentor of yours, Philippe Roubert!"

"Go on."

"All those years ago, when Philippe discovered your relationship with Nadja, he came to me with the information, and I was grateful for that. I made plans to tell your father immediately so we could figure out how best to handle the situation. But, Philippe was adamant that your father should never know. He told me he was very concerned for your political career, that you had come so far in your education that it would be a waste to subject you to public ridicule and rejection for carrying on with an underage girl who was a Gypsy, no less. Had it been that she was merely underage, I think your father would have been able to get over it in time. But it was the combination of Nadja's age and status that really made it impossible."

Amalie looked down. Alluding to her late husband's prejudice made her uncomfortable.

"Continue, Mother."

"Philippe told me it was imperative to keep your affair a secret. I agreed. We decided it best to separate the two of you—send you back to Paris early for a six-week internship with Philippe before you started the Institute. We figured that Nadja would simply resume life as usual with her family in Varna, her secret relationship staying safe with us. There were two members of her father's musical act who were suspicious about your ties to Nadja, so we paid for their silence. We knew that if your actions had been discovered by her community, she would have been banished.

It was not until late November when I saw Nadja again. She came to Aytos Manor very early one morning, crying and scared. Thank God your father was away on business! She was barely eighteen—seven months pregnant and obviously showing. She had been thrown out of her home. The poor little thing had nowhere to go, and I knew that she could only be carrying my grandchild! I didn't know what to do, so I took her in and called Philippe for help. I've always regretted that decision—to involve Philippe Rouber instead of confiding in your father, but up until that time I had little reason to believe that he would ever deceive me the way he did."

"How did he deceive you? What did he do? Tell me every detail!" René demanded.

"Well, Philippe insisted that I take Nadja for a—"

"A what?"

"You know. Oh, I can't even say it. A procedure. An...*an abortion*," Amalie whispered. "God knows I was shocked and so very disgusted with him. He tried to frighten me, but still I refused. There was absolutely no way that I would ever play a role in helping to kill my own grandchild. René, you have to know that I never blamed that young girl for what happened. She was just a child. You should have known better! To this day it makes me sick to think of you, at nearly thirty years old, bedding a child! You were so much like your grandfather."

She sighed, then looked over at Absolon, a native Parisian, and winked.

"That's why I didn't marry a Frenchman," she joked. "I think these things skip a generation. Anyhow, after I rebuffed Philippe, I thought I'd heard the last from him, but I was wrong. He sent a group of his men to Aytos Manor when your father was away again. They tried to intimidate me, Absolon can tell you. First, they said that they would tell your father that I was hiding a pregnant Gypsy at the estate. When that didn't work, they threatened to kidnap Nadja in the night and take her to Czechoslovakia for a forced abortion and sterilization—they used to do that to Gypsy girls, you know. After that, I kept a very close watch over her. Finally, Philippe's henchmen gave up and returned to Paris, your father returned home, and we were freed from his grip, though not for long. Nadja gave birth to Sofi five weeks early, on December 18, 1992."

"So Nadja became pregnant with Sofi right away then....the same month we met?"

"It would appear so. Ah, Sofi was so skinny and long, but surprisingly healthy for being premature. After she was born, Absolon and I made arrangements for Nadja to move to a remote village. It was far enough away from Varna so they could start a new life, but not so distant that we wouldn't be able to keep a close eye on them. I secured a small home for them on the outskirts of Dobrai, one of the Gypsy villages near Tervel, so they could be close to their kind. Believe me, we made sure that they were taken care of."

"Well, why couldn't you tell me then, Mother? Why continue to keep such a secret?"

"I considered telling you at that time, René, but Philippe was still in the picture. He was quite unyielding, forceful even, that Sofi be kept a secret. He wanted to avoid a scandal. It was not long thereafter, of course, that you married Viviane. At the time, I thought things worked out for the best.

When Sofi was not yet five, Philippe returned to Bulgaria with a terrifying threat. He made it clear to me that if Nadja or I told anyone about Sofi, or if Nadja ever attempted to contact you, he would have her killed. I was truly frightened for the safety of Nadja and my granddaughter, so I arranged a position for Nadja with the Laporte's, a wealthy Canadian family of Bulgarian descent, that I met years ago at a gala in Plovdiv. Aidan Laporte was an avid hunter, and quite a sturdy man, with a great enthusiasm for collecting guns. He and his wife, Minerva, were also very kind and without bias, so I felt confident that Nadja and Sofi would be safe with them. Mr. Laporte promised to protect them, if necessary. They hired Nadja as caretaker of their vacation estate and the arrangement actually worked out perfectly well for quite some time. Philippe was neutralized and Mr. Laporte and his wife, being the exceptional people that they are, took great joy in having Nadja and little Sofi around.

At the time, I couldn't understand Philippe's preoccupation with our family's situation—why he was so desperate to destroy Nadja and Sofi. Later, it dawned on me that he was so emotionally and financially invested in your political assent that he would do virtually anything to protect it. If you remember, at that time, you had just made your bid for the National Assembly and both you and Viviane gained instant popularity with the people. It became clear to me that Philippe was living vicariously through you, René. He still does! You had the potential to do what he himself could not. When Philippe made his own bid for the presidency years ago, he didn't have half the support you had. Of course, we all know what happened. He lost in a landslide. In you, Philippe credited himself with personally grooming the future President of France. A leader who would bring our nation back to the ideals of years long gone. The one thing that could have impinged his plan was if some reporter or political hack dug up your illicit relationship. Could you have imagined beginning your political career with such a scandal, René?"

"We would have worked through it, Mother. Politicians get caught up in scandals all the time," he replied bitterly.

"I know that now. But at the time, I could not seem to make Philippe understand. He was so driven—like a madman. There was no stopping him! God only knows what else he did to ensure your political success. I don't even want to think about that! In the end, I managed to convince him that Absolon and I would watch over Nadja and Sofi, and I personally guaranteed that they'd never leave Bulgaria. In return, Philippe promised me that he would leave them alone so long as they were under our control, so to speak. But, if they ever attempted to make contact with you or even set foot in France, he would do anything to silence them."

"Did Nadja know about these threats?"

"No. The girl had enough stress. She was separated from her family and busy raising a small child alone. The Roma in her new village didn't trust her. She couldn't tell anyone about her life or why she came to the town by herself. She was very lonely and so young. It was such a pitiable situation. I knew she was unhappy—how she longed for you and wished she could tell Sofi who her father was. But she was a smart girl. She realized it would only cause more problems.

Over the years, and especially after her time with the Laporte's expired, Nadja became cynical and depressed. She felt as though her life was wasting away. As Sofi grew older, she also feared what the future would bring for her. She started to hold me responsible for her situation and became resentful of her life. In truth, I could not blame her. She felt as though Absolon and I were keeping her prisoner and she wanted more out of life for herself and for her daughter. Admittedly, it was difficult to see Sofi, who was undeniably intelligent and gifted even, attend such an abomination of a school. I believe Nadja thought I should have done more to support my granddaughter and provide her with a better education. Still, I couldn't risk people finding out Sofi's true identity for fear of what Philippe might do— and out of concern for your career. So, I did nothing and eventually, Nadja had enough."

"Sir, if I may," Absolon's mild voice interjected. "I called on Nadja in early December because your mother wanted Sofi to have a special locket of your father's for her sixteenth birthday. When I saw Nadja, she was very distraught and more argumentative than usual. She eventually confided in me that she planned to leave Bulgaria with Sofi to start a new life. She was tired of being under Madame Amalie's constant watch and she wanted more opportunities. Of course, I couldn't blame her for that, but I tried to warn her that if she left, we wouldn't be able to protect her. She either didn't understand or didn't care. Her mind was set. It was the perfect time to give her the locket, as if God had willed it Himself, because unbeknownst to Madame," Absolon looked at Amalie apologetically, "I placed the name and address of Mr. Becerra inside the locket. Since the piece is not obviously a locket and is somewhat of a puzzle to open, I thought I'd leave it in the Lord's hands. If Sofi somehow managed to open it, or if she found herself in trouble and needed to open it, then Mr. Becerra would surely know how to help her find their way to you, sir."

"And that's exactly what happened," said René. "Your decision helped save Sofi's life."

Before Absolon could respond, Amalie interrupted, desperate for her son to understand her motivations.

"René, dearest, please believe me when I say that I never wanted to hurt you or keep this secret from you!" she cried. "Sofi is such a lovely girl, and I knew that you, and Viviane as well, would have accepted her completely. But I could not trust Philippe, and I refused to put the life of my granddaughter at risk! Especially after Rosamonde."

"Mother, what do you expect me to say? I understand why you did what you did, but it's just not enough—not now, at least. The lies you told me and the secrets you kept all of these years have wounded me so profoundly—so deeply. I can't just push it all aside as if it never happened!" René hurled himself from his seat and bounded across the room.

"I get it, I do. I understand why you did the things you did. But for the love of God, Mother, what am I supposed to do with this information now? I can never make up for the time I've lost with Sofi. And I don't know what I'm

supposed to do with you! You are my mother and I can for
give you, but I need time." René threw his hands in the air
"I really can't even think about that now. We've got to deal
with Roubert, that piece of shit. I could kill him for threat
ening my daughter, for treating you and Nadja the way he
did! He needs to be brought to justice for all that he's done
But what justice is there for you and your lies, Mother? For
your deceit?"

Amalie grimaced.

"Forgive me, my son!" she cried. "Everything I've
ever done in my life has been for you! To protect you. To
ensure your happiness! I know I was wrong, but I wanted
only to do the right thing. I'm so, so sorry. You must forgive
me!"

René looked at his aging mother. Her eyes brimmed
with tears and her shriveled hands shook in her lap. He
could never hate her. And he could not put her through such
torment, even if she did, perhaps, deserve it.

"Mother, please calm down. I'm very angry with
you, and you've hurt me to the core, but I can forgive you. I
just need time."

"I'm so sorry..." she blubbered.

"It's alright. Try to calm down."

René glanced at Isaiah and Viviane with an exasperated expression and sighed deeply.

"We'll talk about this more tomorrow, Mother."

As Amalie attempted to get a handle on her nerves,
René's mind was at work. He could not deal with his mother's drama at present. He knew what needed to be done.

"You're confident that Roubert was behind the fire?" Viviane asked hesitantly, interrupting René's thought process.

"Yes, my love, I'm absolutely sure now. Between Mother's explanation and the things Roubert revealed during our argument earlier today, I've put it together."

"Excuse me, but I didn't realize that you and Roubert had a disagreement," Isaiah said. "Did it happen during this morning's meeting?"

"Yes, indeed. That's why Viviane was with me when you joined me later. I'd just finished telling her what transpired."

Isaiah raised his eyebrows, surprised.

"So what did he say to you? What tipped you off?

"We were discussing the expulsion legislation. I showed him the article about the fire and shared my concerns about the mounting incidents of violence against the Roma ever since we introduced the bill. Of course, he didn't want to hear it. I told him I planned to pull it from the Assembly. Then I told him that I was thinking about Nadja and he really flew off the handle. After a lot of his typical ranting and raving, he tried to change my mind by giving me more details about the fire and unreported facts about the two women who died in the blaze. Ultimately, he revealed that he had men watching the South Commune for months, and that the two women who died were a mother and daughter from Bulgaria who came here to France illegally since the mother didn't have a work permit. He insinuated that their status instigated their death, which really turned me off. We then argued about Nadja and things of the past.

Roubert ended up leaving in a huff and that's when I called for Viviane."

"I see," Isaiah said quietly, nodding his head. "It's all making sense now."

"When you joined us later and told me that it was Nadja who died in the fire, it dawned on me. Roubert must've been tracking them this entire time. He implicated himself by his own words."

"That bastard!" Amalie snarled.

She stood up quickly, then put her hand to her forehead and teetered back and forth. All of this was too much for her to take.

"Mother, you need to watch your blood pressure! Sit down. Isaiah, could you get her some water, please?"

"Of course, Mr. President."

"René, my son, what are you going to do about this? Philippe Roubert has to pay for what he's done! I don't care how sick or old he is. He tried to kill my granddaughter and he kept me living in fear for the past sixteen years." Amalie's perfectly manicured hand shook as she held her glass of water.

"Here's what we're going to do," said René assuredly, motioning for his wife to come to his side. "Viviane, I would like for you and Marcel to take Sofi to the Palace so she can get some proper rest. She also needs to be examined by a doctor," he said quietly in French.

René and Viviane looked over at Sofi, who by now was curled into a ball on a chair across the room. She had developed a cough and a slight fever. It was obvious that she was beyond exhaustion, grappling with conflicting emotions of shock and relief now that she finally knew her family's history. She also nursed injuries sustained in the fire the previous night.

"Marcel, since we now know with whom we are dealing, I have no doubt that Sofi should be safe in our apartments, but I still want every precaution taken," he ordered. "Mother, you and Absolon can go with them if you'd like to stay in Paris for the rest of the weekend. If not, then Absolon will take you back to Versailles tout suite."

"Absolon will take me back tonight. You and Viviane must have time alone with your daughter tomorrow."

"Very good. Isaiah, I would like you to brief the security detail on what has happened. Then I'm going to confront that son of a bitch, Roubert. You're welcome to come along."

A triumphant smile spread across Isaiah's face.

"Certainly, Mr. President. Consider it done. And yes, I will come with you. You know I wouldn't miss this for the world."

"I had a feeling you'd say that."

Chapter Twenty-Nine

Moments ago, René and Isaiah were ushered into the grand foyer of Philippe Roubert's townhouse on La Rive Gauche, overlooking the southern bank of the River Seine. Isaiah took a seat on an eighteenth century Rococo walnut settee and looked at his watch. It was getting late.

"Stay here, Isaiah. I've already instructed the guards to wait outside. I want to speak with Roubert alone."

"Of course, sir."

Roubert's housekeeper led René past a formal sitting room and into the dark, wood-paneled study, lit only by a pair of Italian gothic torchères and the amber blaze of a large stone fireplace. Above the mantel hung an oversized portrait of Roubert's late wife, Hillarie, red-faced as ever and just as René had remembered her.

At first, Roubert did not notice René's large frame in the doorway. He was, instead, preoccupied with what appeared to be an old letter. He squinted hard to make out the tiny wording on the page, holding it to the light. When he finally looked up and saw René, he laughed out loud, delighted.

"So, I see you've come to apologize! Ah, but you still look so glum."

Roubert was in fine spirits, celebratory even. René watched as he hobbled towards a small bar area where a half-smoked cigar and a glass of cognac on the rocks were waiting for him.

"Come in and have a nightcap with your old friend before I go to bed. I can't be up all night, you know. Even I can admit that I'm not as young as I used to be."

Roubert chuckled again, but this time, his laugh turned into a powerful cough. After several hacks, he spit a wad of yellow phlegm into his glass and plopped onto a nearby chair. René was disgusted.

"Really, was that quite necessary? Haven't you got a napkin?"

"What do you want from me? I'm an old man!" Roubert lifted one sun-spotted finger and shook it at René. "Wait until you're my age. Time stops for no one. Now, ring the bell. I need another drink."

"Don't bother. I'll pour you another."

René grabbed the bottle of Rémy Martin and took a slow, deliberate swig. He took his time pouring a glass for Roubert, then slammed it down on the wooden bar. It made a thud, which caught Roubert's attention. He turned and watched with curiosity as René walked towards him and purposefully placed the glass of cognac just out of his reach.

"I suppose you're still angry with me, René."

"You suppose right."

"I thought I heard your little puppet in the foyer. At least you had the good sense to leave him there," Roubert said, scowling. "So why did you come?"

"I came to discuss something very important with you. Actually, no. A discussion is unnecessary. I came to tell you something."

"What's that?" Roubert challenged.

"I know what you did. I know what you've done."

Roubert looked amused. He strained to reach his glass, then took a sip of the cognac.

"An accusation! Well, well, well..." Roubert snorted, settling back into his seat. "Let's get on with it, then."

"I met a very interesting person today, Roubert. You'd never guess who." René eyed him sternly, waiting for an answer.

"You'd better just tell me. The suspense is killing me," Roubert answered sarcastically.

"My daughter."

"Your daughter? What on earth are you taking about, René? Good God, your daughter is dead!"

"You know damn well I'm not talking about Rosamonde, Roubert. I'm talking about my eldest daughter. You know. The daughter I had with Nadja."

Roubert's face went pale.

"I don't know what you mean, René," he quickly replied.

"Don't play with me! You know exactly what I mean. I know everything! I know how you and my mother kept Sofi a secret from me all her life. I know how you threatened to kidnap Nadja and have her sterilized, and I know that you kept my mother living in fear all of these years."

"Son, listen to me—"

"I'm not your son!" René roared. His eyes bore through Roubert like a laser.

"René, listen," Roubert said vehemently. "I did those things to protect you! You had a very bright political career, and look where I got you. You're the President of France, for God's sake! That...*situation* you left behind in Bulgaria would have ruined you, and your entire family!"

"Nothing could have destroyed me as much as what I learned today—to learn what you did to me. You know better than anyone the grief we endured when Rosamonde died! You had every opportunity to tell me. But you—*you*!" René pointed hard at Roubert. "You made the decision to play God with my life. How could you do that to me?"

"How could I do that to you? How could you do that to *me*, René? To me!" Roubert spat. "I invested so much time and money in you and your career. I wasn't about to sit back and let it all go to hell because you couldn't keep your dick in your pants!"

René's mouth gaped for an instant, shocked by Roubert's crass audacity.

"Believe me, I knew it was wrong for me to carry on a relationship with a girl so young. I was sick over it for years. But the truth is, I loved Nadja. I truly loved her! It may not have been right, but there was nothing impure about our love."

"Are you kidding!?" Roubert nearly jumped out of his chair. "Your 'relationship,' as you call it, was disgusting and shameful. You knocked up an underage girl. A Gypsy, no less! Then you left her destitute, pregnant, and completely alone!" he screamed. "You were almost thirty years old.

Imagine what a scandal it would have been if your actions came to light! You should be thanking me."

"I would have given up everything to be with her—to marry her. But I never had the chance. You took that away from me! You never gave me the opportunity to explain, to tell you how I felt about her. Not that you would have cared. You never listened to me! After all this time—all I've accomplished—you still treat me like an ignorant child. Do you have any idea what it's been like for me all these years, to have you constantly pressuring me, questioning my every move, inserting your opinion into everything I do?"

"Is that really how you feel, René? So holier than thou," Roubert seethed. "You conveniently forget what you were like back then. Unfocused. Immature. Unprepared. Passionate. Spoiled. You only succeeded in school because of your photographic memory. You needed me. You needed *my* help! I'm the one who bailed you out of the trouble you continually caused for yourself and your family. I'm the one who hid your foolish mistakes! Don't you dare think for one second that I didn't know what you were up to all those years! The countless whores. The pregnancy scares. The Italian bitch from Yale who tried to blackmail you. You never cared for any of those women. You just used them. You are your father's son through and through! He never appreciated your mother, not like I did. You were nothing but a womanizing bastard just like your father and your grandfather before you!"

"How dare you speak about my father in such a way!" René bellowed. "The man wasn't perfect, but you exaggerate his faults. Don't think I never realized that you carried a torch for my mother all these years. You were always lurking around her—watching, waiting for your chance to be with her. But she never gave you the time of day because she was so in love with my father. And now, she despises you! You also seem to conveniently forget that you also had a wife." René pointed to Hillarie's portrait. "What do you think she thought about your...*preoccupation* with my mother!?"

Roubert was quiet for a moment. He could not deny his years of unrequited desire for Amalie.

"I've always admired your mother, that's no secret. She is an excellent woman and was a true beauty. But I would have never acted on any attraction I may have felt for her. Face the facts, René. Your father married beneath him. Before she married your father, your mother's status was far beneath mine. Your father was nobility and he married a singer. You would have been willing to do worse, much worse! You went for the absolute scum of the earth, the bottom of the barrel. You would have broken your precious father's heart, cold as it was, if he knew you were carrying on with a Gypsy!"

"It doesn't matter, Roubert. It was not your call. It had nothing to do with you!"

"It had everything to do with me, you impudent, disrespectful ingrate! What, with all the hopes I had for you —for our country. It had everything to do with me!" Roubert shrieked wildly. "My reputation was at stake. I touted you as the next President of France! I would have been ruined if your scandal went public. You would have taken me down with you, you sex-crazed idiot!"

Drenched with sweat and feral with fury, Roubert could barely breathe from all the yelling he was doing.

"What about the fire, then?" René challenged back.

"What fire?" Roubert wiped his forehead with th
sleeve of his lounge shirt.

"The fire that killed Nadja. The fire that was mean
to kill *my daughter*!"

Roubert did not respond. Instead, he looked awa
like a dog avoiding eye contact with his master.

"You had a lot to say about it this morning, Rou
bert."

"What do you want from me, René?" Roubert re
sponded dismissively. "You already seem to know what hap
pened. What, are you trying to elicit some sort of confessio
out of me?"

"By your own admission, I know that you were re
sponsible for the fire. You said yourself that your peopl
were carefully watching all the Gypsy camps surrounding
Paris. You knew more facts about the fire and its victim
than anyone because your people were running surveillance
I'd wager you knew that Nadja and Sofi were on their way
to Paris before they even left Bulgaria. You were just waiting
plotting your next move!"

"You can't prove a thing." Roubert took a long puff
from his cigar.

"I already did. We've pulled your phone records
Roubert. And of course, I have statements from my mother
and Absolon that detail your deeds over the last sixteer
years. After all this time, you've finally come to the end of
the road," René said victoriously. "Don't you have anything
to say for yourself?"

"What else is there for me to say? Yes, I had Nadja
and Sofi watched and yes, I commissioned the fire. I warned

Amalie many years ago that if she allowed those two to come anywhere near you, I would do whatever was necessary to protect France's interests. And I did! I did it for France!"

"No. You did it for you! You meant only to protect your own interests. You said yourself that you had invested so much time and money into me, like I'm your stooge. Well, I am not your pawn! Did you think that I couldn't do it without you, Roubert? That you are so important that I would have been lost without you? Obviously you forget how powerful my family is."

"*Was*, René. Your family was powerful, but that's in the past! Bulgaria ousted their monarchy years ago, and to the French, your mother is nothing but an antique socialite," Roubert sneered arrogantly. "You would have gotten nowhere if it wasn't for me! I gave you every opportunity, and you nearly squandered it all for a lay!"

"You shut your mouth, Roubert, or I swear to God, I'll shut it for you!"

"You'll do nothing of the sort. You don't have the guts," Roubert choked out. By now he was sweating profusely and his face was white and wraithlike. "You would be nothing without me! You should be on your knees thanking me for what I did. For years I protected your reputation. I saved your poor wife from cruel public humiliation! You're a greater fool than I imagined if you believe for one second that Nadja and that daughter of hers came here to France— to Paris, no less—on a whim! That sneaky Gypsy bitch had a plan. She always did. She wanted to find you and expose you for what you really are, or at least get some money out of you. That daughter of yours was her meal ticket. You're lucky I got to her before she had the chance to destroy everything we've built! As soon as I confirmed her identity, sent my men to the camp right away. They took care of it."

"Did you order them to kill Nadja? To beat her to a pulp?"

"Of course not. I hired those idiot Bulgarians to torch the place with them inside. I'm not responsible for anything happened before the fire. If they wanted to get their kicks in beforehand, that's not on me. Shit happens."

Roubert snatched his glass with a shaky grip and sloppily guzzled his cognac, spilling it on his chin.

"You disgusting disgrace for a human being! How could you talk about a woman and my child that way? Thank God your scheme didn't work. Sofi escaped the fire and with the help of Isaiah, she found me."

"Oh, give me a break!" Roubert hurled his drink into the fire. "Of course I should have known that Jew Boy leech of yours would somehow be involved. He's not on your side, René. He wants your power and he's jealous of your success! Don't think for a minute that you can trust him. His kind cannot be trusted!"

"Isn't that what you said to me all those years ago about the Roma? That 'those people' couldn't be trusted? Who are you to talk about trust? All these years, I trusted *you*. And look where it got me! All the times I was advised to ditch you, to force you into permanent retirement, I stood by you. I made excuse after excuse for you. No more! You are finished, Roubert. Finished! You'll pay for what you've done to me, to Sofi, to Nadja and the other innocent woman who died in the fire. You've failed. You've failed miserably!"

René strode to the door and signaled down the hall. A moment later, Isaiah and three armed Presidential security officers filed into the study.

"It's time for you to come with us," Isaiah calmly instructed. "It's over now."

"How dare you! I'm not going anywhere with *you*," Roubert sneered.

One of the officers tried to help Roubert to his feet, but he resisted. He flailed around like a freshly caught fish and smacked the officer in the neck.

"Get your goddamn hands off of me!" he screeched. "You don't know what you're doing! René! You ungrateful son of a whore! I made you! I—"

Roubert's face turned an eerie shade of alabaster. Sweat poured from him like he had been doused with a hose. He tried to speak, but froze with his mouth open, eyes wide. His cigar fell from his fingers, landing on the Oriental rug below. The right side of his face contorted violently as he gasped for breath. He fell to the floor in a deformed heap.

"Help…" he whispered.

"Oh my God, René, I think he's having a stroke!" Isaiah shouted. He rushed to Roubert's side and yelled to him.

"Roubert, can you hear me? Can you speak?"

The side of the old man's face continued to bend and stretch. René stood motionless in horrified disbelief.

"No! Get up. Get up you filthy bastard!" he screamed in Roubert's face. "You pathetic coward!"

"Dammit, René, calm down, man! Pull yourself together!" Isaiah pushed René away and looked to the guards. "Call an ambulance right away."

Chapter Thirty

The moon's pale yellow rays shone softly on Sofi's delicate features while she slumbered soundly in her comfortable room at the Élysée Palace. Her thick chestnut waves cascaded down her shoulders like a rich mahogany waterfall. Her long, slender hands rested peacefully near her chest, lightly touching her precious cerulean locket.

René lingered in the doorway for quite some time, marveling at the sight of his newly-found daughter. He simply could not take his eyes off of her. He realized this would, perhaps, be his only opportunity to speak with her privately for quite some time. After tonight, a constant stream of people necessary to the role of the President would besiege them, not to mention the press and paparazzi that would undoubtedly stalk them day and night once they got word of Sofi's existence. Not wishing to frighten her, he entered the room quietly and sat at a stool near the foot of the bed.

"Sofi, darling," he whispered, "it's me…your father."

Sofi smiled to herself and stretched. She was surprised to see René, but not alarmed. Gently shrugging off the duvet, she propped herself up on the pillows in a rather prim fashion and carefully smoothed her hair.

"Hello," she said sleepily, attempting to seem alert. "Is everything alright?"

"Yes, my dear, everything is fine. I'm very sorry to disturb you. I know you need to rest."

"It's okay," she replied reassuringly with a half smile.

"How are you feeling?"

"Better."

"Good." René sounded relieved. "I'm here because I wanted a moment alone with you—to talk. Tomorrow will likely be a very busy day. You'll soon see that there will rarely be times when we're not surrounded by many people."

Sofi shrugged. It was difficult for her to imagine what he meant by that since she was accustomed to spending so much time alone.

"I came to tell you that you're safe. I've identified the perpetrator who is to blame for all of our…misfortunes. He's been apprehended. Not only that, the police searched his residence and were able to identify the three thugs he hired to hurt your mother and set fire to your home. Those men were arrested tonight and are in prison. You're safe, Sofi."

Sofi's eyes became dark as he told her the news.

"So, who is this person? How'd you figure out he was the one responsible?"

"There will be plenty of time to explain all of the details tomorrow. I must forewarn you, though, that the press and the public will soon demand information about who you are and what has happened. We must prepare ourselves. It won't be easy for us these next few months, but know you're safe with us. Viviane and I will protect you. I promise that you can rest easy tonight and every night you're with us. I'll never let anything happen to you for as long as I live. You are far too precious to me."

René brought Sofi a sense of security that she had never before experienced. She looked steadily into his face, which was nearly identical to her own apart from her onyx eyes, which she inherited from her mother. She knew instinctively that she could trust René fully, and that the heartache and uncertainty of the past would one day be behind her.

"Sofi, please allow me to express to you how deeply sorry I am for everything that's transpired, and for all the hurt I've caused you. I pray to God that He will take away your pain and make it mine alone to bear. For the rest of my life, I'll work tirelessly to make up for lost time. I'll strive to be the father you deserve—the type of father that Nadja would have wanted me to be."

"You never knew I existed. I know you're not responsible for what happened. Maybe you should've fought harder for Mama back then. But I think I can understand why you felt like you couldn't at the time."

Sofi looked away. A naturally forgiving person, she did not feel animosity towards René, though she recognized he could have made better decisions all those years ago.

"You might feel differently when you know the whole truth—the truth about me, your mother, and the man who was behind all of this. He was someone who was once quite close to me. In fact, he orchestrated my entire political career. I considered him a mentor, a friend. But all this time, he deceived me so treacherously and I was too blind, no—

too stupid to see it. I failed you and your mother. I'm so sorry."

René hung his head in shame. Sofi sat quietly, not sure what to say or do. She did not even know how to address René; her father, the President of France. It was all so strange. In twenty-four hours, she went from living in a trailer with the only family member she had ever known to sleeping in the Presidential apartments of the Élysée Palace face to face with a father she never knew she had.

"I don't know what to say...*Father*?" Sofi tentatively tried the word. It felt strange but somehow right. Leaning closer to René, she reached out to him and gently touched the side of his face, which was surprisingly wet from a tear. He grasped her hand and gave it a kiss. At that moment Sofi wished she had known the love of a father growing up. As if reading her mind, René replied to Sofi's thoughts with a bittersweet smile.

"We've lost so much time. God knows I don't deserve a second chance."

"Father, I don't fault you for what happened. And I want you to know that I forgive you. This entire situation is so difficult for both of us—for all of us. But please, I need to know about you and Mama. I don't know what to think or how to feel about that. You must have cared about her. I mean, you said you loved her. But it's hard for me to believe that. Did you really love her or was I just the unhappy result of a summer dalliance?"

"Dalliance, eh?" René gave Sofi a quizzical look and sighed. "Ah, Sofi, you are quite a girl. Smart and full of surprises." His eyes flashed with a glimmer of amusement, though his sad and remorseful expression remained un-changed.

"Dear girl," he continued, "my relationship with your mother was much, much more than a summer dalliance. Perhaps it began that way, but my feelings for her grew quickly."

René looked out the window and stared at the stars. He was obviously emotional, which startled Sofi. She had never witnessed any man, let alone such a powerful one, openly display such feelings. Then she remembered that her father was half French.

"On the night I first beheld your mother, the moon was as it is this very night—bright and luminescent. In all my life, I'd never witnessed a being so breathtaking as your mother was on the night we met. She was an unearthly creature, so tiny with the darkest of eyes and hair and the smoothest of skin. It was as if she'd stepped out of the pages of a fairytale. I literally couldn't take my eyes off her. She had a bold, captivating voice, but it was so unexpected because of her diminutive frame. I remember clearly that I expected her voice to be high and clear, like a bell. But it was completely the opposite. It was deep and rich...sultry. I was spellbound. She looked like a faerie, but sounded like a seductress. I was lost from that moment on."

René stopped and looked at Sofi as though he had awoken from a dream, like his mind just returned from a faraway land.

"Mama must have been very beautiful."

"She was...inside and out. I loved your mother. You might say it was love at first sight. At the time, I knew she was young, but I didn't know—or perhaps I didn't want to believe—that she was so *very* young. I wish I could say that if I knew her true age, I wouldn't have pursued her. But in truth, it probably wouldn't have stopped me. She was everything I wanted to be— compassionate, unworldly, and completely selfless. I was such an idiot. I should've known she was pregnant! We spent almost every moment we could together. I also should have realized that everyone was lying to me. But I couldn't see it at the time, or maybe I didn't want to. I was a coward back then, Sofi. A disgrace." René put his head in his hands and shook his head. "How can I ever make this right, not for me, but for you? You loved your mother so much and I know you need her. I'm so sorry that she's gone. I'm so sorry for my part in it!"

"Father," Sofi said kindly, "Mama used to tell me that together, we could get through anything. And even though she's no longer with me here on this earth, I know that she's still with me in my heart." Sofi held her hands to her chest. "Somehow, her words seem to have even more meaning to me now. You and I have finally found each other after all these years. Yes, it took a long time, but now I'm here for you just as you're here for me. We *will* get through this. I'm sure of it."

René stared at Sofi incredulously, amazed by her strength and maturity.

"You know," she continued, thoughtfully, "last night, I was convinced that my heart was broken beyond repair. And even now, nearly every waking minute hurts. But you're helping to fix me and my broken heart." She smiled gently at René, who was moved to tears. "You must realize that God allows things to happen for a reason. Of course, it's hard for us to see it now, and maybe we'll never truly understand. But I believe with all my heart that we were meant to find each other. We've got to trust that the Lord will guide us from this point forward. Now that we're together, we can never allow anyone to separate us ever again. So I'll hold onto your promise, Father. And I'll hold onto you...*forever*. You're all the family I've got."

"My dearest daughter, I'm lost for words. But I promise on my life—now that I've found you, I'll never let you go."

Epilogue

As I looked past the crystal clear waves of the Black Sea and across the sky above, it seemed as though the puffy lumps of snow white clouds were nothing more than marshmallows sprinkled across a bright blue canvas. thought about the wonderful time I was having at our family's impressive estate in Varna, Bulgaria. This was the place where my father spent his childhood summers and where he first fell in love with my beloved late mother, Nadja.

Bringing my gaze back to the shore, I noticed my stepmother lounging quietly nearby. I could tell she'd fallen asleep because the book she was reading, which she carefully placed across her legs just moments ago, was now in a heap at her feet. She made no attempt to pick it up, or otherwise move, for some time.

A smile crept across my face as I looked at Viviane. In a short period of time, she'd become my best friend and most trusted confidant. She was the only person on the planet who knew about my feelings for Isaiah Becerra. She comically tried to keep us apart. I think she wanted to avoid a repeat of the past, but she had nothing to worry about. Isaiah was infuriatingly chivalrous.

Father, on the other hand, was wide awake. Dressed casually in a white linen shirt and khaki slacks, he was occupied with some important papers that Isaiah thrust at him just before he boarded the jet back to Paris. He must have felt me looking at him, because he turned his head to me and winked, which caused me to giggle like a kid.

I looked down and touched the gold bracelet that Isaiah gave to me the night before he left. With its beautiful cerulean sapphires, it was a perfect compliment to my cherished locket. Engraved on the inside of the bracelet were the words, *mon rayon de soleil.* Isaiah certainly was my ray of sunshine, too. I wished he didn't have to return to Paris so soon.

I couldn't believe how quickly time passed since the worst day of my entire life—the day my mother was murdered. It took a full year before I could even say the word. I was thankful that the stress and pain of those horrific days following the fire, and the subsequent court cases that garnered so much media attention, were finally behind me. Those times were particularly difficult for my father and Viane, who, on top of being ripped to shreds in the press, felt the same acute hurt I did each time I had to testify.

Despite the agony I experienced when being forced to relive the events of that fateful night over and over again, it was all worth it in the end. The three Bulgarian neo-Nazis that Roubert hired to kill us were tried in Paris, found guilty of murdering my mother and Lulu, and sentenced to life imprisonment. My testimony and statements to police proved to be invaluable to the authorities, and they were able to successfully link the three men to other cases of violence against the Roma. Immediately following the verdict, the men were extradited to Bulgaria and are still in prison there. They're awaiting another trial for the murder of two Roma teens in Sofia and the arson of a Jewish pastry shop in Elin Pelin.

Philippe Roubert faced a very different ending, and though it didn't result in his incarceration, it was strangely fitting nonetheless. After my father learned about his involvement from Grand-mere Amalie, he confronted Roubert at his townhouse with the intention of sparking a confession. However, during the course of their very heated altercation, Roubert suffered a massive stroke and was rushed to the hospital.

As a result of the stroke, Roubert was left unable to speak or move, let alone eat or use the bathroom. His face was permanently twisted into an unrecognizable, grotesque disfigurement, and a myriad of tubes traveled in and out of his body in order for his physicians to administer his most basic needs. Doctors were shocked that his already frail body was able to survive such a violent episode. On the one occasion I saw the man, he was, indeed, a pathetic sight—the epitome of human suffering and the embodiment of fate's cruel hand. Physically speaking, he was in a near vegetative state, but his mind remained intact until his dying day. It was as if his body served as his prison, perhaps the most merciless of all punishments.

After his release from the hospital, he was placed in a nursing home. My father pushed the district attorney to immediately proceed with their case against him. Even though I knew he was responsible for destroying the lives of so many people, I somehow pitied him. He'd suffered enough, so I tried to persuade my father to relent on his prosecution, which he ultimately did. Roubert died before the next spring—miserable and completely alone. He was laid to rest next to his wife, Hillarie, in the Bonaparte Mausoleum in Père Lachaise Cemetery in east Paris.

Shortly after Roubert's death, my father, Isaiah, and I brought what was left of my mother's remains back to Bulgaria, and she was buried in the small cemetery of Sveta Petka, my father's church in Varna. Her final resting place is small yet lovely, just like she was, and lies under the gentle branches of a weeping willow. Little Bulgarian Gentianella flowers, the same as the ones found in our yard in Dobrai, frame her headstone like little white stars scattered across an emerald sky.

In the forty days following her death, I could hear my mother's voice at times, which gave me great comfort, encouragement, and strength; though she sometimes startled me, coming to visit at the most unexpected times. Since then, she's remained quiet, but I know that's because she is finally at peace in God's Heavenly Kingdom. Later that year, we traveled to Matros'ka, Ukraine to bury brave Luluja the Lăutar next to her beloved husband, Andrej.

Though my life changed so drastically due to such terrible circumstances, I couldn't help but feel like it was right for me to come into my father's life when I did. The years of Roubert's domineering and influence caused him to question his morals and personal beliefs. He confided in me that over the years, he lost his sense of conviction, and that his ethics had become muddled. He felt as though he'd finally been given a chance to right the wrongs that permeated his life for far too long.

As soon as news of my existence went public, the media went into a frenzy. I was called every name known to man, but usually the words "scandalous abomination" o "illegitimate half-breed," were involved, which was ver hard for me to bear. Of course, I already knew what the out side world thought about my people. But the revulsion and fear that many expressed were never so pervasive as the were after my father's press conference announcing that was his daughter, and that he and Viviane would be accept ing me into the Élysée Palace. Amid death threats and ru mors of my father's impeachment, I was forced to stay in doors for my own safety for nearly a month. Isaiah came to see me every day during that time. Looking back, I suppose it wasn't quite so bad. I cherished every minute I spent with Isaiah. I think it brought us even closer together.

Although I'll always think of Roubert as a racist and murderous bastard, he was actually right about one thing— the French could easily forgive a President's culpability for producing an illegitimate child, but certainly not an illegiti mate *Roma* child. In fact, it was not until the international media, particularly the American press, took hold of the story that things, thankfully, began to change. Eventually, my father was painted in a more sympathetic light—one of the youngest French Presidents in the history of the nation. known for his wild popularity and undeniable charisma, who was unfairly kept from his child in an evil scheme concocted by those closest to him. Later, when Viviane sat for a special interview with American journalist Barbara Walters, the world finally had the opportunity to see the situation as she, herself, did; as a second chance to have a family. She ex plained that after my little sister's death, she and my father were heartbroken. When I came to them damaged, alone, and needing a family, she accepted me with open arms. She said that I made her feel alive again. I'll never forget her words.

After what seemed like eons, the media circus finally died down and my father got back to his important work. He soon abandoned the increasingly controversial Roma expulsion policy. In its place, he formed a coalition with several Eastern European member states, including Bulgaria, to foster dialogue and devise practical, collaborative solutions on how best to deal with the influx of Roma immigrants from the East. The plan focused on combating the issues that affected Roma back home, like segregation, adult illiteracy, unemployment, and access to public health and housing so that the Roma would not feel compelled to leave their home nations in the first place. Roubert's findings on the activities at the Roma camps in France were integral to this initiative. After the "Roubert Reports" were presented to the European Commission, several member states agreed that more needed to be done to help the Roma and prevent further instances of some of the world's most egregious crimes and human rights violations, including sex trafficking, child marriage, and forced labor. I couldn't have been more proud of my father on the day he addressed the European Commission. After his speech, the Commission adopted a communiqué pushing for the development of national strategies for Roma integration across the EU. Although he received a lot of unfair criticism from his own political party, he stayed strong in his convictions and told the people that it was not reelection that mattered to him, but doing what was right.

That was already more than four years ago, and I'm still astonished by how quickly the time has passed. Though I wished Mama were still here with me, she is forever in my thoughts and in my heart. The time has helped me to move on, as my father predicted. This past year, I finished my second year of study at my father's alma matter, Pantheon-Assas, and I had the honor of being the first Roma student ever admitted to the University. I may pursue law, as my father did, but God willing, I have all the time in the world to figure out what I'm meant to do and what my purpose truly is.

I sat back to enjoy the sweet serenity of the bright cerulean sea before me, finally understanding why my parents loved this place so much. Right here, right now, with my father and Viviane at my side and my mother always close to my heart, there was nowhere else on earth I'd rather be than sitting on the golden shores of the interminable and ever-constant Black Sea.

Acknowledgements

I would like to thank my family, especially my husband, Deffy Mubangu, my mother, Susan Uram, my mother-in-law, Philomena Reynolds, my cousin, Stephanie Sorce, and also my longtime friends, Tabatha Cuadra and Emily Knapp. I would also like to extend special thanks to author Brian Patrick Mitchell and his wife, Cindy, for their guidance and encouragement, as well as to Mitred Archpriest John D. Sorochka, whose life and service is an inspiration to me and so many others. Finally, I would like to thank my high school English teachers for cultivating my love of literature: Mr. David Brzuchalski, Mrs. Carol Datto, Mr. Dave Doud, and Mr. John Hockin.

About the Author

JUSTINA URAM is an author and public interest attorney with degrees from Penn State Dickinson School of Law and Syracuse University's Maxwell School of Citizenship and Public Affairs. *The Cerulean Locket* is her debut novel, inspired by her connectedness to family, ethnic ancestry, love of travel and politics, and study of international law and human rights. She splits her time between her home in the Northern Virginia suburbs of Washington, DC and her historic hometown in Lackawanna County, Pennsylvania. Justina can be reached at www.justinauram.com

Made in the USA
San Bernardino, CA
15 July 2016